WHISKEYJACK

WHISKEYJACK

Hal Barwood

Tracking Terror
a paranormal adventure

Whiskeyjack

This is a work of fiction. The California foothills, national security worries, railroad traffic, and would-be terrorists are all real, but the communities, enterprises, and locations depicted herein are either fictional in themselves or fictional in detail. All the characters and incidents in this fictional world are products of the author's imagination. No resemblance to any real person or the operations of any real organization is intended.

In particular, the Department of Homeland Security and the Union Pacific Railroad would never knowingly allow the untoward events described in this story to occur; they work hard to prevent such things.

Acknowledgements . . .

Many thanks to everyone who struggled with early versions of this tale and offered suggestions and encouragement; especially Barbara Barwood, Jonathan Barwood, Tobias Barwood, Betsy Blanchard, Curt Blanchard, Louis Castle, Robert Dalva, Beverly Graves, Janet Robbins, Matthew Robbins, and Gordon Walton.

Thanks once again to Officer Andy Litzius and Sergeant Dan Maciel of the Placerville Police Department; to KBGE-FM; and to Google, Wikipedia, and the rest of the World Wide Web for offering the author an occasional glimpse of reality.

About the Author . . .

Hal Barwood is a veteran writer with multiple credits in multiple media. Find out more online . . .

www.finitearts.com

Enjoy Marianne Sarzeau's previous adventures in these books . . .

SHADOWCOP

BROOMHANDLE

for

Jennifer & Erin

daughters by choice

Table of Contents

Part ONE

1

"I WANT A BABY."

Marianne Sarzeau, nominally a police officer in Placerville, California, had just returned home to the Sierra Nevada foothills from a secret operation in Ukraine. There, as *Agent Broomhandle,* she assisted Army Major Raymond Bagwell and her father, Army Master Sergeant Emile Sarzo, to debunk rumors of stolen atomic weapons in a faraway land swirling with Russian spies. She was exhausted by Dad's psychic surveillance missions and by her role in FULTAP, the *Full Spectrum Threat Assessment Program.* Chilly weather, bad food, unfriendly strangers, trouble on every street corner. A baby seemed like the key to ordinary life.

Tom Wagstaff, her fiancé, was already in bed. He yawned, scratched his well-clipped beard, and reached out for her.

"Well, okay, M, let's give it a whirl."

What started slowly and romantically with tender kisses soon became frantic. Blouse shed, bra lifted, panties torn off. Hands groping. Squirming and rolling. In a few short minutes they both were finished. Marianne fell aside in a heap. Her eyes fluttered and closed.

Wagstaff regarded her with warm admiration. Fair hair, round face, sharp little upturned nose. Wide lips. Under the lids, dark brown eyes. Under the bedclothes, a shapely torso. From appearances, no one would conclude that this young woman possessed an arsenal of strange powers. But he knew, without understanding how or why, that she did.

When he first met her, four years ago, Marianne was a rookie cop in his tiny foothill town, unsure of herself, alternately timid and reckless. He was astonished by her tale of a ghost that appeared in mirrors — and by her claim that the shadowy form helped her solve a series of murders. He had his doubts, big ones, but he noticed how that case toughened her up, gave her some ambition, sent her off to join Placerville's more professional police force.

For a while thereafter, everything seemed normal. He thought (and hoped) that her odd behavior was a thing of the past, but a year later her ghost returned. It warned that a mysterious plane crash had left her father in a coma.

Dad's secret military outfit recruited her to take over his role, and she soon learned that her peculiar talents were inherited from him. Following a trip to connect with her family's ancient lineage in France, her range of abilities expanded rapidly to include summonings, conjurings, commandments, and magic spells. Or so she said.

Dad eventually woke up, and Marianne took credit for his recovery. Never having personally witnessed that or any of her other exploits, Wagstaff might have been skeptical, but his heart ruled his head, and he took her work on faith.

While he was watching, her eyes reopened.

"Yes?"

This time they moved slowly, caressing each other delicately, savoring each and every moment. They continued making love long into the night.

Next morning she was pregnant.

"I'm pregnant," she announced.

Wagstaff was perplexed.

"How do you know? Did you miss?"

She waved her hands. "I just know."

"Ahh-ha, you've been away for three weeks . . . what about this guy Bagwell, anyway?"

Marianne laughed and playfully smacked Wagstaff's shaggy blond head. "Don't be silly, it's you. You're the father."

"And when did this happen?"

"Last night. Right here in this bed."

"Marianne . . ."

She smiled at his doubts.

"It's a boy. He's going to look a lot like you."

2

GOLDEN HARVEST Labor LLC, its sister companies GHL Distributors and Golden Egg Family Farms, were situated in low hills amid wide fields and abundant oak trees, halfway between Placerville and the Big Valley.

Alejandro Muñoz, the middle-aged proprietor and owner, was at his desk on the ground floor of a stately frame ranch house. He was staring at paperwork and fiddling with a pen while pretending to listen to the urgent appeals of a private investigator.

"My client has been deprived of back wages amounting to thousands of dollars over the past few months. I'm here to collect."

Muñoz dropped the pen.

"Back wages? Your client is undocumented, yes?"

"Yes, but he has rights, like any human being."

Muñoz shrugged. "A delicate situation. Golden Harvest Labor found him a job. For this we receive a fee, pro-rated over three years. It is a normal arrangement. We always work this way. To extract our fee all at once, at the beginning, would be a hardship."

"My client believes he is being exploited. He knows, from conversations with others in his position, that your fees are exorbitant. He wants relief, and I'm here to see that he gets it."

"This man is a skilled vineyard worker, I believe." Muñoz glanced at a notebook open before him. "He trellises, prunes, and trains grape vines. An important job that pays well. A job that we arranged. Our fee is reasonable, I believe, for such a helpful service, and there are no back wages."

The investigator expelled a weary sigh. "Mr. Muñoz, as a Latino yourself who has risen in the world, I hold out the hope you will be sympathetic to someone less well-off who also harbors aspirations here in America."

Muñoz smiled. "Well now, I'm *very* sympathetic. But I'm not Latino, not from Mexico. My family is from Spain. We've been here for a hundred years. I'm as European as you are."

The investigator spread his hands, working to stay cool. "I represent an organization that specializes in tracking down unfair labor practices. Unless we can come to an agreement, at the least you will receive very bad publicity from this dispute. Potential customers will shy away. Allegations of human smuggling will surface. Is that what you want?"

"I don't understand. Your client could be digging onions, but thanks to us, he is well placed. A lucky man."

"True, he has a job that matches his considerable skills. However, just because he is undocumented does not mean that he lacks friends and resources. I must point out that, should we fail to negotiate a settlement here, legal action will ensue."

"Legal action."

"Right. My organization is prepared to file suit. That would bring your smuggling operation, however it works, into public view. It would focus attention. My story — and I know how to tell it — could easily lead to further inquiries, warrants, official scrutiny . . ."

"Really." Muñoz closed his notebook. He managed another tight smile. "Let me think this over. Perhaps I am reacting to your manner and not to the substance of your complaint. Of course, the man in question should be given all opportunities to succeed in our great and inviting country."

The investigator was taken aback by the suddenly conciliatory tone. "Glad to hear it," he mumbled, nodding.

"Give me a few days. I will talk to my associates. I'm sure we can come to an agreeable compromise."

Muñoz pressed a button on his desk, and a fortyish cowboy in cotton shirt and dungarees appeared.

"Meanwhile, why not have a look around? We raise ostriches here. Did you know that a single ostrich egg is bigger than two dozen chicken eggs?"

"No, I didn't. That's some omelet."

"Indeed." Muñoz gestured toward the cowboy.

"Luther Handy, here, is my ranch foreman. He would love to give you a tour."

The cowboy touched his hat.

"Introduce this man to my favorite bird, Sandy Top, would you? She's a sweety."

"Sure thing, boss."

"And call that fool Dingell. I have a job for him."

The lanky foreman nodded assent and escorted the investigator out of the office. Outside, he led the way past glistening white prefab buildings toward a corral where large fluffy birds were milling around.

"Why ostriches? Where's the money in big birds?"

"Feathers mostly. They're like two-legged sheep, they wear their value."

Back in the office, Muñoz returned to his paperwork. After a few minutes a muffled sound reached his ears.

Pop!

3

ROSSI'S Fine Italian Dining was twenty miles south of Placerville, an architectural showplace in upscale Tarvolo. It wasn't far from Wagstaff's newspaper offices in Applefield, and it had been part of Marianne's territory back when she was a rookie cop patrolling the Tri-Town Area. In addition to the food, which was never less than excellent, the place held sentimental value. Last fall Wagstaff proposed on the adjoining golf course.

This evening, a warm one, found them on the patio under a lush canopy of purple wisteria. Marianne was dressed in her police outfit, ready for a long night shift deterring crime, and they were eating early.

Lorraine Wagstaff, Tom's mother and Marianne's best friend, was forced to close her book shop in nearby Ragtown at four o'clock in order to join them. Something about their invitation told her to forget the after-work crowd.

The waiter poured wine, set out a basket of bread sticks.

"*Santé,*" said Marianne as they clinked glasses.

"So? The occasion? Some news?" asked Lorraine, mildly regretful about lost sales.

Marianne and Wagstaff looked at each other. They spoke simultaneously: "We're having a baby."

Lorraine set her glass on the table. She sat up straight. "That *is* news. Sure you got things in the right order? You know, first, put a ring on it, and only then help propagate the human race?"

"Mom . . ."

"Don't 'Mom' me. You guys are engaged. I thought I was going to hear a *date* for a *wedding.*"

Marianne grinned conspiratorially. "You are."

"When, pray tell? Before you show, I hope."

"August," said Wagstaff.

Marianne grinned again. "I'll look like a virgin."

Plates of pasta and chicken marsala arrived. The trio turned to their silverware. After a quiet interval, Marianne renewed the discussion.

"See, what we want to do is keep it small. You maid of honor, and Howard best man."

Lorraine blushed crimson. 'Howard' was Howard Turnbow, mayor of the Tri-Town Special District, and Marianne's part-time employer at his rural radio station. An unexpected autumnal romance had recently sprung up between widow and widower. Marianne and Wagstaff wanted to bless it.

"That . . . that's very nice . . . very thoughtful," spluttered the older woman. She knocked back her glass of wine. "I will be delighted. So will Howard, or I will kick him."

Marianne was pleased. "Now, what about you two senior citizen types? What's going on with your geriatric do-see-do?"

Lorraine waggled her head. "We're maintaining. Things are good. We see each other now and then."

"Every night, is what I hear."

"Not every night. But pretty often. I still keep house in Ragtown."

Wagstaff and Marianne exchanged high fives, suspicions confirmed.

"So then . . . what next?"

Lorraine toyed with her pasta. She gave her dinner partners a coy smile. "We're pretty set in our ways. That happens later on in life — news flash for you children. He's got his businesses. I've got the Book Nook. But things could happen . . . might happen . . . you never know."

▼

Later, after Lorraine had already departed, Wagstaff was escorting Marianne to her car when the future mother abruptly sagged to her knees. She bent over, moaning softly. Wagstaff knelt beside her.

"M — ? Hey, babe, what is it?"

"Uhhhhh, dizzy. World spinning. I may throw up."

"Okay, all right. Want to go back inside?"

She took a deep breath. "No, no. I'll be fine. Duty calls." She stood up, wavering at first. Then she steadied herself. "See? Better already."

"You should call in sick. You can't go to work like this. You can't drive."

"Yes I can. I'm okay, I'm fine."

"Sure?"

She nodded. "Kiss."

Wagstaff knew his headstrong fiancée well enough to know that stopping her would be impossible. He folded her into a tight embrace.

"Call me if this happens again. I'll come get you."

"Don't worry about me, I'm fine. I'm good."

Arriving in Placerville, Marianne swapped her little blue Mini Cooper for an aging Dodge Charger police cruiser, and set out on patrol. The usual swing through the city's neighborhoods revealed no criminal activity. The dispatcher didn't radio any domestic disputes. The homeless camp on the east end of town was quiet. Nobody was dropping lit cigarettes into the tinder-dry grass. Marianne, fighting off her lingering malaise, was grateful for the boredom.

But later on, after nightfall, she was called to a disturbance outside the Hog Heaven Bar & Grille on Main Street. The management had thrown a customer onto the street, and he was yelling and kicking the Blues Brothers statues that flanked the establishment's swinging doors.

Marianne stopped in the lane, flipped on her code three lights, and got out to have a look. Her eyes narrowed when she realized that the malefactor was a raggedy man she knew from previous arrests.

"Bo Dingell. What in hell are you up to now?"

The man stopped kicking. He turned a pale face in her direction.

"Evening, Officer Sarzeau. They threw me out."

"You're drunk, Bo."

"And high too." His eyes were darting every which way. "Foxy-oxy . . . wheee-ooo!"

Marianne detached a pair of handcuffs from her duty belt.

"Hold out your hands. I'm taking you in."

Dingell thrust out his arms, wrists together.

"No, no, pal. Turn around."

Dingell turned his back. Marianne snapped on the cuffs.

"Get in the car." She pushed him into the back seat.

On the way up the hill to the Marshall Medical Center, Marianne called her dispatcher.

"Got a customer. Disturbing the peace on Main Street. Suspicion of intoxication from multiple causes. I'm transporting him up to Marshall on a 5150 hold."

From the back seat, Dingell was objecting. "You can't hold me overnight. What about my truck?"

"It will keep."

"I'm not homeless. I've got a good truck. Two trucks. I've got a job. I can handle a welding torch."

"Not in your condition."

"I done some bad things. I know that. Bad things. But I'm good at my work. I did a whole year in the community college. I can drive, I can weld. I can wrangle animals. I know the river."

"Bo . . ."

"I passed those tests, but then I did some bad things. That's true. And I got drunk. Shouldn't have. Then the oxy. Screwed me to the wall. Never mix your poisons, right, officer? Noooo, bad, bad, bad. You buy stuff, it's all a lie."

"Bo . . ."

"But I'm okay. I'm processing. Facing life. Day to day. I can drive . . ."

"Jesus, Bo, shut the fuck up."

4

FOR WAGSTAFF AND MARIANNE, time spent on the Whiskeyjack River, which wound down from the High Sierra just north of Applefield, was time brought to a halt. Each visit felt like free admission to an eternal realm where the only measures of life were themselves, a blue sky, overhanging oaks, and a lazy current in cool water.

Wagstaff put in long hours each week editing and publishing *The Amador County Courier.* He also taught journalism at Sacramento State and a woodworking class at the community college in Lodi. His getaway hobby was gold prospecting, which he pursued with a gasoline-powered suction dredge. On an off-duty day, Marianne often tagged along.

Today, a hot one in early summer, found the pair in shorts and T-shirts, mounted on nine-foot-long Styrofoam pontoons that paralleled Wagstaff's new Husqvarna pump. They were slowly paddling their way upriver from their woodsy launch site.

The Whiskeyjack figured marginally in California's gold rush, but the miners and their claims were long gone. This suited Wagstaff perfectly. He figured that ninety per cent of the gold available was still there for the taking, hidden among the bends, banks, and rills of the river's almost inaccessible upper reaches. Once he had dredged up a six ounce nugget with his old Honda pump; the strike of his life. He hoped to do even better with the more powerful Husqvarna and was eager to try it out.

But a long morning sucking mud from the river bottom and sluicing it through the suction dredge's onboard sieve produced just a single bright flake. Pennyweight, worth a dollar or two down at Millwood's Gold Rush Emporium in Jackson.

Marianne pointed out a grassy spot on the outer side of a tight bend, and there they consoled themselves with beer, sandwiches, and sex. They were lying on their backs, naked, staring happily at puffy clouds forming, when the conversation turned to Marianne's health.

"Your little moment at Rossi's. Morning sickness already?"

"Or FULTAP overload."

"Mmm."

"I'd be so happy if FULTAP never calls again."

"Agent Broomhandle. You could refuse when Dad crooks his finger, you know."

"No I couldn't. National security. They need people like me — and oops — *there is no one else like me.*"

"Mmm."

"I'd be even happier if *I* wasn't like me. Someone without all my spooky abilities."

Wagstaff rolled to face her.

"You serious?"

"Oh yeah. I just want to be a mom."

"Maybe there's a way. Some magic spell, an intervention."

"I never heard of anything."

"What about your friend Hannah Crowfoot?"

"Doubtful. But who knows? I should talk to her."

At that moment a fluffy bird fluttered across the river, landed at their feet, and began eating the remains of their picnic.

"Look at that."

Marianne sat up. Instead of darting away, the bird flew up and perched on her head. She cringed.

"Hey, no pooping!"

Wagstaff laughed.

The creature daintily pecked at Marianne's hair a few times, then flew off upriver.

"What was that?"

"*Perisoreus canadensis,* a gray jay."

"Professor Bird Book."

"Well, I'm interested in wildlife," said Wagstaff. "Gray jays are rare this far south. And very tame, especially if there's food around. Old time miners called them 'whiskeyjacks'."

"Named after the river?"

"Or vice-versa. Who knows?"

Weeahh!

A loud screech announced the bird's return. It landed nearby and dropped something shiny onto their picnic blanket. Marianne bent to pick it up.

"Look, a belt buckle." Indeed. The object was a small silver buckle, with shreds of leather hanging from it.

"Thanks for the gift, little whiskey thing."

The jay perched on her head, then flew off upriver again. Minutes later it was back with another trinket.

"What now? A metal pen top, just what I needed, how cute."

The jay flew upriver for a few yards, then pirouetted back. It picked up the buckle, dropped it. Flew off, flew back, hopped around near its little offerings. It cocked an eye at Marianne, then took off and disappeared around an upriver bend. But not long thereafter, it was back for a third time. In its beak was a frayed woven bracelet. It dropped the artifact beside the other presents and repeated its sequence of departures and returns.

When the jay flew away and back for the umpteenth time, Marianne's lighthearted mood had faded completely. She reached for her clothes.

"Let's go, babe. Something's up."

Wagstaff reluctantly got into his shorts. They remounted the suction dredge and paddled after the jay.

A quarter of a mile farther upriver they came to a sharp bend where, sometime in a wetter past, the river had carved a cliff into a steep hillside before retreating into its present bed. The jay was fluttering back and forth in front of them, mewing softly.

They beached the dredge on a gravel bar and got out for a look around.

"Over here," said Wagstaff, nearing the cliff.

Marianne pushed through a thicket of ceanothus bushes. "Watch out for ticks."

"Ticks are not our problem, M."

Marianne joined Wagstaff at the cliff face. There the sandstone had been undercut, forming a shallow cave. And in the cave was a pile of desiccated corpses.

The jay flew over and landed on the nearest one. Marianne stiffened. Her skin grew cold.

"Holy crap."

"Yeah," said Wagstaff.

Marianne stood riveted. Then her training took hold. She examined the ragged clothing, took note of a baseball cap with a faded *San Francisco Giants* logo.

"2012 World Champions," she said.

"How many?" asked Wagstaff, stumped by the tangle of bony arms and legs.

"Got me. Quite a few, it seems. God in Heaven."

She fingered a bullet hole in a waxy skull. She reached underneath and fished a pair of cheap sunglasses from the wild hair still growing on it.

"Ugh — ! These poor jerks weren't old time miners, Tom. The remains are new. And they weren't killed at a riverside picnic."

"No?"

"It's a body dump."

She returned to the river bank and scanned the hillside.

"Look, just to the west there. The hill falls back from the river."

"Unh-huh."

"Those bodies didn't get here the way we did. Come on."

She worked her way through the brush until she came to a little-used road angling up the hill away from the river.

"Let's see what we can see."

She led the way up the grade. In a hundred yards the narrow track joined a wider and well-maintained gravel road. They hiked along until they came to another intersection, this one conveniently marked with a small sign.

"N621. BLM road," said Wagstaff, pulling his mobile phone from a side pocket on his shorts. He unwrapped it from a plastic envelope designed to prevent water damage.

"Let's see if we've got a signal. Aha, yes we do. One bar."

"Give me that."

Marianne dialed 9-1-1.

"Hi, there. This is Officer Marianne Sarzeau, Placerville Police. I'm down here in Amador County, in the hills above the Whiskeyjack River. Uh, north side, maybe six or seven miles east from County Road 520."

Pause.

"I'm calling to report a body dump."

Pause.

"Right along the river here. Try Forest Road N-6-2-1. Multiple decedents. I saw at least one bullet hole."

Pause.

"The name is Sarzeau. Not my territory, I know that. And no, technically, we don't have an emergency. But I'm standing at a crime scene with really crappy cell service on a phone that's about to go as dead as these victims. I want you to alert the authorities. Call the sheriff."

Pause.

"Well, okay then, thank you."

▼

An hour later cops were on the scene in force. Somehow, a fleet of police cruisers, SUVs, and emergency vehicles had all made it down the narrow roadway to the river.

Amador County Deputy Sheriff Al Burns was leading the investigation with support from Tri-Town Special District police in the persons of Marianne's former colleagues, Wade Gawley and Ricky Moss, who drove out from Applefield.

"Sarzeau — hit the jackpot, I see," said Gawley. "After Tom writes this up, you'll be famous." He elbowed congratulations into her ribs. She stared at him.

"Jesus, Marianne, you okay? Things like this give me nightmares," said Moss.

A generator was humming. Lights set up on spindly poles brought the scene into blazing clarity for a photographer's pictures. A medical examiner dressed in a hazmat suit was separating the bodies, using a shoulder mike to record his findings.

Marianne and Wagstaff hovered in the background as the pros took over. While they were watching, yet another police car bounced down the steep incline. It parked behind the ambulance, and Officer Desmond Otis, Marianne's partner on the Placerville force, got out. After a quick and nervous peek at the bodies he ambled over to join them.

"Hello, Squeek. Yo, Tom."

"Dez. What are you doing here?"

"You kidding? We haven't had shit this bad since I joined up. Got to take a look."

"But you can't stand blood and guts."

Otis was black, and he liked to look street-wise tough.

"Hey now, I'm cool." He licked his lips. "The victims. How many, you think?"

"Nine, is what I hear. So far."

"Any idea who they might be?"

"No IDs. The ME is checking skull types. Undocumented immigrants, probably."

"Old enough to dry out." He covered his face with a handkerchief and inched forward for another view. "That's a blessing."

"One way to look at it," said Wagstaff.

5

IN A SUMPTUOUS wood-paneled room of the Capitol building in Washington, D.C., the U.S. Senate Committee on Homeland Security and Government Affairs was in session. Senator Lamar Daggett, the committee chair, was throwing softball questions at the Homeland secretary, Bertram "Bud" Quincy, an old friend.

"How would you characterize this past year? Have we had any slip-ups? Any terror events on our soil?"

"No, senator. We're clean. We've been vigilant, and we've been lucky."

"Well, now, I would hardly call a perfect record lucky. I take it that the terrorists have not yet abandoned their jihad on America? You did uncover threats?"

"Yes we did. Most were ill-conceived and failed of their own incompetence. A few were more serious. A combination of intelligence techniques — electronic surveillance, well-placed agents, tips from patriotic citizens . . . taken together they have allowed us to effectively disrupt all attacks."

"The threats were real."

"That's right. Our enemies are active. And so are we."

"I am aware, from the confidential briefings, of the more serious threats . . . they are frightening." Daggett wiped his brow with theatrical emphasis.

"Now, before I turn the questions over to my esteemed colleagues on the committee, allow me to state that we find our nation's safety in good hands — and to congratulate you, Secretary Quincy, and the department you lead, on how well you've fended off these cowardly, murderous, and heinous plots."

"Thank you, Senator. We at Homeland are mindful of our solemn obligations, and we value your positive assessment."

Sitting beside the department secretary was Jameson Sizemore, Quincy's dapper assistant deputy director for Immigration & Customs Enforcement. He was filling in for the undersecretary, who was touring Asia. As Senator Daggett gathered his papers, Sizemore leaned over to whisper in the secretary's ear.

"Hey, boss, all that love. Don't swim in it. The senator and his pals are talking *budget cuts.* We're doing great — yes, and still would be with a lot less dough, so they can fire more missiles into the Middle East."

Quincy held up a finger. "Senator, if I may."

"Go ahead."

"I want to state for the record that our efforts, while successful, have strained our ability to cope. I mentioned luck just now. Should it happen that our Department funding were in any way compromised, we'd need a lot more luck."

"Understood. You make a great case, Bud. I and the members of this committee know what a debt we owe to your excellent work. Tomorrow we'll be hearing from CENTCOM, and those military officers, on the firing line, they'll make a case as well. It's all in the balance."

Sizemore's face compressed into a deep scowl. "We are fucked. Fucked upside down, sir."

6

WHEN MARIANNE woke up in her Placerville apartment, it was 6:00 AM on a day off. She groaned. When she sat up, her head was spinning. She leaned forward and placed her face against upraised knees. She groaned again. Moving slowly and cautiously, she swiveled into a sitting position on the edge of the bed. After a while the world stabilized. She stood up, lost her balance and sat down heavily, bouncing on the mattress, waking Wagstaff.

"What's up, M?" He raised an arm, peered at his watch. "Geez, come back to bed, it's early."

"Can't sleep."

Wagstaff scratched his head. "You okay?"

"Dizzy. I may be sick."

"Get the waste basket from the bathroom."

"Not sure I can make it to the bathroom."

Wagstaff threw off their blanket, skipped into the bathroom, and came back with a little plastic tub. "Here you go."

Marianne dropped her head into her hands. "Yuck. I feel terrible."

"Nauseated?"

"Not exactly. Just . . . woozy."

"Morning sickness? Too soon for that, I read up."

"Or one of my seizures, not sure which."

Wagstaff was alarmed. "You and your seizures. I thought they were long gone."

"Not quite. Every now and then . . ." She trailed off.

". . . when your powers rev up."

"Yeah. There's a connection. And, and, I'm having dreams."

Wagstaff was even more alarmed. "What kind of dreams?"

"Bad ones. I'm being stalked by a monster."

"Christ, M. What is it? What's after you?"

"A big smoky thing."

"A bear?"

"No, it's not really physical. It's a presence."

"You mean, a supernatural presence. Something to do with your abilities, aptitudes, whatever."

"Yeah. Them."

"I think your powers are dangerous. You told me you wanted to get rid of them. Why not do it?"

"It's a big step. I am who I am, you know. A witch."

"Yeah. The strangest person I ever met. Somehow, I fell in love with her."

He leaned over and planted a kiss on her shoulder.

Marianne winced. "Losing whatever it is I've got — I'm not sure I'd still be *me.*"

Wagstaff sat down beside her, looked her in the eye. "I hear you. Even though, to tell the truth, I don't understand you."

He took her hand.

"Now I've been thinking. If you're having seizures, you aren't safe to drive. Officer Otis is going to find out. Your supervisor is going to find out. Goodbye career in law enforcement."

"Tell me about it."

"I'm going to make a suggestion. Don't get mad."

"I'm ready."

"Right . . . so . . . um, if you won't consider getting rid of your magical mojo, whatever that means, at least consider letting science have a look. Might learn something."

"Like what?"

"I don't know what. But I know a guy at State. He's a neuroscientist, has a lot of gear."

▼

"We're doing a symposium next week at U.C. Davis. You — a self-proclaimed witch — you'd be a terrific addition to our panel. This analysis is free if you agree to participate."

Marianne shrugged assent. "Why not?"

She and Wagstaff were sitting on hard plastic chairs in a spartan office on the Sacramento State campus. Unfiled manuscripts were piled high in the corners. The bookshelves on three walls were stuffed with volumes of medical texts, scientific publications, loose-leaf notebooks. A couple of dozen Post-It notes were stuck to the wall behind the desk where Dr. Robert Osborne, Wagstaff's faculty colleague, was ensconced; the research king in his untidy castle.

"Here, sign this."

Sweeping a Rubik's Cube and a Slinky aside, he pushed a sheet of paper across the desk.

"What is it?"

"The Pendleton Foundation, my grant guys. They're nervous about lawsuits and possessive about intellectual property. Without them I couldn't do anything. Any discoveries I might make, well, Pendleton wants to own them."

"They see money in this?"

Dr. Osborne grinned. "They're naïve." He picked up three small rubber balls and began juggling them as Marianne read the terms.

"All right, Doc. I'm yours. Have at me."

She signed on the dotted line.

Dr. Osborne led the way along a corridor, into an elevator, and down three flights into the basement, where a well-equipped lab awaited.

Over the course of the next three hours Marianne patiently endured a dozen wires glued to her head, a sonogram that revealed the size and shape of her brain, and a functional MRI inside a claustrophobic tunnel the size of a casket.

"What do you want me to do in here?"

"I dunno, something magical," said the good doctor, raising his attention momentarily from a computer display filled with wiggly lines.

"Call your ghost, M," suggested Wagstaff.

"I haven't seen him for months. I don't know if he's still around."

"Try."

"I need a mirror."

Dr. Osborne gestured, and a young assistant mounted a small mirror inside the tunnel.

One of Marianne's unusual attributes was the ability to communicate with the spirit world. Her particular supernatural contact was what students of the occult call a 'virtual visitor,' a ghost that only appears in mirrors. After many encounters, she had identified the apparition as her former police chief, Hector Ibañez, now deceased.

"Okay, here goes. Show yourself, Mr. G."

Dr. Osborne stared at his wiggly lines, looking for some change, but saw none.

"That was me without my talismans."

A year before, on a trip to France, Marianne had found a small chunk of granite in a Celtic tomb, connecting her with an ancient family heritage. She reached under her blouse where it was dangling from a leather necklace and gripped that in one hand. Then she gripped Ibañez' old police badge in the other.

"Okay, I'm calling. Boogey switch is on. Ghost? *Hey, you!*"

Dr. Osborne recoiled. "Hey you? What kind of a summons is that?"

"Sometimes it works."

Her ghost flickered briefly into view in the mirror, then disappeared. A voice in her head scoffed at the proceedings.

I'm not interested in stunts.

Afterward, Dr. Osborne paged through the experimental results on a computer monitor. He was bursting with pride and excitement.

"Pre-frontal lobe, it lights up as expected when I asked you about arresting a thief. Straightforward decision-making. You're probably an excellent police officer. That's what I would expect. That's what Tom told me, and the data confirms his good judgment."

"What about seizures?"

"I don't see any indications here. But look at this — the anterior cingulate cortex when you talked to your visitor, ghost, or whatever you think you saw just now. Wow. Hot, hot, hot. And the electro-encephalogram . . . it will take me a week to puzzle out this pattern." He pointed to a sharp spike that appeared among the squiggles at regular half-second intervals.

Marianne snorted. "Now I'm data points. How uplifting."

7

THE LONG BEACH, California, Office of Homeland Security Investigations was housed on Ocean Avenue in a pink granite structure that looked like a fancy hotel. There, Special Agent Jaromir Pavlov was staring out a third story window at a bad view of the harbor, idly watching a container ship pull into port.

A well-dressed woman knocked sharply on the open door of his tiny office and leaned in.

"Hey, Jerry, call for you."

Pavlov swiveled around in his chair to face her. "For me? Whatcha got, Ginger?"

"A guy at Home Depot thinks he's discovered a terrorist plot."

"You're kidding."

"Nope."

"Why pick on me?"

"Because you like this stuff. It's not as if you're overloaded with cases this week."

Pavlov frowned. "Or any week."

Pavlov was a black sheep in the department, a loner, a loose cannon. His superiors were careful not to assign him anything that carried political implications or opportunities to appear on local television.

"Okay, shit, put him on."

Ginger returned to her desk and punched a button. Pavlov's phone rang.

"This is Agent Pavlov. Who's calling?"

The voice on the other end was larded with self-congratulatory vigor. "Dick Kettleman, Mr. Pavlov, up here at Home Depot, the regional offices. You will be amazed at what I'm going to tell you."

"Kettleman? Home Depot?" Pavlov was making notes. "Amaze me."

"Well, sir, I manage the electrical department, and I buy for most of our Southern California stores. I've been going over some recent purchases — suspicious purchases, very suspicious — and I think we have a secret terrorist Al-Qaeda sleeper cell plotting against us right here in LA. What do you think of that?"

"I don't know what to think. Is this some kind of conspiracy theory of yours?"

"No sir."

"Does Home Depot sell guns and bombs now?"

"No sir, we surely don't."

Pavlov rattled a pencil on his desk. "Tell me the punch line."

"What we do sell are smoke detectors."

"Smoke detectors."

"That's right, sir. And, in the past two weeks, we have sold three hundred and twenty-five smoke detectors from seven different stores in the same local area. That's probably triple our usual inventory turnover, and here's the kicker — the customers paid in cash."

"Really. Sounds to me like somebody is putting up an apartment building."

"No, a contractor would buy directly from Kidde, the manufacturer, on a purchase order or previously established corporate account." Kettleman paused dramatically before continuing. "Do you see the pattern? These sales occurred in batches of twenty-five from each store, all on the same day. And then last week, it happened all over again. Twenty-five more from six of the same stores."

Pavlov leaned back in his chair and stared at the ceiling.

"Any other plots you've uncovered over there?"

"Well, I do keep an eye out. I'm a Marine, retired now, but — *semper fi*. I read the papers, and I hate to see the U.S. of A. getting pushed around by your jihadis and your terrorists. But plots? This is a first."

"How long have you been buying electrical products for Home Depot, Mr., ahh, Kettleman?"

"Fifteen years."

"I'm guessing you know your job. So, if you think this is unusual, it's unusual, okay? Grant you that. But I don't understand how smoke detectors could be involved in a terrorist plot."

"Radioactivity."

"Beg pardon?"

"Smoke detectors contain a small amount of radioactive material. That's how they do their detecting."

"You sell these things to ordinary customers, right? Dads and moms. How dangerous can they be?"

8

MARIANNE traded a day off with Dez Otis, got up late, showered, and prepared herself for a performance onstage. Wagstaff drove her down the hill and through Sacramento to Davis. By the time they found the Stroud Conference Center on the sprawling university campus, and a parking place within five blocks, they were running late.

Signs in the hallways pointed to Room 101. They pushed open a door and found themselves in a handsome amphitheater with curved rows of seats descending toward a stage where four learned men were sitting behind a long table. The assistant dean of the biology department was standing at a lectern. The session was already underway.

"Welcome, everyone, to U.C. Davis and to our monthly seminar on *Frontiers in Neuroscience.* Today we're going to vary our format just a little and discuss some of the deeper mysteries of the human brain. As you know, neurobiology has made tremendous strides in the past ten years. What do we know? A lot. What's left to learn? A lot more. Here's Dr. Rakesh Batterjee, our program director, to explain . . ."

The speaker took a seat at the side of the stage, and a brown man at the table waved, leaned forward, and pulled a microphone close. A hundred conference attendees clapped politely.

"Good morning, all. 'Pride goeth,' as the Bible says. Neuroscientists like me are proud of our achievements. Were we all wired up with our latest tech here, we could actually watch our minds consider the matters our panelists will put before us today. The question is, would we see thoughts in action? Trace their paths through the jungle of neural connections? Decode their meaning? Or, are we fooling ourselves? Ready for a fall?"

Wagstaff tugged on Marianne's hand, urging her to step forward and take up her seat. She resisted.

"I'm nervous. What did I let myself in for?"

"Don't be nervous. Only two of these guys are actually famous."

"Thanks, now I'm really nervous. I'm never going to do this again."

Dr. Batterjee raised an arm toward his colleagues. "So without further ado, say hello to my fellow panelists, Dr. Isaac Lunenberg, professor of neurobiology at Stanford" — the young man beside Dr. Batterjee nodded — "Dr. Milton Falkopf, professor of psychology at U.C. Berkeley" — a pudgy man in his sixties waved — "and Dr. Robert Osborne, associate professor of neuroanatomy at Sacramento State."

More applause. The audience felt blessed to be in the presence of such distinguished scientists.

"Now, please welcome our special guest, Ms. Marianne Sarzeau." Dr. Batterjee looked around the room, suddenly aware of an awkward problem. "Is she here?"

Marianne croaked out a groan and took her place among the academics. Dr. Batterjee was much relieved.

"Ms. Sarzeau is a police officer in Placerville. But that's not the reason she's joining us this morning. She is also a self-proclaimed . . . *witch.*"

There was a collective gasp from the audience.

Marianne waved sheepishly. "That's me."

Scattered applause. The audience was uncomfortable.

"I imagine that our guest has a very different perspective on mental activity than we do. What can you tell us, Ms. Sarzeau?"

Marianne surveyed the room. Of the hundred people in the audience, she noticed only a scattering of women. On the panel beside her, only men.

"Hi, everybody. I'm Marianne. I have a vagina. I just want to get that out there."

Nervous laughter.

"I'm not a 'self-proclaimed witch,' actually. It's more like Alcoholics Anonymous, I finally had to admit it. And people like me don't usually use that word. No warts on my nose, no black hat. No black cats either. We like to call ourselves 'adepts'."

Dr. Batterjee interjected. "A nice neutral description. Fair enough. What is it that adepts can do that the rest of us can't?"

Marianne squirmed around in her chair. "Well, uh, some of that is classified information. Secret fraternity stuff."

"Magicians never explain their tricks," griped Falkopf.

"Just kidding, doc. Some of us make potions, others cast spells, some see auras, and, uhh" — she paused, remembering the little gray jay on the river — "some of us, we have our familiar animals."

"Potions?" asked Dr. Batterjee, eyebrows raised.

"I stay away from those."

"Auras?"

"My father is the aura king. I can see other adepts, sometimes, when I'm cool, calm, and collected."

"What sort of spells?"

"They vary. Last year, believe it or not, I ran into some kids who could put you to sleep."

"Hypnosis," said Falkopf, "it's well-documented in the literature."

"Sleeping? I'd like to see that," chorused Lunenberg. He gestured to the audience with a mischievous grin. "How about it, out there?"

Laughter and applause. Cries of "go for it!" and "right on!"

Marianne scowled.

"Hear that? Let's see you put me to sleep."

Marianne turned fierce eyes upon the young professor. "You drank a lot of coffee this morning, I take it."

He laughed and raised his hands in protest. "On second thought, no thanks. I'd rather stay awake."

"I'll do it," volunteered Osborne. "But first, glue on the wires. Let's show our audience what's going on."

Marianne sat back and permitted technicians to stick a dozen sensors to her head. A digital projector flashed the result, a loose weave of wiggling lines, onto a gigantic screen behind the stage.

Marianne tapped a finger against her head.

"All right. A spell. These things have no real power on their own, but they help to focus attention. As does this small stone I'm wearing." She held up her granite talisman for all to see. She gripped the stone tightly, waited for the characteristic tingle it always produced in her hand, then pointed toward Dr. Osborne.

"Now then . . ."

> *Your eyes that shine, awake and bright*
> *Shall lose their luster — shut them tight!*
> *Nod thy head unto thy breast;*
> *Prepare thy soul for quiet rest.*
> *Thus I charge by thorn and flower;*
> *Bend your will to my sure power!*

On the screen behind Marianne, neural spikes jumped up out of the background rhythm of her ordinary brain waves. Osborne's eyes fluttered. He slumped forward. His head tilted down to the table. Falkopf grabbed his water glass to prevent a spill.

"Bob? You okay?"

Marianne was almost as shocked as everyone else. "Uhh, this is just one of several different sleeping spells. Like most, it's old and sort of old-fashioned. You know, who writes couplets anymore, ha ha?"

"Bob, wake up."

Murmurs of disapproval from the audience, suddenly displeased and suspicious. Marianne held up a hand. "It's okay, it's not a curse. I'll bring him back."

> *Sleeper, drifting far away,*
> *Heed my call and greet the day.*
> *Raise your nodding head from dreams;*
> *Seek the sun, search out its beams.*
> *Let lively purpose touch your brow;*
> *Obey this witch and wake up now!*

More strange spikes on the video projection. Osborne shook himself and sat up with a jolt. Dr. Batterjee cast an eye to the stunned audience and, acting to recover control of the seminar, fashioned a giddy smile. "Whoa there. Long night, Bob?"

Osborne managed a wave and a nod. He looked dazed.

The attendees were on edge. A few people laughed nervously. Others clapped to signify their astonishment. Standing in the back of the amphitheater, Wagstaff smiled. Marianne's antics filled him with pride.

"That — that was pretty cool," said Lunenberg. "But Bob here? He looks a little green. Glad I ducked the challenge."

"Yes, very impressive," sniffed Falkopf. "But science is nothing if not skeptical. Let's remind ourselves — Ms. Sarzeau is really Dr. Osborne's guest. He picked her. Without wishing to give offense or belabor an ugly possibility — they might be working together to fool us all."

Dr. Batterjee intervened to keep the discussion civil. "Now, Milt, you saw those spikes on the EEG? Where have you ever seen them before?"

"I didn't really notice," grumped the older man.

"Never, that's where. Either we've got a technical fault in our system, or we're looking at new data."

Osborne seemed to regain his faculties. "New data, definitely. There's more. Marianne casts an occasional spell, but that's not all. Her main and most unusual ability is communication with the spirit world."

"Really, Bob," said Lunenberg. "Don't push it."

Marianne held up a hand. "It's true. I know a ghost. I'll show you."

"This is ridiculous," said Falkopf.

Dr. Batterjee, however, was smiling with suppressed glee. "Here's our chance, gentlemen, to test our knowledge and our theories. Exactly what this little gathering is all about. Ms. Sarzeau's claims are obviously impossible. Or . . . . . . let's find out."

"Here's the deal," said Marianne. "I don't see *ghosts,* just one, my former police chief, who died investigating a drug ring a couple of years ago. And he's kind of shy — he only appears in mirrors."

Osborne held up a mirror attached to a little stand and placed it on the table before Marianne.

"I don't always make contact, and when I do, the bad news is — you probably won't see him. Disappointing, I know."

She displayed her two talismans. "To help me focus, I use these objects. The chief's old police badge, and the stone I already showed you."

Marianne gripped her talismans tightly in each hand and stared into the mirror.

"Hello, Chief, wherever you are. Help me show these people what's really going on."

As she spoke, her brain waves changed. A dense pattern of spikes rippled across the screen. But her ghost did not appear.

"Okay, nothing so far. When this happens, I have to *command* his presence, like so —"

She opened her mouth to yell at the mirror, but before she could make a sound, there he was, a shadowy form moving in the glass. A voice in her mind made the spikes in the overhead display double in size.

"What do you think you're doing, Miss Cutie Pie?"

"Ah! There you are. Hello, I'm demonstrating you." She turned the mirror toward the audience. "Anyone see him?"

Grumbles of negation from the onlookers.

"You should be more careful."

"I know, you like privacy, but it's okay. Wave to the crowd."

"You are being very foolish. We are not alone."

"No, we're not. It's a seminar. Lighten up."

"What if others can see?"

"Others? What others?"

Marianne squinted into the audience. Her ghost vanished.

"Whoops, he's gone."

Dr. Batterjee shrugged disappointment. "That was brief. Anyone out there spot anything?"

"We recorded the brain wave spikes. We can analyze them in detail later," said Lunenberg. "But I'd like to point out the sequence. Cortical signals propagate one way during observation, and reverse themselves when the subject is imagining something. We see this all the time. But here, unless I'm mistaken, the pulses are traveling both ways at once. Overlapping. That's unusual in my experience."

Falkopf shook his head. "I saw nothing, because, most probably, there was nothing to see. Instead of occult powers, I suggest that our guest here is simply a capable woman whose personal rituals coordinate separate and discrete parts of her brain — parts that most of us can't control — thus enabling her to establish a rare kind of expertise."

Marianne looked hurt. Lunenberg regarded her sympathetically.

"What, may I ask, persuaded you to join us today?" he wondered. "What were you hoping to get out of this?"

Marianne removed the sensors from her head one by one. "I was hoping a group of smart guys like you might know how I could get rid of my powers, if that's what they are."

"Why on Earth?"

"Being an adept is not that much fun, doc. I'm going to be a mom, and I'd like to be a normal one."

None of the esteemed researchers had the slightest idea how to help. After politely allowing each of the panelists to express some inane pleasantries, Dr. Batterjee called the seminar to a close. Wagstaff pushed through the departing crowd and hugged Marianne.

"You were great, M. Wow. They'll be thinking about this for a while."

"Let's get out of here," she said, looking grim.

As they moved toward the exit, Marianne became aware of a faint glow in her mind.

"Uh-oh, my ghost warned me."

"What?"

"Others. I sense another adept."

"Where?"

"Not sure."

Outside, nearing Wagstaff's big Toyota FJ Cruiser, a scrawny man in jeans and a ragged sweat shirt bounded after them. He tugged awkwardly at Marianne's sleeve.

"Wait, wait up."

Marianne turned around. Her face fell.

"Bo? Bo Dingell? Jesus, what are you doing here?"

Dingell removed a dusty baseball cap and stared at Marianne with frank admiration.

"I saw your ghost."

"No way, José."

"Oh yeah I did. In that mirror there."

"You? You've become an adept? Since when?"

Marianne forced herself to relax. Sure enough, the glow she had noticed was emanating from the unkempt creature confronting her.

"I woke up. It happened all at once, right after you arrested me. I don't drink anymore. Don't do drugs. I cleaned up my trucks."

"That's great, Bo. Stay out of trouble."

"I can see things now. In a different way. Colors, kind of. And you, you're green. Thought I should tell you, thought you'd like to know."

9

LATER, in her Placerville apartment, Marianne dragged Wagstaff into the bathroom.

"So you agree with that guy Falkopf. I'm just a chick who knows how to meditate."

"I didn't say that. You're putting words in my mouth."

"Let's try our own little experiment. Science in action."

She gripped Chief Ibañez' police badge and stared into the mirror. "Oh-ho, Mr. Ghost, show yourself. I need some help with my future husband." When nothing happened for a few seconds, she shouted *"Hey you!"* for good measure.

"Whoa, not so loud, M. The neighbors . . ."

After a few more seconds, the mirror darkened, and a ghostly shadow faded into view, obscuring the couple's reflections.

"Marianne . . ."

"Okay, Doubting Tom, here he is."

"Unh-huh. I worry about you, babe."

Marianne ignored the remark.

"Question, Chief — after we talked earlier today at that stupid seminar, I ran into a guy who made me jumpy. He's a half-wit slacker, a minor criminal or maybe worse. Usually when we cross paths he's drunk and disorderly, a real pain in the ass. Now he claims to be an adept. How could this be? What's going on?"

"I don't know."

"But you warned me about him."

"I sensed a presence. It was vague."

"Ask around, will you? Talk to your ghost buddies. I don't like this."

"No buddies over here, Sarzeau. But I will make inquiries."

Marianne's tension level dropped a notch. "Can't ask for more than that."

"Who's there with you now?"

"Uhh, Tom Wagstaff, my guy. Don't worry, he can't see you."

"But you wish he could."

"That would be a big help in the true love department."

"Sorry, you know how it works. I don't make the rules."

The ghostly image evaporated. The mirror cleared. Standing beside her, Wagstaff was white as a sheet.

"Tom?"

"Yeah?"

"You okay?"

"I saw something."

"Really?"

"Yeah. For just a moment. A blurry shadow."

She hugged him, bestowed a grateful kiss.

"So now you don't have to believe in me anymore. You *know.*"

Wagstaff walked back and forth in the small space between sink and toilet. He hammered a fist on the now vacant mirror.

"Listen, M. Let's say it's all true. My God, the supernatural! Like in fairy tales."

"Right."

"Well, fairy tales are stocks of wisdom packaged up in simple stories. And what do they all say? Don't fuck with the universe. Bad things happen."

"Like what?"

"Like your seizures, your woozy spells, I don't know."

"Hmm."

"You've got to lose these powers. Be normal. You said it yourself."

"But no one knows how."

"Got to be a way, gotta try."

"I'm ready. Unless it's going to kill me, or our unborn son."

"Come on, Marianne, don't be ridiculous."

"Ridiculous? I'm Ridiculous? Oh — are we having a fight? Is this what married life is going to be like?"

"Hey, ease up . . . I just want you to be safe and sound."

▼

Summertime in Placerville.

Blue sky above the tree-lined hillsides. Temperature in the nineties. The living was easy, but parking was not. Tourists in shorts and T-shirts on their way to and from the High Sierra were crowding Main Street, clogging the sidewalks, claiming every available patch of asphalt for their cars, vans, and SUVs. Irritated locals were forced to patrol the side streets, muttering curses as they searched for remote places to drop their rides. Had Marianne been on duty, she would have been able to ticket a lot of violators.

Instead, she was in the Golden Goose Omelette Shoppe, her favorite café, having lunch. Wagstaff was with her, and after a while a flustered Lorraine joined them.

"I parked behind the Pantry in their lot. All I could find, in spite of strong language I haven't used in years. I hope no one notices," she said.

"We ordered already."

Lorraine checked the menu, ordered a scramble with red potatoes and mushrooms. As the waitress poured iced tea, she noticed the subdued mood of her companions.

"You're awfully quiet today. What's the latest? Seen the doctor? Pregnancy confirmed?"

Marianne nodded. "Unh-huh. I'll pop in about eight months." Wagstaff remained silent.

"All right, you two. Something's wrong. What? What is it?"

"Nothing. Pregnancy is tough. I'm sick every morning."

"Witchery, that's what's tough," said Wagstaff.

Lorraine sat back. She looked from one to the other, trying to decide who was responsible for the obvious tension.

"You know, marriage isn't all milk and honey. The secret is respect. Respect and, uhh, constant adjustment."

"Tom wants me in therapy."

"I never said that."

"No, but that's what it amounts to. As if being adept was just a bad habit."

"Hey, no fair. I saw that blur."

"Whoa, boys and girls, wait a minute." Lorraine's eyebrows knitted together in envious dismay. "Tom, you saw Marianne's ghost?"

"Just a ripple in the mirror, but it convinced me."

"Damn, I never have. When you two make up you can pity me."

"No big deal. Don't worry about it," said Wagstaff.

"I won't. In fact, until I saw your long faces, I was feeling pretty good."

Lorraine's sly smile signaled a secret ready to burst forth.

Marianne leaned forward. "News? You and Howard?"

"As a matter of fact . . ."

"Hey! Tell us!"

"Howard has proposed. I said yes. We're going to tie the knot at his house on the Fourth."

"Wow, you guys are moving fast."

Lorraine grinned.

"I think Howard's worried we don't have a lot of time."

"Nonsense."

"Anyway, we want you two to stand up for us. Marianne maid of honor, Tom best man."

Part TWO

10

NEXT MORNING Marianne was up before dawn strapping on her gear. Dark blue blouse and pants. Radio mike on her shoulder, .40 caliber Glock 22 on her hip. Placerville Police cap fitted over her hair, which she had swept back and tied into a ponytail.

Given her sensitive stomach, she avoided her usual cup of strong coffee, and munched dry toast instead.

She leaned over and kissed a sleeping Wagstaff lightly on the cheek, tucked her little 9-mm Beretta PX4 Storm into an ankle holster, and was out of the apartment and down the stairs, ready for another day fighting crime in Placerville.

At the station she ran into Officer Otis, also arriving for a day on patrol.

"Morning, Dez. Got anything on our body dump?"

Otis shook his head. *"Nada.* It's all sitting with the Amador sheriff's boys. If they had made any progress, we'd hear whoops and hollers."

After a dull hour rolling through town in her police cruiser without being called upon to deal with a single traffic violation, domestic dispute, drunken parolee, or drug abuser, she circled back to the department, sat down at a desk and made a phone call.

"Al Burns, please."

"Morning, Amador County Sheriff's Operations, Burns here."

"Hi, Al — Marianne."

"Officer Sarzeau. How are tricks in Placerville?"

"Quiet. Boring, if you want to know. I'm calling about the body dump down there on the Whiskeyjack. I'm the one who found it, and I was wondering . . . any good news for me?"

"What a scene. We've got piles of evidence, but no suspects."

"Theory of the crime? Time of death? Any indications?"

"The victims were all shot, looks like one at a time over a period of years. But no bullets, so no ballistics. No IDs either, but I think you already knew that when we were all down there sorting out the bodies."

"Yeah. So, what's the plan of attack?"

"To tell the truth, we don't really have one. We made sure the story got reported in the papers. The *Bee* did a piece. I interviewed on Channel Four. Hell, your friend Wagstaff published an account in the *Courier,* right?"

"You're waiting for a tip."

"That's about it. Meanwhile, I've got a drowning on Upper Bar Lake to worry about, and a head-on collision down where 520 meets Red Hill Road."

"I know that intersection. It's a bad one."

"Three fatalities."

"Look, Al, since the body dump investigation has stalled, mind if I take a look?"

"Tell you what — you can have copies of the pictures, the ME report, and so on. Get your barf bag ready."

"Duly warned. Thanks. If my sharp eye spots anything, you'll be the first one I call."

Marianne hung up the phone and breathed a sigh of relief. Getting cooperation with another law enforcement agency was always tricky.

Later in the afternoon Marianne and Otis were bumping downhill in the ruts angling off Forest Road N621, approaching the Whiskeyjack River. Marianne was at the wheel, and Otis was sorting through a stack of photocopies.

"Where'd you get these?"

"I drove down to Jackson. Burns made copies."

"Hard to look at."

They stopped on the flat shelf of land between the cliff face and the riverbank and stepped out for a look around. Otis was nervous.

"Why are we here?"

Marianne was uncertain of the answer. She felt curiosity, a sense of the crime's injustice, and a little touch of dread that she wanted to overcome, like scratching an itch.

"I don't think this case has Al's full attention. Maybe his team missed something. And . . . I need a witness if anyone claims I screwed up a crime scene."

She worked her way through the brambles to the undercut hollow where the bodies had been found. Nothing out of the ordinary remained to be seen. She bent over and moved slowly back and forth, examining the weeds and gravel.

"What did they miss that we might find, huh? Answer me that," grumbled Otis.

"An ID or two would be nice, don't you think? Something to jump start the process?"

"Good luck, partner. I was watching, they scoured the place."

"You're right. Worth a shot, though."

She led the way back to the police cruiser, laid out the photocopies on the hood, and began thumbing through them.

"Looks like the victims could be Mexicans. Undocumented aliens, or members of a gang."

"Not all." Otis fingered one of the pictures, the sharply focused profile of a man's head. The flesh was still intact, except for a ragged depression above the ear where a bullet had penetrated. "This looks like a honky dude to me."

Marianne's lip curled. "Yuck. And he hasn't been dead too long."

"Let's get out of here," said Otis. He was bouncing up and down on the balls of his feet, very ill at ease.

"What's biting you?"

"I know you can see ghosts and shit. What if the dead guys left their ghosts here? What if they don't like us?"

"I don't sense any ghosts, Dez. Jesus, calm down."

Weeahh!

While they were studying the ugly pictures, a little gray jay flew out of the trees and landed on Marianne's cap. It pecked at the Placerville Police logo. Marianne grinned.

"Hello, there."

She dug into a pocket and produced a handful of peanuts. The jay hopped onto her fingertips and hungrily stuffed them into its beak. Otis stepped away from his fellow officer in alarm. The bird flew away out of sight.

"What the fuck?"

"It's a jay. A whiskeyjack."

"Like the river?"

"Same name anyway. That little bird, or another one a lot like it, is how I found this place."

"You're kidding."

"Nope. I thought he might still be around."

"How do we know there's not some kind of ghost inside?"

Marianne was getting set to object, then thought better of the idea.

"Maybe you're right. Maybe it is a ghost."

"Jesus Christ."

The bird reappeared, carrying a dime in its bill. It dropped the coin on the stack of photocopies, scurried around the hood of the car, then fluttered away into the trees.

"Uh-oh."

Soon it was back again, this time carrying a shiny tie clip. It dropped the thing beside the coin. Otis picked it up. The bird ran across the hood, flew up, and pecked Otis' hand. Otis dropped the clip and leapt backward.

"Hey, hey, hey, bird. Get the fuck away from me."

Marianne couldn't stop herself from laughing at Otis' discomfort. She retrieved the tie clip and examined it.

"No initials engraved or anything. Damn."

Weeahh!

The jay was back yet again with yet another trinket, this one dangling from a little steel ring. Marianne held out her hand, and the bird dropped it into her open palm.

"Thanks, little guy."

The jay seemed to make a bow, then flew away upriver.

Marianne held the shiny item up for a close look. It appeared to be the souvenir reproduction of a military dog tag. A pair of crossed flags were embossed on one side, and an enigmatic inscription was engraved on the other . . .

MC3RKN
This Dog Hunts

"What about it, Dez? Look like an ID to you?"

Otis was amazed and troubled by the strange business he was witnessing. "A key fob. Some guy with fond memories of his military service, you ask me."

"Hmm."

"Shit, Squeek, it's stuff like this that keeps me awake at night. I hate to hang around with you."

11

"AUNT IMOGEN?"

"Yes, who's calling?"

"Hi, it's Marianne."

"Mary Ann. Good heavens, how are you?"

"I'm fine. How's life in Georgia?"

"Not too bad. We had a tornado last week about twenty miles west of here. And it's hot. The humidity makes the air feel like a blanket."

"I'll bet. Hot here too."

The awkward pleasantries being exchanged on the telephone reflected Marianne's estrangement from her aunt; a woman, she had learned, who was involved with her father both before and long after he married her mother. A bitter divorce resulted, and Mom moved to Louisiana, where she died in the aftermath of Hurricane Katrina. A year ago Marianne figured out how to forgive her father, and was now trying to forgive the woman she had lived with all through high school in Sacramento.

"Listen, I'm sorry I haven't written or anything — I'm looking for Dad. I understand you two are in touch."

"I was told the secret's out . . ."

"Can I talk to him?"

"We don't actually live together, you know."

"I know. Dad explained. Got a number?"

"Yes, but he's out of the country. I don't know where, and I couldn't tell you if I did."

"How about Ray Bagwell?"

"They're together, running down bad guys, I suppose. But you know all about that, you're part of the act now. Agent Broomhandle." She chuckled.

"Yeah, that's my asset label. Damn, I need some help."

"Here's what I've got."

She recited a telephone number. Marianne promised to keep in touch, they both professed their love, and the call ended on a conciliatory note.

Marianne stared at the number. She had never heard of the mysterious area code 789. She dialed, was greeted by a dour robot, answered a long sequence of queries about her business by pressing numbers on her keypad, and wound up listening to Bagwell's voicemail message.

"Hi, Ray — it's me, Broomer. I need some help with an ID from a case I'm working. Here's the skinny: looks like a military dog tag, but it's really just a key fob. One side has a little crossed-flag insignia. There are no serial numbers, but the other side shows an inscription: *M-C-3-R-K-N* — Initials? Why the '3'? — and the phrase *This Dog Hunts,* some kind of motto, maybe. Army man? What in the world am I looking at?"

▼

Marianne was eating a solitary lunch on the shady deck outside her second-floor flat in the Golden Nugget Apartments when Bagwell called back.

"Broomhandle?"

His voice crackled.

"Hi, Ray. Any news from American TV & Appliance?"

"Yes. Here . . ."

Whistling interference in the phone line interrupted him. Marianne pulled the receiver away from her ear and waited for the awful noise to subside.

"Ray?"

". . . here's what I've got — the letters M-C-3-R-K-N? Most likely an abbreviation for *McCracken.* The crossed flags indicate Signal Corps. Looks like you've got yourself a retired Army intelligence officer — name, McCracken, *Floyd.*"

"McCracken — of course, the three Cs. But Floyd? Nobody names a kid 'Floyd' anymore."

"Someone did."

Another howl echoed through the connection.

"Where are you, anyway?" asked Marianne.

"Didn't you hear that? In the wind, as always. Where the Kalashnikovs roam. It's Midnight."

"How's Dad?"

"He's good. We're wrapping up."

Marianne thought for a moment.

"What else? If McCracken is retired, what's he doing in my body dump?"

"Can't tell you much. It's a security deal. Don't want to step on

Homeland's toes."

"Homeland Security? Why not?"

"Asset protocol. Look, if you need to follow up, call Homeland down in LA. Long Beach, actually. Investigations & Customs Enforcement. Ask for Jerry Pavlov."

"Pavlov?"

Another burst of windy static effectively cut off all communication. Marianne put down the phone, opened her notebook, and wrote down the name.

12

IN LONG BEACH, Jerry Pavlov was bent over his desk, doodling. At his left hand was a list prepared by his Home Depot informant, itemizing the details of each store that sold multiple smoke alarms for cash; seven in all. At his right hand was a paper map of Los Angeles' eastern suburbs printed from his computer. He was looking at the list and circling the locations on his map. Telegraph Road in Commerce; Whittier Boulevard in Pico Rivera; Washington Boulevard, Whittier; La Mirada Boulevard, La Mirada; Alondra Boulevard, Paramount; Firestone Boulevard, Downey.

Thus plotted, the store locations formed the perimeter of an almost perfect circle with a five mile radius centered on the City of Downey.

"Hmm."

He stood up from his desk and strolled over to the window, watching water traffic while he mulled the situation. Downey. Some bozo or bozos operating from Downey knew enough to use several sources to cover their tracks, but were too lazy to vary the distances involved. Amateurs. At first he was inclined to dismiss the whole thing, which appeared to be a harebrained scheme, if it was even a scheme at all. But the more he thought about it, the more he thought there might be a connection to other hostile actors. The problem was — where in Downey were these morons hiding?

He was still standing at the window several minutes later when his phone rang.

"Yo, Ginger."

"Hi, Jerry. Got a call coming in from some chick in the sticks wants to talk to you. She's working on a murder case."

"Is she a reporter? Tell her to call the cops."

"She *is* a cop. She says it might involve Homeland personnel."

"Oh fuck. All right, put her on."

"Hello, Agent Pavlov?"

"Speaking."

"This is Officer Marianne Sarzeau, Placerville police. I have discovered a murder victim up here in the foothill wilderness named Floyd McCracken. I've done some investigating, and I have learned that Homeland may be involved. What do you say?"

Pavlov frowned at the phone. "Who told you to call me?"

"Another security agency gave me your number."

"Oh sure. Who?"

Marianne thought it best, for the moment, to be coy. "Sorry, my information is confidential. I've been told to button my lip. Does the name mean anything to you?"

"McCracken?"

"Floyd McCracken. Ex-Army intelligence."

"I don't personally recall that name." He was staring at his Home Depot list, still pondering the smoke alarm problem. "But I'll check around the office."

"Please. You're my only lead."

Pavlov tapped his map. "Sarzeau is it? A cop, right? Sworn to the oath?"

"Yes indeed. You bet."

"All right then, officer, tell me this — why would anyone buy three hundred and twenty-five smoke alarms for cash? What would you do with them?"

It took Marianne a while to grasp the notion. "I don't know, detect a lot of smoke?"

"I doubt it."

"Is there a black market? Are they illegal over the border? Good God, smoke detectors? Is this how Homeland spends my tax money?"

"I'm laughing too, but I'm having a slow threat week."

"Wait a minute. Aren't those things radioactive? I mean, that's what people worry about, right? You're safe from burning to death, but you stare up at the ceiling at night — that little green light is on — you're getting zapped."

"Maybe so, at some tiny dosage."

Marianne paused to consider the matter further. Then, "You're Homeland, right? So you're worried about terrorists."

"That we are."

"Think dirty bomb."

Pavlov grunted. "Not much dirt for a bomb. I'll call you back if I get anywhere with your victim's name."

"Counting on it."

▼

Marianne was standing under Placerville's iconic bell tower writing a ticket for illegal parking when Pavlov's call came in on her personal phone.

"Sarzeau here."

"Jerry Pavlov."

Marianne crumpled the ticket and shooed the relieved motorist away in order to concentrate.

"What's the scoop?"

"Here's what you need to know — Floyd McCracken is — was, anyway — a civil rights lawyer and private investigator up there in the Big Valley, trying to make life work for a bunch of illegals."

"Undocumented, you mean. That's how we refer to them," said Marianne, paying respect to political correctitude.

"Right, un-fucking-documented. Anyway, he's tied into a non-profit activist group, the *Bracero Brotherhood Dot Org*. They're a 501(c)(3) company based in Lodi. Bleeding hearts. But this guy — he's also a spy for us."

Marianne almost shouted aloud. But then she calmed down and adopted a more demure tone.

"Oh really."

"We were hoping he might help us track down the *Fast Pass Gang*."

"Huh?"

"That's what we call them. Because they move fast. Criminals mostly. One day we've got them under surveillance in Mexico City, and a week later they're on the streets of Chicago. They've got money, and they've got a ride."

"No more tunnels under the fence?"

"So twentieth century. Listen, there might be a connection here. Maybe McCracken was onto the smugglers and their methodology, and that's what got him killed. Any ideas?"

"Not a one. Sorry."

"I'm looking for the faintest hook."

"I'll check with the team, best I can do."

"Appreciate it."

13

NEXT MORNING Marianne was on the phone to Al Burns again, repaying his favor and hoping to earn another one.

"Hey, Al, I figured out the name of one of the murder victims in our body dump."

"Sarzeau. Glad to hear it."

"Got a pen?"

"Shoot."

"Floyd McCracken. He's a lawyer, ex-Army, private investigator for one of those activist groups working with undocumented aliens."

"Unh-huh."

"The Bracero Brotherhood. Down in Lodi."

"That's great, Sarz. A break. I'm writing it down."

"Thought you'd like to follow up."

Marianne waited nervously for Burns' reply, hoping her personal involvement from the beginning trumped her obvious lack of jurisdiction.

"We will, we're on it. But just at the moment, we're also hot after a meth operation down the hill a ways. My boss is all over my ass."

"Understood, gotta stay with the priorities."

Deep breath.

"Mind if I have a chat with the Braceros?"

"Go ahead. Let me know what you find out. Victim ID or not, that case is cold as a turnip."

▼

Marianne scoured the online search pages and discovered that the Bracero Brotherhood offices were located on East Lockeford Street in the northeast corner of Lodi, fifty miles south of Placerville. She found a telephone number and called, but the woman on the line spoke only in rapid and unintelligible Spanish. After several repetitions, she thought she heard the name, *Señora Carrasco,* and maybe *aquí esta tarde.*

"This afternoon?"

"Sí."

She had an appointment scheduled with her obstetrician in Shingle Springs just before the lunch hour. After some thought, she decided to use that as an excuse to be away from her normal patrols for half the afternoon. So, following a routine examination and some happy talk from her doctor, she drove down to Lodi in her department wheels. She was hoping for another break in her case, or failing that, a terminal breakdown of the creaky Dodge Charger she loathed but could not seem to drive into the ground.

She pulled into the gravel parking lot of a whitewashed Quonset hut at Tokay and Lockeford on the east edge of town. The Bracero non-profit was housed between rundown stucco buildings. A dubious legal aid office stood on one side, and a seedy urgent care clinic on the other. All the signs were in Spanish. Across the road, table grapes were ripening in a vineyard that reached to the hazy horizon. The nearest tree was blocks away. Valley heat threatened to roast Marianne as she made her way to the company entrance. It made her feel queasy.

Inside, the high curved ceiling lifted some of the heat away. But without air conditioning, Marianne was still broiling in her police uniform.

"¿Te puedo ayudar, señorita?"

The woman behind the linoleum-covered counter appeared to be in her late teens.

"Speak English?"

"¡Señora — la policía!" she shouted.

An older woman came hustling out of a back office, prepared for confrontation. When she saw Marianne, relaxed and smiling, she smiled too.

"Buenas tardes, how can I help you?"

"I'm investigating a series of murders up in the foothills — cold case — but we've identified one of the victims. Someone named Floyd McCracken? Ring a bell? We think he worked for you."

The older woman's face fell. "Mr. McCracken, he is dead?"

"'Fraid so."

"I am so sad to hear this news."

"I'm sorry to bring it. Maybe, with your help, we can at least nail the people who killed him."

The woman shut her eyes while she absorbed the information. Then she turned to a filing cabinet, yanked open a drawer, and busied herself sorting through papers.

"Mr. McCracken was our friend. He was fierce about justice, and volunteered his services to us, but we did not employ him."

"Do you possibly have a record of his last job?"

The woman removed a sheaf of papers from the filing cabinet. She read from a report. "Golden Harvest Labor LLC. On Latrobe Road."

"Latrobe? Which end?"

"South, near Jackson."

"Got it. Thank you very much, *muchas gracias,* this is a big help."

The woman adopted a stern pose.

"This company, these people, they are *bastardos.* They fix up jobs for my *hermanos,* and they steal their money. And they threaten them to shut up about their smuggling operation. They have *no* honor and *no* shame."

"Hmm. So they smuggle people into the country?"

"We believe that is so."

"McCracken was looking to go after them?"

"We are preparing to sue, to bring them to face the law."

Marianne scowled. "Isn't that a tricky business? Some of the people you represent are, uh, undocumented themselves, right? People who needed some smuggling?"

"That may be true, I cannot say. But even the undocumented have rights. The courts have ruled on this. It is, ah, what do you say? *Probado en el tribunal* — settled law."

"Good luck, then."

Marianne returned to her police cruiser feeling upbeat and excited. The detective at work! Thoughts of pregnancy and witchcraft were far away, banished by pride. She reached for the door handle, and suddenly her world was spinning. She gripped the handle tightly, cracked the door open. She attempted to slide into the driver's seat, but bent over and vomited instead.

"Ohhhhhhh . . ."

She leaned against the fender, breathing hard. It took some time for the world to come back into focus, for her stomach to calm down. She addressed the embryo growing inside her, which she had learned that morning, was about to become a full-fledged fetus.

"You in there. You are big trouble, know that?"

In response, she thought she detected the tiniest kick and heard a little cry.

▼

Marianne sat in her cruiser for ten minutes before she felt well enough to drive. Then she powered up her hated Charger and roared away into the foothills.

A few miles outside Jackson she turned north onto Latrobe Road. This minor highway was the main artery between many a foothill town and the state capital, and it was also the location of many a ranch. Some of them were funky reminders of bygone days, whose dilapidated buildings and junked automobiles testified to a rougher era. Others were playthings of the wealthy, shining examples of modern architecture and the latest animal husbandry techniques, as startling and well-kept as Big City mansions. When she arrived at Old Sacramento Road, she swung downhill, moving out of the surrounding trees into open country.

Golden Harvest Labor LLC was housed in a spacious complex together with Golden Egg Family Farms, an ostrich-raising operation. Their territory abutted a long line of oak trees on one end and a suburban housing development far away on the other.

Marianne cruised past the main entrance and parked at the gate of a dirt access road. She got out and surveyed the premises. Golden Whatever was neither funky nor a plaything. Several large corrals enclosed fluffy two-legged animals she took to be ostriches. A maintenance yard contained old trucks, tractors, a backhoe, plastic storage tanks, and numerous farm implements. Several large prefab metal buildings, painted white, served as barns and workshops. Beyond them she could see a three-story farmhouse standing inside a ring of tall poplars. The peaked roof was studded with gables. Gingerbread details decorated the veranda that encircled the entire building. The house was nicely painted in mustard hues with white trim, and it was at least a century old.

She flicked on her radio and called in to Placerville.

"Hello, Sarzeau here. Doctor's appointment is over. I am pregnant for sure. Tell Officer Otis I will be back inside the city limits in one hour."

She was skirting the truth, confident that she was going to get away with it. But just as she hung up her mike and started onto the ranch property, Otis' voice blared out over the speaker on the Charger's roof.

"Hey, Squeek, what the fuck? You've been gone all day. How long does it take for your doctor to issue a free pass?"

Marianne groaned and toggled the mike.

"Dez, Marianne. Take it easy on me. Feeling sick, woozy, throwing up."

"I heard that's what happens to pregnant women, but it's bullshit. You're screwing around with that body dump business."

Marianne clicked her tongue. "Got me. Keep it quiet, okay? But just so somebody knows, I'm scouting out Golden Harvest Labor LLC. I just ID-ed one of our victims. He is — was — a private eye working for one of those activist groups. I'm standing at his last-known location, Latrobe Road near Old Sacramento."

"Want backup?"

"I'll be okay. I'm in the colors, I look official, no one will mess with me unless I go crazy."

"You are crazy, so watch your ass."

"Roger that."

She clipped the mike back on the dashboard and set off across the fields. As she moved, ostriches in the nearest corral raised their heads. Some trotted away, but three approached the fence and matched her pace. One of them leaned over and attempted to peck her cap.

Between corrals, a lane wide enough for a tractor opened up. She turned onto the dirt track, walking obliquely toward the ranch buildings. As she drew nearer she spotted a couple of rusty cargo containers. An old motorhome and a moldering fifth-wheel trailer were standing nearby, looking forlorn.

Beyond the ostriches, another corral held a pair of black and white llamas. Marianne was admiring their eyelashes when an old Jeep Cherokee outfitted with oversize tires rolled up. The door opened and a lanky cowboy stepped out. He held up his hand, palm out, to intercept her.

"Hold it, officer. This is private property."

Marianne regarded the fellow with cool detachment. "And who are you?"

"Luther Handy, ranch foreman. May I ask your business here?"

"You certainly may. I'd like to talk to anyone on the property who can tell me about a man named Floyd McCracken. Would that be you?"

▼

The ranch proprietor rose from his desk and shook Marianne's hand with a welcoming smile as Handy escorted her into his office.

"Officer Sarzeau? From Placerville? You're a little out of your way down here in the county, aren't you?"

"Your name, sir?"

"Alejandro Muñoz."

"The owner of this place?" She waved a hand. "Ranch, farm, business, whatever?"

"Golden Egg Family Farms, that's right. I am the owner."

"And do you also operate a labor contracting service from this location? Golden Harvest Labor?"

Muñoz leaned back in his chair, slowing himself down to deal with a perceived adversary he might have underestimated.

"Well now, officer, yes we do. We are one of the three largest labor contractors north of Fresno."

"Thank you. Obviously, we're not in Placerville. I'm here today assisting my colleagues in the Amador County Sheriff's Office. We are — jointly — investigating a series of murders. Corpses have turned up in a body dump along the Whiskeyjack River."

"That sounds ugly."

"It is. Some of the victims have been dead for a while. You don't want to look."

"No indeed, Ms. Sarzeau, I lead a sheltered life. What on Earth gave you the idea that my company, or any of my employees, or myself for that matter, could possibly have to do with this?"

"Most of the victims appear to be Mexicans or Mexican-Americans. Even when bodies are all dried up, as these are, forensics can often determine ethnicity by skull shapes."

"Go on. I smell a hook coming."

"Yes, sir. One of the victims doesn't fit that description, and we have obtained an ID. Floyd McCracken. He was a private investigator working for an activist group based down in Lodi, the Bracero Brotherhood."

"The Braceros? What a useless bunch of do-gooders — if you'll pardon me for saying so. They are their own worst enemy, challenging every company and organization that tries to help California field workers. As my company does."

"According to the Bracero records, Mr. McCracken's last known investigation involved your company, seeking back wages on behalf of a Bracero client."

Muñoz appeared to consider the information. "I don't know. I've never heard of this McCracken fellow, never met him. Luther, is this something you were handling?"

The cowboy shook his head. "No, boss. Can't recall the name."

Muñoz leaned forward for emphasis.

"As you may have heard, we contract for labor in all the local almond groves, vineyards, tomato patches, arugula fields, you name it. We have never withheld anyone's wages."

Marianne pressed on. "What do you pay them?"

"Depends on the job. We have common laborers, foremen, various specialists, backhoe operators, carpenters, welders, grapevine trimmers."

"You pay into social security and tax withholding?"

"Of course we do."

"Can I see?"

"See what? Our records are private." Muñoz spread his hands to show how business demands blocked his genuine desire to help. "To see them, with all due respect to law enforcement, that would put us at a competitive disadvantage against all the other contractors. You would need a subpoena."

"Understood."

Muñoz' face darkened. "And, to protect ourselves and our business, I must admit and warn — we would resist through our legal staff. We have excellent legal representation."

"Right. Thanks for your time."

Muñoz nodded, and Handy led Marianne out into the sunshine.

"You want to be careful around ostriches, officer," he said. "They can kick pretty good."

"I'll remember that," Marianne replied. She wasn't surprised to be so easily foiled, but she was feeling surly. "You should too."

14

SOMEWHERE in the eastern suburbs of Los Angeles, a pair of scruffy young men exited a modest stucco house at the midnight hour, locked the door behind them, climbed into a dilapidated camper truck, and drove away.

Inside the truck, the passenger was staring at his smartphone, studying a map. "Where are we going again?"

"Berdoo," said the driver.

"Oh yeah. Turn on I-5 south, then, and take 91 east."

On the 91 freeway, the driver frowned. Had they covered all the bases?

"Got the number?"

"Yeah, right here." The passenger pointed at his own head.

"And the date?"

"Yeah, 12, unless we hear different on the scanner. Don't sweat, we're ahead of the game by a couple of days."

"Are you sure?"

"Sure I'm sure."

"How?"

"My mind's working just fine, so that's how I'm sure."

"Where's the note?"

"Um, well, there is a note, but it's in my work shirt."

"What the fuck?"

"In the closet. It was covered with that damn dust."

"You dumb shit, they'll figure it out."

"Don't call me a dumb shit. No one will find the house, and if they do, no one will understand a thing."

"You better hope. Got your piece?"

The passenger reached under the seat and showed off a Czech CZ 75 SP-01 9-mm automatic pistol. The driver nodded approval.

The pair drove on into the outer suburbs, heading for Riverside and San Bernardino.

15

MARIANNE was in the early hours of a night shift. So far, the most exciting event was her stop for a caffeine boost at the Coffee Depot. She had learned from her doctor that a couple of mugs — 200 milligrams of caffeine — would be okay, and she was facing what looked to be a long and boring night. No domestic disputes, no thefts, no drug overdoses, nothing more serious than minor traffic violations had so far marred the tranquility of Hangtown on a hot summer's eve.

But around ten-thirty a call came in. Somebody had triggered the burglar alarm at the Stop 'n' Shop. She motored up Main Street, turned onto Mosquito Road, then onto Broadway, and proceeded east to the location. She parked in the lot beside the local 76 gas station and got out to have a look around, doing her best to ignore the alarm, which threatened to wake the dead. The parking lot extended all the way around the store, and she started an inspection tour. While she was walking, the alarm stopped ringing. By the time she backtracked to the storefront, the owner and a security truck were both on the scene.

"What have we got?" she asked.

The owner was apologetic. "False alarm. I might have set it off when I was closing up."

Case closed.

Marianne was returning to her patrol car when she noticed a faint glow intruding on her thoughts. An aura, the sign of an adept. She stopped and scanned her surroundings. Except for the departing owner and security guard, the area was quiet, devoid of any human presence. She waited for a few minutes, hoping the mental glow would dissipate. But it did not. She couldn't be sure, but the source seemed to be coming from behind the store. She freed a can of pepper spray from her duty belt and cautiously moved around the building to check out her suspicion.

Nobody there. Nothing but bins full of cardboard boxes and dumpsters loaded up with trash. She examined the rear door. There were marks on the jamb where a screwdriver or pry bar had tried to force the latch. When? This evening or a week ago? Could mere tampering have set off the alarm? She didn't know. She lit up her flashlight and aimed it into the trees sheltering Hangtown Creek. Nobody showed up in the beam.

She was halfway back around the building when she heard footsteps coming along behind her. She whirled around, hand on the butt of her Glock.

A scrawny man clad in a dirty T-shirt and oil-stained jeans loomed out of the shadows.

"Bo Dingell? Holy crap, you scared me!"

"Evening, Officer Sarzeau. Marianne."

"Where were you hiding?"

"In the bin with the boxes."

"What are you doing here? Are you following me around? Are you drunk?"

"No, ma'am, I am not following you. I admire you. And I don't drink anymore. Don't do drugs. I'm on the straight and narrow now."

"You and what twelve-step program?"

"Don't need a program. My angel straightened me out."

"Oh sure. You tried to break into the Stop 'n' Shop."

"Just because I knew you'd show up." Dingell's eye were roving around every which way. He licked his lips. "My angel admires you too. He wants to meet you."

Marianne was conscious of Dingell's aura shifting rapidly between red, yellow, and green. When she concentrated, it settled back into a smoky red-orange.

"I see your aura, Bo. Yours or your so-called 'angel's.' It's red. You don't really want to be friends."

Dingell took a step forward, reached out to snag Marianne's arm. A shot of adrenaline coursed through her body. She raised her can of pepper spray and gripped the little stone amulet under her blouse.

"Stop where you are! I *command* you!"

Dingell stopped in mid-motion. His shoulders went slack.

"Now listen. You and your 'angel' better keep away from me. Understand?"

Dingell nodded weakly.

"Lemme hear you say it."

"I understand."

"You don't, I'm going to take you in again. Jail time, got it?"

"Yeah."

Marianne turned on her heel and started for her car. Dingell sheepishly followed. She turned back to face him. She pointed to the street.

"Bo. Walk away."

"Sorry, it's just that . . . my angel . . . he's awfully hoping to get to know you better."

"You go that way, I go this way. Is that clear enough? Or do you want a ride to the station?"

Dingell shook his head. He was still shaking and muttering as he shuffled down Broadway.

Marianne got into her patrol car and drove off.

Dingell watched her go, fingers clenching and unclenching. "Let me know when you'd like to get together."

16

IN LONG BEACH, in the hazy light of a southern California morning, Jerry Pavlov was staring at his computer screen, studying a roster of names thought to be potential threats against the United States. He was particularly intrigued by two who had just this morning popped up on the threat board — *Simon Hatch*, a Brit, and *Yannick Brunel*, from France. Europeans converted to Islam, known jihadis, both on the American no-fly list, and both now spotted in Mexico City. Pavlov doubted they wanted to cause trouble in Mexico and thought it likely they had a plan in mind to cross the border. He ran a query through the Homeland database and discovered that Hatch and Brunel were both members of an Al-Qaeda offshoot designated AQ-4 by American intelligence agencies. What, he wondered, was their plan? What were they up to?

He was nursing his third cup of coffee and pondering the matter when Ginger relayed a call from Dick Kettleman, the smoke alarmist from Home Depot.

"Pavlov here."

"Agent Pavlov, glad to catch you in your office. This is your lucky day. You will not believe your good luck."

"Try me."

"Well sir, you remember those smoke detectors I'm worried about? It turns out there was another purchase, twenty-five more to be exact. This was at our Pico Rivera store, bringing the total there to fifty."

"Unh-huh."

"You see? Fifty from each of seven stores. Same days, same totals. What we already talked about. They all match up."

"If you say so."

"How about this? This is the good part" — Kettleman slowed for dramatic effect — "the sale was not for cash. Instead, just this once the purchase was made by a cell phone using near field communication technology."

"What?"

"You've seen the ads on TV? You put your phone right near the terminal at the register, and — *bip* — transaction completed. You're thinking, 'so what'? But now, hold onto your hat, I have the phone number."

Pavlov leaned forward in his chair, suddenly feeling lucky indeed. He grabbed a pencil.

"Give me the number."

Kettleman read off the digits twice. Pavlov wrote them down, started making phone calls.

▼

An hour later, an inquiry to the Homeland Border Protection Office over by the airport came back with a name to go with Kettleman's number — a woman named *Ghani Mansour.* She did not reside in Downey, however, as Pavlov was hoping. Instead her address was over in Culver City, on the other side of the county. Pavlov cursed, sensing a dead end.

Just to be sure, he opened up the Homeland database again. With Ginger's help formulating the proper queries, he discovered that Ms. Mansour had a brother, *Adi Mansour,* and that the man was connected, albeit peripherally, to the AQ-4 group. Connected to Hatch and Brunel, it seemed.

Aha.

17

MARIANNE and Tom Wagstaff left the Apple Ranch restaurant down in Applefield in a mellow mood. Ordinarily the place was shunned by the locals as a tourist trap, but Wagstaff needed to work on the next issue of the *Courier*, and Marianne was due for another night shift twenty miles north in Placerville. An early dinner of steaks, fries, and apple pie was the solution to their scheduling problem. They strolled along under the oak trees lining picturesque Main Street holding hands. After three blocks dodging out-of-towners, they turned into the local park. The former apple orchard was the source of the town's name, and developing fruit was already loading down the boughs. In another month or two deer would sneak out of the nearby hills to snack on the windfalls.

They meandered through the gnarly old trees to the water feature, a life-size bronze statue of a gold prospector. A trickle of water flowed from his pan into a pool at his feet. One hand held up a large nugget for inspection.

"He's having better luck than we do," said Wagstaff.

"But it's just bronze. We find the real thing."

"Every now and then."

Marianne was about to reply when she jerked to attention, startled by a voice in her head.

"Hello? You there? Can you hear me?"

"M? You okay?"

"I heard a voice."

Wagstaff looked around in alarm. There was no one within hailing distance. No one in sight. "Your ghost? You've talked to him here, in this pool."

"I don't think so. Doesn't sound like him."

She stood frozen, holding her breath.

"When you get sick, it's not my fault."

"There it is again."

"What? Who?"

Marianne's mouth turned down in a wry pucker. "Not sure. Someone is denying responsibility for morning sickness."

"I love you. We'll talk more later."

"Now it's gone."

"That's very weird."

"You said it." Marianne shuddered.

"Weirder than usual, anyway." Wagstaff scratched his beard. "Life with you is an adventure."

"Brrr. As if I needed another way to make my skin crawl."

Suddenly, a wave of nausea washed over Marianne. She staggered. Clutching Wagstaff's hand to prevent a fall, she sagged to the ground in slow motion.

"Ohhhhh, crap . . . I feel like shit."

"Morning sickness at five PM? Are you going to throw up?"

Marianne didn't reply. She glanced up at Wagstaff. His outline against the sky was jagged and luminescent. The statue in front of them was changing colors, vibrating through the spectrum. She dropped her head into her hands.

"Worse. Urrhhhh . . . having a seizure."

Wagstaff sat down beside her, draped an arm around her shoulder.

"Hey. Lean over here."

Marianne tilted herself into his arms. She was shivering uncontrollably in spite of the balmy weather. Then, as suddenly as the attack started, it stopped. The jaggy edges and their prismatic hues faded. Wagstaff's face came back into focus. The statue darkened to the color of ordinary bronze, stylishly oxidized in shades of green.

Marianne jumped to her feet.

"Whoa, gotta jet. Shift starts at six."

Wagstaff stood up slowly, brushed himself off. "You're not going anywhere. We can sleep at my place tonight. Then . . ."

"I'm fine. These things come and go."

"Come on, M, you know that's not true. You're a mess. Not safe to drive, not safe to patrol the streets — what if you have a seizure while you're trying to arrest a bank robber?"

"No one robs banks in Placerville."

"Just saying. Or an aggressive drunk. If anyone on the force finds out, you'll be on administrative leave. At best."

Marianne gritted her teeth. "I am not quitting my job."

"All right, let's move the discussion forward. Multiple voices, talking to you. Scaring you. Are they really, or are you having hallucinations?"

"I'm pregnant. That's all," pouted the mom-to-be.

Wagstaff flapped his arms in frustration. "Are you kidding? Anyone else hearing voices would be ready for a diagnosis. I think it's your damn powers, they're doing something to you, warping you."

"You know all about my powers. I warned you."

Wagstaff took her hands in his. "I'm worried about you, M. You need to talk to a doctor."

"You mean therapy? See a shrink?"

Wagstaff looked hurt. "Of course not. I don't actually think you're crazy, so don't accuse me. I meant, like, a neurologist. A specialist."

"Like your science pal Osborne and his buddies? They know less than you do. I will figure this out on my own."

Wagstaff pressed on.

"What about what's-her-name, Hannah Crowfoot, your mentor?"

"She's not my mentor, she's a grumpy old woman, and I've already got an obstetrician."

"She knows a lot of stuff no OB ever heard of."

Marianne angrily spun herself around, arms spread wide.

"Okay, Mr. Prosecutor, I will make an appointment to see Dr. Crowfoot. Satisfied?"

Wagstaff inclined his head in a miserable little nod.

18

IN WASHINGTON D.C., Jameson Sizemore was in his office at Homeland Security headquarters, being briefed on a new case that was picking up steam in Los Angeles. A pair of underlings were there with PowerPoint slides on their laptops and paper charts on an easel.

Dylan Roche, a casually dressed young man, rolled up his sleeves and touched a map of LA on his computer screen.

"Here we go. One of our agents in Los Angeles has discovered that known terrorist operatives associated with the AQ-4 group have recently purchased — for cash — several hundred smoke detectors, here in the vicinity of Downey, California, with the evident purpose of constructing some sort of dirty bomb."

Ruby Judson, a black woman in a trim business suit, brought up a slide showing mugshots of two scruffy men.

"On the left, Adi Mansour. To the right, Irfu Tayeb. These are the suspects. In spite of those names, they're American. We've been watching them for a while. They both have police records for minor infractions, but up until now they have given us no reason to take them seriously. More like fans of jihad than jihadists."

Sizemore fingered his elegant tie, shot his cuffs. "Where is this going?"

Roche nodded to acknowledge his superior's impatience. "Takes a sec to set this up, sir." He brought up a slide of his own. On it were several images of a different pair of men, each photographed surreptitiously while walking the streets of a foreign city somewhere.

"A link to other AQ-4 members, known to be a real threat based on activities in Europe, has been tentatively established. These men are now in Mexico."

"Names? IDs?" asked Sizemore.

"Right. Simon Hatch and Yannick Brunel. Our friends at GCHQ believe they teamed up to burn that London bus. You remember, sir? Right there in Piccadilly? Some of the passengers were badly burned."

"Go on."

Judson took over. "The question is — how shall we deploy assets to counter this threat?"

Sizemore's attention was wavering. He glanced at his own laptop to check the day's appointments.

"What threat? Smoke detectors?"

"That's right, sir. They contain radioactive material," said Judson.

"What? How much?"

Roche flipped through his PowerPoint presentation until he had the facts visible in bold-faced type. "Well sir, each detector contains three thousandths of a gram of Americium 241. It's an artificial element, number ninety-five, with enough power to ionize the air in a little detection chamber. But, individually, as you probably know, these things are consumer products and therefore harmless."

Judson displayed a photo of the units in question. They looked like little flying saucers. "They emit alpha particles, which are mostly stopped by the plastic housing you see here."

"That's it?" Sizemore felt his morning wasting away.

"They do have a half-life of 432 years, and they do emit approximately one percent of their energy as gamma rays."

Sizemore rolled his eyes. "Dirty bomb? This one sounds like a dud. How many of these detector things are out there?"

"It looks like three hundred and fifty, if the Home Depot inventory is reliable."

"And how much total — what is it? Americium? — are we talking about?"

Judson picked up a magic marker and did some math on the easel. "Three hundred fifty times oh-point-oh-oh-three, gives us" — she circled the total — "just about one gram. One twenty-eighth of an ounce."

Sizemore stared incredulously at his staffers. "One gram. Your plot is nothing more than a childish fantasy."

"We don't see it that way, sir. These guys are working hard. They might have access to other sources of radioactivity. There is potential for harm."

Sizemore swiveled his chair to stare out the window. The capitol dome was visible in the distance, rising over nearby rooftops. He thought in silence for a while, making his assistants very nervous. An idea slowly took shape. He swiveled back to face them.

"Congress doesn't think we need to be so vigilant. They'd rather spend our tax money on drones and missiles — smack the bad guys before they get here."

"That never works," said Roche, flashing his departmental loyalty.

"Experience proves it," echoed Judson.

Sizemore smiled. "I agree with our elected representatives."

"Sir?" Roche was appalled.

"Fiscal responsibility. We don't want to be wasting money the military so desperately needs." He tapped the blotter on his desk with a decisive fingertip.

"So here's the deal. We keep an eye on these clowns, if it doesn't exert us, and let events take their course. That way we'll find out about their operation. If the two European dudes get into the country, we'll arrest them."

"That's all?" Judson was shocked.

"Yes, all. Let things unwind, see where they lead us, assuming these jokers actually try to detonate a gram of harmless smoke detector stuff."

Both assistants started to protest. Sizemore waved them away. "Get me the LA SAC, I'll fill him in."

19

WAGSTAFF drove Marianne down to Angels Camp in his big yellow SUV. The sixty-mile trip was accomplished in a strained silence. The betrothed couple, already expecting a child, were hardly speaking.

The northern end of town was all new, an endless line of unattractive roadside businesses clinging to California Route 49, the main highway. Marianne roused herself.

"Here's the Save Mart. Gotta stop for a care package."

"Is this necessary?"

"If we don't want the old lady to bite us."

Wagstaff pulled into the parking lot and waited while his fiancée did some shopping. She came back to the car loaded down with heavy bags.

"Okay, this will please her."

They motored on into the tree-lined historic district, where second story verandas sprouting from historically significant brick buildings crowded the road. Marianne pointed, and Wagstaff turned off into Bush Street.

Hannah Crowfoot was an elderly Native American adept, a crotchety old woman who had helped Marianne get in touch with her own remarkable powers. Her house was a ramshackle cottage at the end of the street. Its poor state of repair was softened by a tangle of shrubs and vines. Roses and jasmine blossoms imparted a genteel ambience.

A sign on the door read, *Readings & Spiritual Advice.* Marianne led Wagstaff up the steps, bit her lip, and prepared to knock. She was leery of the criticism that always accompanied a visit. She was also afraid that the old woman was near death's door. She most certainly did not want to be around when the end came.

A year ago Ms. Crowfoot had been rendered unconscious by a trio of Pakistani adepts intent on military sabotage. As a result she had spent a week asleep in her favorite chair, dehydrated, malnourished, left for dead. It had taken months to recuperate, aided now and then by Marianne's encouragement. Now at last she was her old self again, full of grit and vinegar. Marianne was irrationally fearful of her penetrating gaze, unhindered by the cataracts that threatened to blind her.

A little side table stood in the foyer. A tented sign beside a brass bell read, *Ring for Service.* Marianne rang the bell.

As usual, some time went by before they heard footfalls creaking on the stairs. Then a pudgy hand swept a curtain aside, and a rotund old lady stood before them, clad in a shapeless green smock. Wild gray hair framed a fleshy face. Thick glasses magnified the hazy eyes that examined them.

"Ahh, it's you. The young adept."

Marianne swallowed. "Hannah, this is Tom Wagstaff. We're engaged, I thought he should meet you."

Ms. Crowfoot offered a hand. Wagstaff forced himself to shake it.

"I brought you some stuff," said Marianne, pushing past the awkward introduction. "A bottle of pinot grigio, a couple of bottles of sparkling water and a quart of cranberry juice — gotta drink those liquids — a bag of rice, packages of Chinese food you can microwave if you don't want to cook, carrots for vitamin A, ice cream — I hope you like peanut brickle — and look here, a roast chicken hot out of the oven." She pulled the items out of her bags one at a time and set them down on the table. Ms. Crowfoot watched the show with obvious satisfaction.

"Thank you, Marianne."

Wagstaff opened his wallet and offered a fifty dollar bill.

"You don't have to pay me anymore, not after saving me from those kids."

Marianne and Wagstaff exchanged a knowing glance. "That's very kind, but you can use the money, right?"

The old lady shrugged, folded the bill, and stuck it in a pocket.

"Follow me. I see from your glow that we have a lot to talk about."

They settled themselves in Ms. Crowfoot's consultation room, herself in an old leather easy chair, her visitors on hard wooden stools.

"Tell me, what's the trouble? You are all knots inside."

"I can't sleep, and when I do drop off, I'm having bad dreams. I'm also having seizures again — seeing those multi-colored jaggies like I used to do."

"And you're pregnant," noted the old woman. "Without benefit of wedlock," she added, showing off her eerie smile.

"You can tell?"

"Your aura makes it obvious."

"It was Marianne's idea," said Wagstaff. "We're getting married in August."

"I should hope so. Nowadays, you young people . . ." She trailed off, considering the situation, apparently listening to something.

"Your baby — a son, yes?"

"You can tell that too?"

"I don't need ultrasound. Is he talking to you?"

"How could he? I'm not even two months pregnant."

"It's not uncommon among powerful adepts — female adepts, anyway."

Marianne blanched. "I did hear a voice, just this week. That was my son? He didn't want to be blamed for my morning sickness."

"I doubt what's bothering you is morning sickness. Tell me about your dreams."

Marianne thought about her midnight experiences, trying to recall details that seemed to be hiding behind a fog of anxiety. "These dreams aren't exactly vivid, like some are. I'm standing around someplace. It's gray and hazy. Orange light. Things like spidery umbrellas here and there. Trees, maybe? I can't be sure. Then a monster comes up out of nowhere and tries to catch me." Marianne paused to collect herself. The memory was disturbing. "You know how you try to move while you're dreaming, and you can't? So I'm thrashing around in bed and wake myself up."

"That's all you remember?"

"It's enough. It's scary."

"You skipped the important part. What kind of monster?"

Marianne closed her eyes and tried to find words for her vague impressions. After a long silence, she made an attempt. "He doesn't want me to see him. He's doing something to prevent it. But I see a shape. I feel his presence, his anger, his hatred" — she blushed — "and his lust."

Wagstaff regarded Marianne with something like awe. His familiar partner was suddenly a stranger.

"It would help to know *some* of the details," complained Ms. Crowfoot. "You said, 'he.' Is this monster a *he,* do you think?"

"Pretty sure."

"Flaming?"

"No fire. *Smoky* is the only way I can describe him."

"Visible eyes?"

"Dark holes."

Wagstaff shifted his weight. "What we were hoping, Ms. Crowfoot, is you could tell us how M can lose her powers. Become a normal woman."

Ms. Crowfoot dismissed the idea. "Become *normal?* Whatever that might be. Is that right, Marianne?"

"Being adept is a rough ride. I just want to be a mom."

The old woman lifted herself out of her chair and moved to her bookcase. She pulled down several volumes and placed them on the table in front of her visitors. She leafed through the pages.

"The lore is sparse on this topic. You might be able to lose your talents, but it won't be easy, and the idea is so unusual no one bothers to explain how it's to be done."

Wagstaff flipped through the pages of the oldest book, noting the engravings of animals and plants, the recipes for potions, the litanies of spells. "Hey, M, you negated the powers of those Pakistani kids last year."

Marianne sighed. "Yeah, with fire and brimstone. I don't want any burn scars, thank you very much."

Ms. Crowfoot picked up Robinson's *Native Methodologies and Practice, Revised Edition.* "Wait, here's something — a lot of weed might work, or peyote if you can find some, or a very small amount of datura. To enter the trance state. And then, when the drug takes hold, you need to chant a *dispersal* spell."

"Dispersal?"

"That's right. The powers exist, they cannot be destroyed. But, it says here, you can send them off in separate ways with the right spell."

"How would I find a dispersal spell?"

"I don't know. I have never had the slightest interest."

"And if I do this, what will I be like afterwards? Still me? Will I know myself?"

Old lady Crowfoot cracked her eerie smile. "The chance you take, my dear."

Marianne studied the text. "I've still got some datura."

"Call your friend Ray Bagwell, babe, get him to jive up some dispersal instructions," advised Wagstaff.

The spirit woman shook her head. "You're dreaming about a monster. Your seizures have returned. You're sick, but your unborn son is right — it's not his fault. A warning — none of this is natural. An unholy spirit is on the prowl. If I were you, the last thing I'd be thinking about is losing my powers. I'd be whipping them into shape to confront the beast."

Part THREE

20

IN LONG BEACH, Jerry Pavlov was on the telephone with his supervisor.

"Where did this come from, if you don't mind my asking?" said he.

"Above. High up."

"How high?"

"Washington. They want us to lay low, so you're out of it."

"But, wait, this could be hot, I'm onto something —"

"Don't argue with me, Pavlov. I've got my orders, and now you do too. Smoke detectors? Please. We'll find another case for you, equally exciting."

"I'll bet."

Pavlov jammed the phone back in its cradle. He stood and paced his tiny office, trying to work off his frustration with the Homeland bureaucracy. His mind was racing, imagining events far away in space and time; events that endangered the peace and tranquility of his country. Ginger appeared and brought him back to Earth.

"Here's your new assignment. In writing, I notice, delivered a little quicker than usual." She grinned. "Looks like their trust in your professional attitude is . . . limited."

Pavlov snatched the paper. "Medical malfeasance? Are you fucking kidding?"

"The dentist identified in the complaint is suspected of treating illegals and billing Medicaid."

"Good Christ. Just where is this monument to waste, fraud, and abuse doing his frauding?"

"At the bottom of your sheet there." She pointed to an address in Inglewood and returned to her desk.

Pavlov folded the order into a paper airplane, stepped to the far side of his office, and flew it into his wastebasket. He resumed pacing, talking to himself. He reached into a pocket and withdrew a pack of Marlboros.

Ginger poked her head back in. "So you're frustrated. Angry. Don't you dare light up a cigarette inside this building."

"Me? Fuck no."

He set up like a basketball player making a three-pointer and launched the pack into his wastebasket, where it landed on top of the work order.

"He shoots, he scores."

He paced some more, thinking and muttering. Then he sat back down at his desk, opened his mobile phone, withdrew the SIM card, inserted a different one, and punched in a call.

▼

Marianne was talking to Ray Bagwell, somewhere across an ocean, looking to obtain a magic spell from her military colleague. The Army major who ran field operations for FULTAP had a poetic side, having translated many of her spells from Old French and invented others. He was confused by the request.

"Why dispersal?"

"I want to lose my powers, and old lady Crowfoot says they can't be destroyed, only scattered."

"Oh."

"And keep it simple. I'll have to recite it while hallucinating under the influence of marijuana or peyote or datura."

"You can't be serious."

"Yes I am. Totally."

"I'm not sure I want to get into this, Marianne. You lose your powers, your dad and I lose an important asset. Think it over."

She was about to insist when her office phone rang. "Damn, wait a sec." She put him on hold to take the call.

"Sarzeau here. Help you?"

"Officer Sarzeau. How nice to hear your voice."

"Who is this?"

"Jerry Pavlov."

"Oh, the Homeland guy. Thanks again for the McCracken ID."

"Happy to be of service. Hey, listen, I've got a problem."

Marianne was cautious. "What kind of problem?"

"Smoke detectors."

"Those things. Mild radioactivity. Long shot for a dirty bomb."

"Right, that's right. Well, I've been pulled from the case. Assigned to something else."

"Bummer."

"Life goes on. I've got a lead — a name, but no address. I thought . . ."

"How do I fit into this? I'm just a local cop."

"Mmm. The fact that you know anything at all about McCracken's covert activities tells me you're *not* just a local cop. I don't know what you are. What I was hoping was this — you could follow a phone number and tell me where some of the calls were made. You know?"

"No, I don't." She sounded genuinely puzzled. "Why don't you do the work?"

"I can't use our methods or resources, I'm off the case. Look, here's the phone number" — he read off the digits — "Write it down."

"Writing . . ."

"See if you can track it for me."

"I doubt this will get you anywhere," said Marianne.

"Make a few calls, who knows? Someday I'll return the favor."

Marianne thought she was listening to a kindred spirit, a reckless fool willing to try anything.

"Stay tuned, Mr. Pavlov. This may take a while."

She returned to her call with Ray Bagwell, but he had hung up. She called him back. The usual squeals and pops accompanied the encrypted satellite connection.

"Broomer . . ." He sounded sleepy. The difference in times zones probably meant he was in bed with a bad novel.

"Hey, I'm back. Forget the dispersal spell, Ray. That guy in Homeland you steered me to — Agent Pavlov — has a phone number he wants researched. Any chance American TV & App can take a look?"

"What's the number?"

Marianne read it off.

"Let me talk to my friends at our favorite store."

Twenty-four hours later, Bagwell left a message on Marianne's voicemail. "Broomhandle. Can't really talk tonight, duty calls. Check your email."

Marianne listened to the message when she passed through the department offices during her lunch break. The news prompted her to take a look at her email, and that prompted her to place another call to Los Angeles.

"Agent Pavlov? I have a cell tower for you, where the last known calls from your phone were relayed. Ghani Mansour's phone, right? The Cell ID is 499-634-771. It's new, just went up, in Downey."

"You are good, Sarzeau."

"Here's the GPS — 33.942257 north, 118.106727 west. Not too far from you, right?"

"Over where I-5 and the 605 cross."

"Also — what's your email?"

"Um, better use my personal address, jpav@lightfiber.net."

"Check your mailbox. This unit made calls to just seven other phones from that tower, all of them throwaways, all connected to the same tower. Sending the dump."

Pavlov was impressed. "That was quick. How did you do this?"

Marianne didn't know how much Pavlov knew about FULTAP, or how much he should be allowed to know. "Oh, we've got a good database up here. I'm well wired," she lied.

Pavlov was not taken in. "You certainly are," he said.

21

PAVLOV left his office in a thoughtful mood. He swung by Ginger's desk.

"I'm off to the dentist if anyone wants to know."

"Make sure you floss."

He then stepped into an elevator and rode it down into the basement for a conversation with Ike Stoneman, the fellow in charge of the department's stockroom.

"Stone, my man, I need some advice."

The stockroom clerk was old and thin and sharp. "Always ready. Any topic. I am a walking encyclopedia."

"Here's a test for you. What if I want to detect radioactivity in a house somewhere? Somebody playing with smoke detectors?"

"Not so easy. Tell me why."

"Why do you think? Terror potential."

"Smoke detectors? They don't scare anybody."

"What if there are a *lot* of smoke detectors?"

Stoneman thought about the problem. "Hard to pick out. Each one contains a minute amount of Americium 241. So there's radioactivity, but just barely. Americium emits alpha particles."

"What are they?"

"Ionized helium nuclei."

"Sounds dangerous to me."

"No, no. Those things are stopped by almost anything. Paper, plastic, human skin. Americium? Just don't breathe the stuff."

"I'm talking about hundreds of smoke alarms, all together somewhere. I'll be in a car. What do I need?"

"Let's see. An AN/PDR-60 alpha probe might work . . . if you drive real slow with the windows down."

"Got one handy?"

Stoneman held up a finger and ambled away into a storage bay. After a few minutes rummaging around in there, he returned with an aluminum case in hand. He placed it on the countertop, raised the lid, and withdrew a small metal box covered with dials and switches. He demonstrated its controls, showed Pavlov how to aim the sensor wand that was attached to the unit by a curly cord.

▼

By early afternoon Pavlov was sitting in his departmental car, a Ford Crown Vic, on Firestone Boulevard in Downey. He was eating a McDonalds chicken & bacon McWrap and munching french fries while he fussed with an app he had just installed on his smartphone: something called TowerTalk, a tool recommended by Stoneman. When he made a call, the app was supposed to identify the cell tower he was connected to by dropping the image of a pin on a little map.

It took him a while to get the hang of it, and another twenty minutes driving around to connect to the cell tower identified by Marianne. It was smaller than most, not much more than a telephone pole with upright slabs of antenna jutting out, half-hidden between palm trees on Florence Avenue.

Pavlov then drove back and forth through the network of residential streets, annoying Ginger with frequent telephone calls.

"Haven't you arrested that dentist yet?"

"I'm circling the block. He's out to lunch. No patients. I'm bored."

"You're not really anywhere near that guy, are you?"

"Don't let that get around."

"Jesus, they'll can you."

"Not yet, not yet."

Pavlov's excursions and phone calls eventually revealed that he only remained connected to the correct tower when he was within about a quarter mile, vastly cutting the amount of territory he needed to search.

Now he rolled his windows down, flipped switches on his alpha probe, and drove through the neighborhoods, making a slow survey of the modest stucco homes lined up under palm and lemon trees.

He crisscrossed the streets branching off Florence all the way from I-5 to Lakewood Boulevard. It took him more than half an hour.

After rolling up Fairview and down Matlock, he proceeded south on Rio Vista, turned east on Halsey for a block and then north on Chatham. Nearing Florence again, his probe beeped and lit up.

"Ding dong."

Among the houses large and small, he spotted one on the east side of the street that was not as tidy as the others. He kept going. The probe stopped beeping and blinking. Just before Florence he turned around and glided south again on Chatham. When he drew alongside the not-so-neat house the probe beeped again. He drove on for another block, turned around, and parked.

Pavlov sat in his car for a while, thinking things over, then made another call to his associate.

"Okay, Ginger, I have the dentist office under surveillance. I see no patients, but am waiting patiently for them to show up."

She giggled. "You — patient?"

"Gotta be. It's quiet here in Downey."

"You're in Downey?"

"10246 Chatham Street — Isn't that the address you gave me?"

"Jerry . . ."

"If I don't respond in a reasonable amount of time — half an hour, say — that's where you send in the troops. Got it?"

"Downey, Chatham, troops. I'm rooting for you. Don't do anything dumber than usual, please."

He checked the loads on the SIG Sauer P229R automatic pistol he carried under his jacket. Then he locked his car and hiked back to the house he had spotted, carrying the alpha probe. As he approached, it beeped and flashed.

At the house next door a thin old woman in a wide straw hat was weeding the garden planted along her picket fence. Pavlov showed her his badge.

"Homeland Security ma'am. Any idea what your neighbors here might be up to?"

The woman stood up, brushed dirt from her pants, gave the adjacent house a disdainful look. "That place, what a shack. The owner should sell, it's ruining the neighborhood."

"It's a rental?"

"Never for more than a couple of months. And the tenants! Frankly, I think there's termites and vermin. Skunks in the crawl space."

"Are you friends? Ever try to borrow a cup of sugar?"

"Heavens no. The latest trouble showed up a couple of weeks ago. Two men. They had beards. Lights on all night. Then, they drove away in some rickety old camper truck."

"When was that?"

"A couple of days ago. Two or three days. Sorry, memories don't last long anymore."

"Any make on the truck?"

"I couldn't tell a Ford from a fart, young man. It was old and rusty. The camper shell was covered with mildew."

"Yeah, well, this is helpful. Any information helps. Nice garden you've got here."

"Thank you."

She went back to work, and Pavlov walked back to his car. There he opened the trunk and pulled out a portable Makita drill. He fitted a 3/8-inch metal-cutting bit into the chuck.

Then he returned to the rundown house and knocked politely.

"Avon calling . . ."

He waited for the socially correct amount of time, then knocked again.

"Fuller Brush man. No? How about, Downey permits, here to discuss your pool application? Fuck. Nobody home?"

A tumbledown fence separated the back yard from the street. He opened a gate and walked through to the rear of the house. There he knocked on the back door. Hearing nothing, he hammered it with a toe. Still no response.

"Maybe you've fallen and can't get up. I'll save you."

He fired up the Makita and drilled into the deadbolt. After waiting for the bit to cool, he drilled the door lock. Flicking away the metal shavings, he threw the bolt, lifted his knee, and pushed hard. The door sagged open, and the Homeland agent slipped inside.

The house was empty, and it was a mess. Pizza boxes were stacked up on the kitchen table. Dishes were piled high in the sink. Soda cans were crammed together on the countertop. The refrigerator contained a gallon of sour milk, unopened cans of Dr. Pepper, and slices of salami in a plastic pouch. Pavlov's alpha probe was beeping regularly.

The living room furniture consisted of three fold-out canvas camping chairs. A small portable TV set was on the floor in front of them, tipped on its side. Surrounding the cast-iron fireplace, a relic of nineteen-forties housing décor, were piles and piles of smoke alarm boxes.

Pavlov examined one of them. Empty. He threw it down, accidentally knocking over one of the piles. An avalanche of cardboard boxes skidded across the floor.

Pavlov gave each room a cursory glance, scanning them with his alpha probe, which continued to beep at a steady rate. Then he made his way into the attached garage. There, stacked against a wall, were the smoke alarms themselves, three hundred and fifty of them. The covers had been snapped off and were piled on one side, the frames and broken circuit boards on the other. Plastic ceiling mounts and nine-volt batteries were gathered in piles of their own. He picked up one of the circuit boards. He hardly knew what he was looking at, but the little detection chamber appeared to have been pried open.

Nearby was a huge mound of colorful paper, the ripped-open remains of 'safe-and-sane' fireworks: fountains, spinners, poppers, and pinwheels. Enough to celebrate the Fourth of July in Big City style. Pavlov's alpha probe was beeping rapidly, sounding an elevated warning.

On a worktable attached to the garage wall were cardboard mailing tubes, an empty baking soda box, and more fireworks debris. Sitting nearby was a Waring cocktail blender. Pavlov fingered the cardboard, imagining bombs made from the gunpowder contained in the fireworks.

Then he turned to the cocktail blender. When he brought his alpha probe near, the dials pinned and the beeps became an hysterical buzz. He jumped backward.

"Whoa. They weren't making margaritas in this thing."

22

A SUMMER EVENING in Applefield.

Marianne shared a pizza with Wagstaff and his glamorous assistant Kari in the *County Courier* office, munching in silence while her companions discussed page layouts. Wagstaff assessed the sparse collection of ads and agreed to write a filler article on Tri-Town traffic. Marianne looked on without much interest. Then, not long before sunset, she drove her Mini a mile south of town on Copper King Road to KVIG, the local FM radio station.

A year earlier she had feared Kari Hamilton as an unstoppable rival for Wagstaff's affections, but after she did some matchmaking with a handsome shop owner in Placerville, her rival became Kari Frey, a married woman. Marianne smiled at her accomplishment. She was uneasy about her own impending marriage and, while thinking of ways to improve relations with her fiancé, was singing old love songs as she motored along the road.

She had a fine voice, the reason she was hired as a police officer in the first place. The crusty chief of the Golden Hills Tri-Town police force was impressed by a candidate who would sound good reporting road conditions on radio 1610 AM. Marianne's other qualifications were in order, she had her degree from police school, but her pipes were what nailed that first job. Months later, Howard Turnbow, KVIG's owner, recruited her as a substitute disc jockey based on the same warm and sultry contralto.

She turned onto the property and rolled slowly down the long gravel drive to the cinder block studio. Three-foot high call letters bolted to the wall were glowing neon orange against the evening sky. A red hazard light atop a tall mast in the far corner of the lot was blinking on and off. Not exactly the dazzling splendor of Big City showbiz venues, but more than presentable up here in the foothills.

KVIG was only a Class-A station, limited by FCC regulation to six thousand watts, barely enough power to be heard in Jackson, the Amador County seat, and not near enough to reach Lodi, a mere thirty miles away in the Big Valley. Although Turnbow knew next to nothing about popular culture, he was an astute businessman, and he knew how make his feeble station into a successful enterprise. The previous owner had let it languish as his health failed. After he died, Turnbow bought it from the family estate and revived interest by hiring consultants to put it on the internet. More people heard KVIG on their computers and mobile devices than over the air, many of them from hundreds of miles away. Next, he signed up a programming service, Spin-O-Matic, Inc., to automatically select the country and alternative rock songs that went out to his listeners, giving the station a hip contemporary feel. And finally, he employed disc jockeys like Marianne to take requests in the evening. If anything, she knew less about popular culture than Turnbow, but that wasn't the point. Each request that came in adjusted Spin-O-Matic's playlist, subtly shaping KVIG's output to the taste of its audience.

Inside the building, the dimly-lit space was wide open, with a tiny bathroom walled off in one corner. Racks of electronic gear were mounted along the walls, their status marked by a galaxy of red and green LEDs.

Marianne took a seat at the desk, scanned through the new advertisements, adjusted the boom arm on the microphone, and recorded a series of testimonials with professional charm. Inwardly she approved some of the sponsors and disdained others. Occasionally she was amused, as she was tonight by the appeal from the Apple Ranch restaurant. Bessy Strathwaite, the owner, had long refused to advertise on KVIG, but seemed to feel it was politically necessary now that Turnbow, a business rival, was mayor of Applefield and the Tri-Town Special District.

With ads out of the way, Marianne dug around in the files, selected one of her many introductions, and slotted it into the list of songs notching upward on her computer display. A few seconds later the intro popped up between a pair of arrows:

"This is The Golden Girl of the Golden Hills, coming to you from *The Vig* — K-V-I-G — in Applefield, California, at ninety-three-point-one on your FM dial. It's seven o'clock."

She was on the air.

The first song up was *Lucky,* a collaboration between Jason Mraz and Colbie Caillat that gently celebrated leaving home and returning to a true love. She was tapping her foot to the beat and humming along at first. Then, at the second chorus, her eyes moistened as she considered her own relationship. Just when she was feeling sorriest, a voice from nowhere interrupted.

"I'm going to need a name. Have you thought about it?"

Marianne almost jumped out of her chair. "Who are you?"

"Hi, Mom. It's me."

It took a dozen heartbeats for Marianne to realize that she had heard the voice, tiny but insistent, once before. She recalled old lady Crowfoot's identification. "Mom? Mom, is it? You claim to be my unborn son."

"That's right. That's me."

"And you deny making me sick."

"Sometimes it's me, but sometimes . . . something else."

"Unh-huh. You won't be born for months! How did you learn to talk?"

"I listen."

"Of course. Ha ha, silly me."

"Well? A name. What's the story?"

Although still worried that her own mind was tricking her, Marianne started to relax. After all, she told herself, she had heard other, equally strange voices. "This is what I get for being adept. How about, 'Jack'? I was thinking . . ."

"Not a chance. Try again."

"Your father mentioned 'Norman,' after his grandfather."

"Norman? Normal Norm? That doesn't sound like me."

"You are one picky fetus. Tom loved his grandfather."

"Forget it."

"In that case, we'll have to do some thinking. Got a request?"

"Not yet. I might, though. Talk to Dad. Cold silences are as bad as fights."

"What, now you're a marriage counselor?"

"Hey, I've got a life riding on this."

She felt the presence of her unborn son recede as *You Or No One* revved up, Chrissie Hynde's melodic refusal to fade into rock and roll history.

Marianne was making coffee on the station's little hot plate when the first request came in. She leaned toward the mike.

"Hello, this is your Golden Girl. Make a request, we do the rest."

"Evening, Golden Girl. I understand you play golden oldies now and then."

"Yes we do. What's on your mind? Something hot on a hot summer night?" Marianne scowled. The voice was familiar, and it surprised her.

"Howard? Is that you?" she blurted.

"I'll call back."

The phone went dead. Marianne carried on as if nothing had happened. A glance at the playlist inching upward revealed the next song, *The One That Got Away,* one of Katy Perry's big hits. "Well, folks, our caller got away, but this song did not."

As soon as the music started playing the phone rang again.

"Marianne."

"Howard?"

"Yup."

"So you tune in sometimes. I wondered."

"I listen to all your shows."

"That's, wow, that's very flattering."

"I've said it before, I'll say it again — you could be on the air full time if you wanted."

"But I don't want. I'm still a cop."

"I know. Listen, I have a request, it's for Lorraine, and I want to know if she's listening. Can you call her and makes sure she tunes in?"

"Okay, next song."

"Don't tell her I love her or anything, just play *Love Me Tender* — from me."

"The old Presley tune. Even I heard that one."

"Ancient, but it holds up."

"You want to do this live? Listeners hear your voice?"

"Never. You should noodle in the details for me. But wait, don't use my name."

"I can hear you blushing."

"Call Lorraine."

Heavy piano chords signaled *Stay*, Rihanna's moody hit. While the pop star's throaty voice warbled the opening lines, Marianne called Lorraine and persuaded her to tune in KVIG, lightly dodging an explanation.

When *Stay's* last bars faded, Marianne opened up her mike.

"Now we have a request from a gentleman of few words, someone who wants Elvis to explain his feelings. This track goes out to Lorraine, from an admirer. I heard him say, 'don't use my name,' so his identity is a mystery. Here's *Love Me Tender*. You know, folks? I think he means it . . ."

Elvis crooned, the track ended, and the phone rang again.

"Golden Girl at your service."

"Hello, this is Lorraine. I think that song you just played was meant for me. It's a wonderful tune, even though it's as old as I am."

"Looks like someone out there has a crush on you," said Marianne.

"It's no mystery — it's that scoundrel Howard Turnbow."

"Whoa, you're giving the guy away."

"I'd like to return the favor. If we're going to get all sentimental, play *Can't Help Falling In Love* for him."

Hear that, folks? Lorraine's admirer is Howard Turnbow, and I know a secret too — he's the owner of this radio station. How about that? Rumor has it these two are getting married pretty soon, if Elvis has it right . . ."

At 11:00 PM, Marianne turned the station back over to the automated playlist coming from Spin-O-Matic's data center somewhere. She had experienced bad moments on two separate occasions just outside the studio, so she checked the little Beretta in her ankle holster and gave the station grounds a careful inspection before she shut and locked the door.

Away from Applefield's streetlights, the sky was infinitely black. The Milky Way arched up over the eastern hills, striping the heavens with powdered silver. Embedded among the stars there, Cygnus the Swan flew high overhead. Marianne stood at her car for a moment, gazing upward, wondering if the source of her unusual abilities was up there among the stars, or as conventional belief would have it, in another and darker world altogether.

She opened the driver's door, was about to drop into the seat, then hesitated. She pulled out her phone and called Wagstaff, walking around her little Mini as she waited for him to pick up. After four rings, he did.

"Guess what, our son was talking to me. Again."

"Is this good or bad news?"

"I know you think I'm hallucinating, the victim of my super powers. Maybe you're right."

"Damn, M, this is scary."

"Tell me. Now he wants a name. And he wants us to settle our differences."

"Yeah, well, I'm down with that. You know how I feel."

"Unh-huh. Look, it's late, I'm on duty tomorrow, so I'm going back to

Hangtown."

"Right."

"Just thought I'd call and let you know."

"Thanks. Got it."

"So, good night."

"Good night."

As she pulled out of the drive and headed north on Copper King Road, she came upon an old pickup truck parked in a gravel turnout. It didn't register at first, but in driving past she felt the momentary pressure of a reddish glow in her mind. She glanced at her rear-view mirror: when she was a few hundred yards beyond, the truck's lights came on, and it pulled onto the road behind her. Gradually, it crept closer. Now the reddish glow was a steady force, pulsing behind her eyes.

To be sure the truck was actually tailing her, when she arrived in Applefield she turned up Digger Creek Road, drove three blocks, turned across T Street, turned again down Juniper and back onto Main. The truck stayed right behind her. She was pretty sure who the driver was, so she pulled into a parking spot, lifted her Beretta out of its holster, and stepped into the street. The pickup pulled in beside her little Mini. Bo Dingell emerged and shambled over to chat.

"Nice night, huh, Marianne?"

Marianne hefted the Beretta so Dingell could get a good look.

"What the fuck, Bo? I told you to stay the hell away from me."

"I know you did. Just want to show you I'm friendly. Don't mean no harm."

His aura was flickering red to blue, as if conflicting forces were at work in his probably addled brain. Marianne frowned. "That's fine, Bo, just great. Now listen up: this behavior, unwanted attention, you're stalking me. I'm going to get a restraining order if you show up just one more time."

"Oh, don't do that. I'm not *stalking* anybody. I just want to introduce you to my angel."

"I don't want to meet any of your imaginary friends, Bo."

"He's not imaginary. He's looking out for me, and he would like to look out for you too." He took a step forward.

She waggled the Beretta. "I've got all the protection I need, right here."

"Don't be like that, hostile and all. My angel has feelings like everybody, and you're hurting them."

His aura settled into the red.

"Get back in your truck. Drive away."

Dingell shuffled forward. "You shouldn't treat me so bad, I'm in touch with powerful spirits."

"One more step and I'll shoot you."

Dingell seemed to sober up. "That would be murder, since I am not a threat at this time."

"In the leg, maybe hit your knee. Might hurt. It won't kill you."

Dingell stopped. His fingers were twitching. He opened his mouth, tipped his head up, and let loose with a bone-chilling howl.

Marianne was startled by the performance. She rocked back on her heels and grabbed the little stone chip under her blouse. Her hand tingled.

Dingell grinned at the effect he had on her.

"Get in your truck, I *command* you!" she barked.

Dingell shivered. "I'm going."

"Get the fuck out of my sight."

"I'm going, going, don't worry, I done some bad things, I been around dead people, sure, but I never killed no one. Don't mean nothing, don't mean no harm."

She waited while Dingell backed out of his parking spot, turned his truck around, and drove off.

Marianne watched him go. The red glow of his aura faded gradually, along with the taillights of his rattletrap truck. Marianne shuddered.

When she was sure he was gone, she returned to her own car and drove around the corner to Wagstaff's office.

"Hey you, change of plan, I'm going to crash here tonight."

Wagstaff was staring at his computer screen, still busy with next week's *Courier.*

"Join you soon as I finish this," he said without looking up.

23

AN HOUR before dawn, Marianne woke up alone on Wagstaff's couch. She threw off the scratchy blanket, sat up, and fluffed her hair. In the bathroom she was washing her face when her world started spinning.

"Gahhhh . . ."

She vomited into the toilet, recovered, gargled with a slug of Wagstaff's mouthwash, then vomited again. Yesterday's pizza stared back at her from the toilet bowl.

"Ugh."

She ran a hand over her abdomen. Still trim, pregnancy invisible.

"Hey in there, is that you? Stop making me sick."

"Not me, I'm not doing anything."

"So you say."

She waited for the visual jaggies to signal a seizure, but instead her senses cleared, and her stomach settled down.

"Woof."

She gargled again and checked her watch — still early. After waiting for a few minutes to be sure the episode was over, she threw on yesterday's clothes and headed out.

Wagstaff was slumped over his desk, sound asleep. She touched him on the shoulder, got into her Mini, and drove across town to Applefield's little park.

The eastern sky was showing some color as sunrise approached, but the diminutive streetlights decorating the park walkways were still lit. Marianne hiked through the apple trees to the bronze prospector statue and stood before the pool, where an underwater lamp illuminated her troubled face. This was her go-to spot for serious consultations with her virtual visitor, and she wanted some answers. She took Chief Ibañez' old badge in one hand and her stone amulet in the other.

"Hey, Chief. Got a minute? I am a mess, talk to me."

An early morning zephyr rippled the pool surface, nothing unusual. She was about to resort to her *hey you* command, when an undulating shadow darkened the water. It wavered, nearly disappeared, then solidified into the shape of a man. An eerie but familiar voice spoke to her.

"Marianne . . ."

As always, the ghost's presence rattled her. She bit her lip, forced herself not to flinch.

"Good morning, Chief, if that means anything over there in Spookville," she said, trying for levity.

"You're pregnant," replied the ghost. *"Congratulations."*

"You know about that?"

"The news is out. It's good news."

"Except I'm sick all the time, having bad dreams, seizures."

"With an unborn son to protect."

"Yeah. All while being stalked by a crazy moron who has suddenly become adept. I'm tired of all this crap. You were going to make inquiries . . ."

"I did. You never called."

"You sound like my aunt — I'm calling now."

"This isn't a joke, Miss Smarty Pants. Your friend Dingell is not stalking you. He's just the avatar for someone else."

"What are you talking about?"

"Dingell is nothing but a weak-willed criminal who has lost all self-esteem. An easy target for a demon's purpose."

"I don't understand a word."

"Better try. A creature from my world is reaching for you. He's using Dingell to do it."

"Creature? What creature?"

"A demon. He senses your powers. He has many of his own and hopes for more. He wants what you've got."

"Shit. He's planning to steal my powers? Hey, he can have them. I'll give them away."

"Not so fast. This guy is a raging maniac. Your only defense is your powers — you'll need them all."

"Why? Why me?"

"Two reasons. First, he knows you have doubts about yourself. He thinks you're easy prey."

"Number two?"

"You are, by far, the most powerful adept he has ever come across."

"You've got to be kidding. I hardly understand anything I do."

"Most potential, then. Untapped, sadly for you, but for him — a good harvest. Show some spine. You are more than you know."

"Yadda yadda, thanks for the pep talk, coach. I just want out."

"You don't really have a choice. He's going to attack. Don't make it easy for him."

"You mean, I'm stuck, stuck being a weirdo . . ."

"You're in mortal danger. And I'm just an ex-cop floating around — I can warn you, but I can't help you."

"Come on, you the man. My man. Or, you know, whatever you are."

"I'm going to introduce you to someone."

Marianne was trying hard to grasp the incredible situation. It made her feel stupid. "Oh boy. Another ghost."

"Not a ghost. A power spirit. But this one is on your side. He'll keep an eye on you."

"He has eyes?"

"Oh yes. Now get ready, because . . . I'm going to drift away."

"No no no. Not now. If I'm in trouble, now's when I need you."

"It can't be helped. I'm destined for other things."

"What things?"

"I could never explain, so don't ask."

"You can't say goodbye. You can't leave. This is terrible." Marianne's eyes were clouding over.

"No, Golden Girl, it's all good. Keep your head high, be a good cop."

She sniffled, then caught herself, inhaled, and stood up straight. "So this demon or power spirit — whatever — whoever — does he have a name?"

"Yes. It's Wiiskaedakioushouchag."

"What?"

"WII-SKA-EDAK-IOO-SHOO-CHAG."

The water in the pool rippled, and the shadow faded. In its place a less clearly defined shape appeared, surrounded by bubbles that percolated upward from the depths and popped noisily on the surface. The water seemed to boil. Waves sloshed back and forth, spilling onto the sidewalk. The shape grew, writhing within the pool. Then a smoky form erupted from the water. Fiery eyes regarded her from within the vapor. Marianne shrank back in horror.

"Fear not. You have seen me before."

Marianne's heart was thumping. She willed herself to stand her ground, fighting off a powerful urge to turn and run.

"How? When? Where?" she stammered.

"From the beginning. Think back. When you conjured me I was harsh with your father."

"Back in Arizona. That was you?"

"Yes. Then, on the river, I showed you the remains of your fellow men."

"That little bird."

"A manifestation."

"Unh-huh. What about the cat on my doorstep? Last year, the one who brought me my owl feathers?"

"Myself as well."

Marianne nodded inanely. She was trembling, but starting to regain her composure.

"Why is this happening? What about Chief Ibañez? He's been my guy, you know? All those spooky weather reports . . ."

"I recruited him for you. We are allies, part of a larger self. I knew you would listen to him."

"And he kind of knew about charades. Back when we couldn't talk."

"He knew. I do not."

"It was you all the time? Behind the scenes?"

"Yes."

"Shows you what I know." Marianne sagged. Tears were forming. She blinked them away, scuffed the sidewalk with a toe, and smacked her hands down hard against her thighs.

"Those science guys I talked to, they think this stuff is all in my mind, some sort of delusion. Maybe it's true. Maybe I'm completely nuts. Are you a delusion?"

"You decide. The thinkers are half right — your mind is the key. Our worlds connect through it. You are a portal."

"Wow, a supernatural cell tower. Why me? Why bother about my problems?"

"No spirit should overpower the rest. Leave it at this — I have an interest in you and your family. It goes back centuries."

"But your name — Wiska-doo-dah. I can't wrap my tongue around it." She was sniffling. She wiped her nose with the back of her hand.

"How am I ever going to call you?"

"I am Wiiskaedakioushouchag."

"Like I said, a mouthful."

"I know it is hard for mortals to pronounce. Call me Whiskeyjack."

24

IN SOUTHERN CALIFORNIA, Jerry Pavlov was making a second trip to the Downey safe house on Chatham Street. Unanswered questions were bothering him, and he hoped a more thorough search would turn up some clue, some lead, some tiny way of latching onto and defeating the evil plans of would-be terrorists.

He drove by twice, just to survey the place. Then he parked and knocked on the neighbor's door. The thin old woman he met on his previous foray appeared on the doorstep.

"Hello, young man," she said. "Did you catch those criminals next door?"

"No ma'am, not yet."

"Are they going to tear down that dreadful house? It's an inducement to crime."

"Inducement?"

"Free hideout, gives people the wrong ideas. Tear it down."

"I think the courts might want to rule on that one. Don't swing your wrecking ball just yet."

"Hmph."

"We are trying to get to the bottom of this case, however lax we may appear. And what I'm wondering is, anything suspicious going on here? Anyone show up? That old camper truck, maybe?"

"I would have seen it. The place is dead. The landlord hasn't even come around to see the wreck he owns. Maybe he's dead too. Maybe those tenants shot him."

"I'll look into that. Thanks for your time."

"I hope you catch them. They all deserve life sentences for the mess they've made."

Pavlov nodded politely and escaped from the interview by tying a surgical mask over his nose and mouth. When she saw it, the woman retreated inside and slammed her door.

Pavlov walked around to the rear of the safe house, pulling on latex gloves as he moved.

Once inside, he lit up a powerful flashlight and began a thorough examination of the premises, photographing everything as he went with a small digital camera.

Nothing of interest in the kitchen, the living room, or the bathroom. He toured the garage again, but found nothing there either. Nothing anywhere, except piles of smoke alarm boxes and smoke alarm parts.

He turned to the bedroom, which was connected to the rest of the house by a narrow hallway leading past the garage. Nothing to be found in either of the rickety bedside tables. He opened the bureau drawers, found a pair of socks. He slid open the closet door. A shirt was hanging from one of the plastic hangers. He removed it, still on its hanger, and looked it over. Nothing notable, except lack of style — it was pink and green, with little crocodiles and palm trees printed all over the fabric. He wasn't that stylish himself, but still he winced. Now he knew something about the opposition — one of them, at least, had very poor taste.

He replaced the shirt on the closet pole, then yanked it back off. A rustling noise alerted him to something in the shirt pocket. He reached inside and retrieved a small scrap of paper. It was a cryptic note. Just a few letters and question marks, scrawled in pencil:

G H L

B-line — ? KMX— ?

He aimed his camera, set the focus for macro, and took a photograph.

▼

Back in his office, he stared at the display on his little camera for a while, then opened up his computer and did some research on privileged government websites and databases. After twenty minutes, when he thought he had the information he wanted, he punched a call into his personal mobile phone.

"Hello, Hicksville."

"This is Sarzeau."

"Marianne?"

"Who is this, please?"

"Jerry Pavlov."

"Well, hello, there. Find your smoke alarms?"

"Yes I did. In the safe house I was looking for, based on your cell tower info. Thanks again for the input."

"Hey, there, we try to help."

"Today I've got something else on my mind."

Marianne adopted a wary tone. "Mmm. I hear another favor waiting to be asked."

"Yeah, might be a big one. My smoke alarm pals are gone, but they left a note in the house. Not much to go on, just a couple of words and a bunch of initials. G-H-L is what stands out for me."

"Unh-huh. G-H-L."

"I thought . . . you've been so helpful . . . maybe you could decode this for me."

"I don't have a clue."

"Me neither, but your identified murder victim — McCracken? — he was working for those alien rights activists, the Bracero Brotherhood."

"Yeah . . ."

"And, unknown to them, he was trying to uncover the Fast Pass Gang for the Home team."

"Yeah . . ."

"Who was he after?"

A lightbulb went on in Marianne's head. "Wait a minute. G-H-L — that could refer to Golden Harvest Labor, that was McCracken's last known investigation, I checked."

"G-H-L — tah-dah! I think the note refers to that company, right up there in your neck of the woods."

"Uh-oh, what's on your mind? I don't think I want to know."

"To me, it looks like McCracken was closing in on Fast Pass. That's probably what got him killed. Let's say G-H-L does in fact mean Golden Harvest Labor. If that was his target, then — somehow — those people are tied up with the ridiculous terror plot I'm onto."

Marianne was intrigued but doubtful. "Coincidence? Either that or you're a lot luckier than most of us."

"Take a look at that operation for me, okay? I can smell it from here."

"For your information, already done."

"What?"

"I already scoped out the place, quizzed the owner. I agree — it stinks, but I don't know how to prove a thing."

"Take another look, okay? Scout around."

Marianne bristled. "No can do. I'm a cop, sworn to uphold the law. I would need probable cause and a warrant."

Pavlov gritted his teeth. He glanced at his computer screen, where the results of a database query were still on display.

"Wait a minute, lady. Local cops don't have terrorist telephone numbers. I've been doing some research. How did you identify McCracken? Military intelligence, I swear. Your dad, spelling Sarzeau with an 'O,' is a spy, nominally stationed at Fort Benning, but that's just a mail drop for his unit, which I believe is something called FULTAP. How'm I doing?"

Marianne grunted noncommittally. "I can't talk about it."

"No? I also notice you've been traveling overseas. Passport in the name of" — he read from his screen — "Mary Ann *Sarnoff?*"

This revelation annoyed Marianne. "Where do you get off checking my passport?"

"Ha, I'm Homeland. I don't even have to make a request for that. I conclude that you are working with your dad, who is a spook. A real one. FULTAP. Psychic surveillance. You're like him, spooky powers, right? *Agent Broomhandle.*"

"I can neither confirm nor fucking deny."

"Now listen, we're not looking for a conviction in court, this is intelligence work, not law enforcement — something you already know about, in spite of your tight lips."

Marianne relaxed a little. She felt violated by Pavlov's intrusion into the details of her life, but couldn't help admiring his investigative skills. "All right. Busted. What do you want from me?"

"Find out all you can about G-H-L. Somehow, they are involved in smuggling aliens into this country. Aliens who are planning to do bad things."

"Oh man, I am scheduled for night duty. I will have to lie and cheat and sneak my way out of Placerville."

"Get your ass in gear, lives are at stake. Who knows how many?"

25

MARIANNE made herself a cup of weak tea, grabbed a handful of tasteless crackers, and wandered out onto her deck. Almost noon and already hot. She leaned against the railing, mulling Pavlov's problems and the possible connection to the body dump she had discovered. While she was munching and slurping, Wagstaff emerged. He was lugging a backpack.

"I'm off. The *Courier* needs me."

"When will I see you?"

"Depends. It may be an all-nighter."

"I'm on duty tonight, so fine."

"Right."

He gave her a perfunctory kiss and started down the stairs.

"Here's something," she said, calling after him.

"What?"

"My ghost, the blur you saw? He's gone."

"How do you know?"

"He told me."

"Does this signify a return to normality, like you hoped?"

"Don't I wish. But no, not exactly. He appointed a guardian spirit."

"What? Who?"

"He's not human. His name is 'Whiskeyjack.'"

"Like the river."

"So it seems."

"Jesus, M. The weirdness never stops." Wagstaff resumed his departure. "Just don't join a cult or anything, and we'll be okay."

"Roger that," she replied, watching him go. She was enjoying the hot weather, glad that her next shift, in heavy police blues, would take place much later in the cool of the evening.

Shortly after Wagstaff's big yellow SUV drove out of sight, an inner voice cut through her idle thoughts.

"Hi, Mom."

Marianne's heart skipped a beat. But as inexplicably strange as it was to hear the voice of an unborn child, her even stranger experiences of the past couple of years gave her some perspective. She smiled to herself.

"Whoa, it's you, the kid, talking again. What's on your tiny mind today?"

"I can tell you're planning on taking some big risks. You, my mother to be. That worries me."

"I'll be careful. I always am."

"You can never be too careful. You need Whiskeyjack by your side. You need spells."

"Unh-huh. Spells I've got. Whiskeyjack? Except for the introduction, I've never seen him."

"Try your mirror."

Marianne returned to her apartment, entered her little bathroom, and faced the mirror. She tightened her hand around the stone talisman under her blouse.

"Okay, there, Whiskeyjack, whoever you are. Let's talk."

Nothing but her own face showed in the glass. Not a blur, not the faintest ripple. Her hand was tingling. She waited for a few seconds, just to be sure she was obeying the proper protocol.

"Hey, you with the long name. I've been advised to make contact. My advisor seems to know what he's talking about — God, he's *talking!* — so where are you?"

She waited some more, but saw no changes in her frowning image. She fetched Chief Ibañez' old police badge out of her purse and held up both of her magical artifacts in a ferocious grip.

"Whiskeyjack? *Hey you!*"

Another long wait. The abrupt summons, which often worked with her virtual visitor, had no effect.

"Maybe you're asleep. Do you sleep over there? Or maybe you're busy. Don't let me interrupt anything important, ha ha."

She waited some more, waving her hands and tapping her feet. But finally, overwhelmed by impatience, she gave up.

"So much for guarding me, Mr. Guardian."

▼

Out on the deck she nibbled on crackers while leafing through her book of spells. Last year, chasing her heritage in France, she had acquired an old leather-bound book from her French cousins. Ray Bagwell had it translated by computer and later touched up the spells. The result was a long and dense PDF file, filled with strange observations, confusing instructions, and secret knowledge, which she had printed out on Wagstaff's inkjet.

While she was reading, a small bird flew across the grounds of the Golden Nugget Apartments and landed beside her on the porch railing. A gray jay. Marianne was surprised and pleased.

"Hello, little guy. Have I seen you before? Do we know each other?"

The bird hopped along the railing in her direction. She frowned. At close range the thing looked ragged and flustered. It was carrying a large nut in its bill. It tipped its head down and dropped the object near her hand.

"What's this? An acorn."

The bird pushed the nut forward with its bill.

"Is this a gift?"

The bird pushed the nut again, then wobbled, crouched down, closed its eyes, and slowly toppled to one side.

"Oh my God, you're exhausted. Where did you come from?"

The bird didn't stir.

Marianne ran into the kitchen, poured water into a cup, grabbed a handful of almonds from a can she kept ready, and returned to the deck. She placed the cup on the railing, gently picked the bird up with both hands and held it above the water. She could feel a beating heart through the worn feathers. After a moment the bird's eyes re-opened. It plunged its bill into the cup and drank, splashing water everywhere. She placed the bird back on the railing and opened her hand, revealing the almonds. The bird studied them without moving.

"Oh, too big?"

She cracked the almonds into little pieces. The bird hopped into her hand and hungrily plucked them up. Then it flew up and landed on her shoulder.

"Whoa, you are being very friendly."

The bird nibbled her ear.

"Careful, there."

The bird hopped down onto the railing and tottered back and forth. Marianne ducked into the kitchen again, refilling the cup with water and replenishing her nut supply. When offered, the bird ate and drank, still desperately hungry and thirsty. When the almond chips and water were gone, it cocked its head and stared at her.

"You're a messenger, right? All the way from the river, I bet."

The bird stared.

"The acorn is an amulet."

Weeahh!

The bird flew away in the direction it came from.

Marianne examined the acorn. It looked completely ordinary. She closed her hand around it. She couldn't help noticing a subtle warmth.

"I'll be damned," she said.

In front of the bathroom mirror again, she gripped her granite chip in one hand and the acorn in the other. "Whiskeyjack!" she said.

Her image in the mirror blurred. A ripple started in the middle and spread toward the corners. A smoky form ballooned outward and billowed up in front of her.

"Marianne. You received my gift."

"The jay. Another manifestation?"

"Yes. He is valiant."

"I need to do some investigating. Might have a lead on those dead bodies we found on the river. My son is worried about that."

"You should be worried too. The work is dangerous."

"Well then, Guardian Spirit Thing, what's your advice?"

"Spells. Make sure you have them close at hand, in your mind, ready to declare."

"I have a book that's filled with spells. I can't begin to learn them all. What kind of spells?"

"Invisibility would be useful."

"I've never spotted that one."

"It's in all the books. It's a classic."

She raised a finger to inquire further, but the smoky shape evaporated.

She growled a complaint and returned to the deck with her spell book. After skimming through the pages for long minutes, she came across something called *Obscurity*. She read aloud, repeating the incantation over and over:

> *. . . won't be heard . . .*
> *. . . won't be seen . . .*
> *. . . can't be found . . .*

26

MARIANNE was dressed in blue and ready for battle by 5:30 PM. She drove her Mini downtown, parked, signed in, exchanged greetings with Dez Otis, who was also on night duty this week, and rolled away in her Dodge Charger, off to deter, detect, and halt whatever crime might disturb the peace and tranquility of placid Placerville.

The designated homeless encampment on the east end of town was quiet and nearly empty. Its usual residents were out on the road, she theorized, energized for travel by the comfort of warm weather. The various seedy apartment complexes in the northside canyons were free of domestic disputes. She knew that would change once really hot weather shortened tempers. On Main Street she crossed paths with Otis outside the Hog Heaven Bar & Grille. Nobody was drunk enough to cause trouble this early in the evening, but frequent checks were mandatory, just in case. The two officers waved and continued on their separate ways. In Little Mexico, the radios were loud, but the guns were silent.

Teenagers fled the city park on Benham Street as she cruised by, causing her to stop, get out, and take a look at the grounds. Dirty syringes left by drug users were a constant problem, and sure enough, she found one in the grass beside the basketball court.

"Oh man, bring back OxyContin," she said, being careful not to stab herself.

She deposited the thing in a little sharps box she carried under the front passenger seat and resumed her patrol.

After the second uneventful pass through town and a half-hearted drive through the hillside neighborhoods to show the flag to the middle classes, she judged the hour was right for some real sleuthing.

"Where do you think you're going?" asked her unborn son.

"I'm on a case," she replied as she motored up the hill onto Route 49, heading south.

"Aren't we supposed to be patrolling Placerville?"

"You mean Peacefulville? That *we* are."

"You're risking your job and our safety because you're bored."

"Not another word, you little monster. *We* have work to do."

Marianne would never admit it, not even to herself, but her son's accusation made her uneasy. Maybe he, or some part of her own mind masquerading as a fetus, was right; maybe she was bored. Or dissatisfied. Or restless. Or something. Riding herd on the good citizens of Placerville wasn't really much of a challenge once she grooved into the city's police routine, a task she had accomplished, without apparent effort, more than a year ago. Maybe becoming an ordinary mother was not the way to shape her life. Evasive thoughts about the future tumbled through her mind as she sped along the highway.

Twenty miles later, in the tiny town of Plymouth, she turned west onto Old Sacramento Road. Five minutes after that she crossed Latrobe Road, continued downhill past the Golden Egg Family Farms complex and parked in a gravel turnout a hundred yards beyond the main gate.

Light was fading from the western sky as she emerged from her vehicle. She stood beside it for a while, waiting to see if her arrival would trigger a response. But all was quiet. She checked the loads in her Glock and in her Beretta, told herself to remain calm, and hiked back along the highway toward the ranch buildings. Soon she came to the dirt farm road she had used on her previous visit. She swerved onto the track and continued between the ostrich corrals until she had the main buildings in view. She was worried about motion sensors, but no bright lights flared, and no one challenged her.

Getting directly to the ranch's barns and sheds meant traversing the yard near the main house, and a single lamp on a very tall pole cast just enough light to make that path look risky, so she climbed a fence and started across one of the ostrich corrals. Almost all of the ostriches were gathered in one corner of the enclosure, nestled down and sleeping, but one curious beast stood up, separated itself from the rest, and trotted over, matching her stride. Marianne picked up her pace. The ostrich did the same. It leaned forward and nipped playfully at her hair.

"Hey, go to sleep, you stupid bird," she hissed.

The ostrich made ready to deliver a kick, but Marianne leaped onto the fence, clambered up, and threw herself over before the blow struck.

Now she was in a storage yard. In addition to the aging tractors and farming equipment, she saw a couple of derelict recreation vehicles squatting on flat tires. She thrust her flashlight through an open door of the nearer one. A quick inspection revealed a gutted interior. Seats, storage cabinets, beds, kitchen appliances, and bathroom fixtures were all missing.

She moved on to the second RV and found it in the same condition: aging on the outside, empty on the inside; a hulk.

"Hmm. These things sure aren't smuggling anyone," she muttered.

She continued on, passing the weatherbeaten shipping containers she had seen on her previous visit, and approached a prefab metal building with an arched roof. Rounding the corner she observed another shipping container across the yard. This one was up on a truck bed, and it was gleaming with a new coat of bright red paint. A large white logo on the side read *BEE-LINE* in stylish block letters.

She pushed her flashlight against the window on the end of the prefab building and squinted inside. There in the beam was yet another shipping container with an opening cut into one side. Seats, a stove, a sink, several storage units, a tiny shower stall, and a toilet, all salvaged RV furnishings, were stored nearby. Power tools were arrayed on work tables. A plastic curtain hung from a metal frame surrounding the container, furled in a corner at the moment, but ready to turn the shop into an automotive paint booth.

Marianne was absorbing the view when she noticed a faint reddish glow invading her mind. She flicked off her light and peered around the corner of the building. A big truck tractor was rolling down the long ranch driveway. She ducked back out of the headlights' glare.

The truck stopped in front of the newly painted shipping container, and the driver jumped out.

"Bo . . ." breathed Marianne. "What the fuck . . ."

Dingell it was. He checked the trailer hitch on the truck bed, reached under the chassis and unfolded a step ladder. He placed it beside the container, climbed up and pushed on the large *B* in the logo. Marianne's eyes went wide as a metal portal, fitted exactly to the outlines of the tall letter, pivoted outward, revealing an opening big enough for a person to step through.

"Holy crap," she murmured. "A secret door."

Marianne watched in amazement as Dingell disappeared inside. An interior light went on. She could see RV seats and a kitchenette through the opening. A small hatch opened up near the roof, revealed by a square of light shining through. She heard a gas-powered generator start up, run for a minute or so, then stop. The little hatch closed. The light inside went out. Dingell reappeared, swinging back onto the ladder. He closed the portal and dropped to the ground. Marianne was hypnotized by the show. She wondered how the opening, so precise, was made. Lasers? Welding torches? Could Dingell, that shambling wreck, have done the work?

Dingell had a foot on the step to the truck cab when he paused and looked around. Marianne froze. The man raised his head and sniffed the air like a dog. He started walking slowly in her direction.

Marianne eased herself away from the prefab building and retreated toward a shed alongside the nearest ostrich corral. There, thirty yards away, she huddled under an overhanging roof.

Dingell continued to move warily toward her, evidently able to sense her position. The glow of his hostile aura was scrambling her thoughts. It made her feel dizzy, then nauseous. She bent over and vomited into the dirt.

"Ughhh . . ." she moaned.

Dingell perked up his ears. He turned and marched back to the truck, snatched a flashlight out of a cab door pocket, and turned it on.

Marianne wiped her mouth on a sleeve. Dingell's flashlight was playing over the yard, swinging back and forth. The beam passed right over her, but her dark uniform seemed to conceal her presence. Or maybe not. Dingell was moving her way again. The glow of his aura was pulsing with menace. Marianne scowled, struggling to remember something. After what seemed like hours she separated the words of her new spell from the red haze filling her head. She grasped her talisman tightly and muttered the lines in a shaky whisper:

> *Stop up your ears, I won't be heard;*
> *Avert your eyes, I won't be seen.*
> *Ignore my place, I can't be found;*
> *Be not aware, I am not known.*
> *Think thee I be far away,*
> *Far from where you stand today.*

Dingell paused. He stared vacantly here and there, then snapped off his flashlight and returned to his truck.

Marianne waited for the engine to start before allowing herself to exhale.

After lining himself up with several small turns and moves, Dingell backed under the trailer hitch and hooked up the container. Marianne watched the procedure with great curiosity.

"What's your plan, Stan?"

Dingell threw his rig in gear, made a wide turn through the ranch yard, and headed for the highway.

Marianne ran forward to watch which way he turned.

"Left, he's going left," she said. She lit up her flashlight and sprinted back toward her police cruiser, racing down the dirt track between corrals, heedless of being seen.

▼

Marianne floored the accelerator of her cruiser and roared off eastward on Old Sacramento Road. Dingell and his container were nowhere in sight. She zoomed past the Latrobe Road intersection and drove another half mile before she began to doubt her tactics.

"Where is that guy?"

She pulled over and stepped out onto the roadside. She forced herself to relax by drawing deep and even breaths and staring up at the stars, which were shining brightly in the country-dark sky. After a little while she became aware of Dingell's red aura, moving away southward behind her.

"Christ! He went down Latrobe!" she said.

She made a hasty one-point turn and backtracked to Latrobe Road. There she caught up with Dingell as he turned east onto California Route 16. She followed discreetly, staying well out of sight, relying on her ability to detect the man's peculiarly strong and hostile aura.

Just before the Route 49 intersection, he turned southwest onto California Route 124. Marianne was beginning to wonder about his destination.

"Shit, Bo, where to?"

Not far beyond Ione Dingell picked up California Route 88 and continued downhill toward the Big Valley. He was driving conservatively, and it took him the better part of an hour, rolling sedately through Dogtown and Waterloo, to reach Highway 99 outside Stockton.

"You're not going all the way to LA, I hope."

Marianne was ready to quit. Already, far from home and her own jurisdiction, she felt herself sliding into another life, moving farther and farther away from becoming a normal mom.

"Ten more miles, Bo. Ten more miles and you're Pavlov's problem, not mine."

But Dingell was not heading for LA. When he reached Lathrop, a Stockton suburb, he veered off the highway onto French Camp Road, moving west. After a mile he turned south onto Airport Road, then west again on Roth Road. She watched him turn into a drive paralleling railroad tracks and trundle off toward an endless array of containers waiting to be loaded on trains or trucks. She pulled up at the sign, which read:

UNION PACIFIC RAILROAD
INTERMODAL FACILITY

Marianne drove slowly down the long drive. On one side was a parade of big steel boxes, some of them on truck beds, some on the ground. On the other side were railroad tracks. In between were tall gantry cranes to load and unload. Some of the boxes were arriving, others departing. Some had begun their journeys as far away as Shanghai and Rotterdam. Marianne had just come in contact with the modern way to move the world's goods, in sealed containers adapted for travel by ship, train, and truck.

When she reached the southern end of the operation, Dingell had already passed through the transfer office. She could see him swinging around to position his truck under one of the cranes. She parked out of his sight and, moving stealthily, wove her way on foot through the container maze to his load. Dingell was unhooking his truck when she drew near. He paused when he finished the task, suspiciously looking this way and that. Marianne was wondering if he could detect her presence.

"Marianne? That you?" he called out uncertainly, slowly removing his work gloves.

Yup, he seemed to know she was there. She shrank against a steel container wall. Her stomach was doing flip-flops.

Dingell wasn't convinced, however. Maybe her spell was still working its magic. After a few moments he shook himself, climbed aboard his truck tractor, and drove off the way he came.

Marianne watched the vehicle recede into the distance, then hiked across the gravel and photographed the cargo doors. Then she moved around to the side where the portal had appeared. She could not see the seam. She reached up and ran her fingers along the lower half of the letter

B in the *BEE-LINE* logo. She could just barely feel a narrow slot marking the edge of the secret door. Impressed, she walked thoughtfully along the tracks to the transfer office, where lights were burning.

"Hello, there." she said to the night manager, a middle-aged man with a comfortable paunch. He was wearing a red T-shirt and bib overalls. He stared at the young policewoman over his reading glasses.

"Yes? Well now, look at you, you're a cop. What can I do you for, officer?"

"I'm a long way from home, so I don't have any authority, but I'm tracking a container that just arrived, and I'm hoping you can tell me all about it."

"Maybe, maybe not. ID?"

She opened her wallet and showed him her Placerville ID card.

"No, no, I trust the law. Container ID."

"Sorry. Not sure. I took a picture."

She showed him the photo on her little digital camera. He studied it for a while, punched keys on his keyboard. The information he uploaded took some time to percolate through the railroad's computers.

Marianne was getting antsy. "Do I need a warrant?"

"No, ma'am, I don't see the harm. I'm against crime, and so is my railroad. What evil deeds are we talking about?"

"Don't know yet, could be anything."

"Unh-huh, got it, police business, mum's the word. Okay, then, look here — *GHLU 687621 1* — that top row of letters and numbers on the door there, see?" He pointed at a corner of the photo. Marianne nodded without understanding.

"The first three letters are the company name. And that name is, wait a minute" — he scrolled through a list — "that name is *GHL Distributors,* an LLC registered in, uh, Jackson, looks like."

"Where's it going? Got a destination?"

"Mexico Direct. Intermodal ramp in Nogales, drayage from there to Mexico City."

"Good lord." Marianne was getting excited. "This is great, this is important. Um, any idea what the cargo might be? Or is it just, you know, empty?"

"The manifest says ostrich eggs. Ostrich eggs and ostrich feathers."

"You're kidding."

The man pointed at his screen. "That's what it says."

"Ostrich eggs? What are they good for?"

The man thought it over. "Could be they're empty shells. Send 'em to Mexico, decorate 'em up, send 'em back, sell 'em in gift shops. Engraved views of Aztec ruins, or what the hey."

"Is there a market? I never heard of such a thing."

"Lady, there's a market for everything. That's why this here facility is full of all these big boxes." He swept a hand around to encompass the entire yard and all twelve hundred shipping containers stored there.

"You know a lot about this stuff, and I know zippity-doo. Can I call you if I get stuck?"

"Sure, but you'd do better to check with customer service in Omaha."

"Why Omaha?"

"That's where all our trains are controlled. Harriman Dispatch Center, the Bunker. Think of air traffic control, but no windows. I was there once." He reached into a drawer and withdrew two business cards. "This is me, Barney, and this is Molly C. I know her, and she's a doll. Talk to her."

Marianne looked at the cards. The Union Pacific shield logo and the slogan "Building America" were printed above the names: *Barnard Durham* and *Melissa P. Caspian.* There were phone numbers. Marianne stuffed the cards into her blouse pocket.

"Thanks, bro."

▼

Back in Placerville, an hour later while cruising through town, she crossed paths with Otis outside the Hog Heaven. They were each keeping a watchful eye on that notorious source of bad behavior. Otis signaled with an outstretched hand, and Marianne, going the other way, pulled her car alongside.

"Where you been, Sarzeau? I haven't seen you all night."

"Oh, down in Little Mexico. Out on Missouri Flat, here and there." She waved nonchalantly. "Quiet tonight."

Otis frowned. "Yeah, very."

"Well look, I'm going to swing through the canyons. Meet you at the Coffee Depot."

"I dunno about you, Squeek. You're up to no good."

"I'm just rolling and patrolling."

Cars were lining up behind them.

"Right, Coffee Depot," said Otis with a skeptical smirk.

They drove away in opposite directions. Marianne, heading downhill, turned behind the Buttermilk Pantry and parked in the lot. There she lit up her smartphone and made a call, the fourth time she had tried the number that evening.

"Ahh, hello . . ?"

The voice sounded drowsy and confused.

"Agent Pavlov?"

"Who wants to know?"

"It's Marianne Sarzeau."

"Unnhhh . . . Sarzeau . . . whassup?"

"You sound foggy. Is this a bad time?"

"No, no, wide awake. What's on your mind at this hour? Christ, it's after midnight."

"I tried to call you earlier, but you didn't pick up."

"No, kind of . . . busy."

Marianne grinned. "Okay, big guy, what's her name?"

"Um . . . . . . Ginger."

"Is she cute?"

"Cute enough."

"I see. Okay, then, if you can concentrate on work for a minute or two, I've got some news that will ruin your date."

"I'm listening."

"I was checking Golden Harvest tonight, like we talked, and discovered one of those containers outfitted like a fancy RV."

"What kind of container? Plastic?"

"Are you drunk? A cargo container. Steel box. Size of a bus."

"Oh yeah."

"There's more — a nutball who's been stalking me works for those guys. He's a criminal with a record. Hiring him? That's shady right there. He showed up in a big truck and towed the thing down to Lathrop, where the railroad has a yard set up to put containers on the tracks."

"Unh-huh."

"Where do you think it was going?"

"Is this a trick question?"

"Mexico."

"You don't say."

"I observed a livable interior in that thing. Seats, some kind of kitchen. They're building another one in a shop with parts from a couple of gutted RVs I also saw."

Pavlov seemed to wake up. "Now *that* is interesting."

"I also did some googling. Did you know that trains can come from Mexico into the USA without clearing customs until they reach their destination?"

"Yes, behold the glory of NAFTA. Your conclusion?"

"I think Golden Harvest has more of these chariots. Your Fast Pass Gang is migrating to America by riding the rails."

Pavlov mumbled something unintelligible.

"Sorry if I wrecked your evening."

"Are you kidding? News like this is better than sex."

"Tell that to Ginger."

27

AT FOUR O'CLOCK in the afternoon of July Fourth, friends and family of Lorraine Wagstaff and Howard Turnbow gathered on the spacious lawn behind Turnbow's grandiose Tarvolo mansion for a wedding.

The mayor of the Golden Hills Tri-Town Special District was a wealthy man, and a catering army had been busy for days sparing no expense to make sure of every detail. Many of them stood waiting for the guests in white shirts, black vests, and sharply creased pants.

A tent canopy had been erected in the middle of the lawn. Wooden folding chairs were set out in rows on the hardwood floor beneath it. Lavish bouquets of lilies, orchids, and hollyhocks were suspended from cast iron stands in silver vases all across the yard. They lined a paved walkway from the house to a lattice-work gazebo at the edge of the property. This ornamental structure, covered with white-painted gingerbread, surrounded by roses, and topped by a golden weathervane, had been constructed especially for the occasion.

Turnbow's home was the first one built in the upscale gated community that was Tarvolo. As one of the development's principal investors he got first choice of the lots, and his choice was a good one. The building sprawled across a knoll overlooking the Tarvolo golf course. Fifteen rooms, a pool, and a three-car garage. Maturing oaks softened the appearance of massive stucco walls. The waters of Upper Bar Lake glistened in the distance.

The guests arrived in waves, looking bright and breezy in their summer clothes. Cousins, nieces, and nephews of the bride and groom. Turnbow's brother, wife, and their grown children. Lorraine's college roommate. All the locals. Marianne's former police colleagues Ricky Moss and Wade Gawley were there in suits with string ties. They were ushering guests to their seats as instructed, without regard to family connections. Dez Otis appeared in his police blues.

The afternoon was hot, and soon men's jackets were hanging on the backs of chairs. Women fanned themselves with the occasion's little programs, nicely printed by Tom Wagstaff.

After inevitable delays for last minute grooming, Dominic Fabriano, the Tri-Town chief of police and the man chosen to officiate, led Wagstaff and

Turnbow out to the gazebo, where they turned and waited for the bride and her maid.

Upstairs in the master bedroom, Lorraine was fussing with her clothes and makeup. Marianne was there to help her motherly pal.

"I'm a wreck. What a joke, getting married at my age," said Lorraine, throwing up her hands.

"Come on, you're beautiful. Howard will be dazzled. I'm dazzled," Marianne replied.

"Now that this is really happening, I'm not sure we shouldn't have left things as they were."

"Don't be silly."

"Who knows how much time we have? One of us is going to be widowed all over again."

"Boy, are you cheerful today."

"Just looking for some sympathy. Getting older, it's hard to look ahead."

"Then don't. Help me worry instead — my ghost is gone," said Marianne, changing the subject and looking for a little sympathy herself.

Lorraine stopped fluffing her hair. "How do you know something like that?"

"He told me. Off to 'other duties' . . . in some galaxy far, far away, probably."

"I would think that's a relief. You're always nervous about him."

"Yeah, true. But he introduced me to someone else, a guardian spirit."

"What?"

"Yup."

"You've seen him? What does he look like?"

"He's not human. Think Smokey the Bear. Sort of. Except you can see through him and his eyes glow."

"Whoa. Spooky."

"Tell me. And, whoa, it turns out I conjured him last summer with Dad, and when he appears on our side of the line, he's a flaming monster."

"Good gracious. Does this spirit have a name?"

"Whiskeyjack."

"Like the river?"

"Weird, huh?"

The Tailings, a local country rock band, had their gear set up under the tent. At a signal from Fabriano, the keyboardist jammed his hands down on a chord, and *Here Comes the Bride* blasted out of huge loudspeakers, nearly deafening everyone.

Marianne preceded Lorraine out of the house. She was wearing a lightweight lavender dress, held up by spaghetti straps. She cast rose petals from a silver platter as she strutted to the gazebo.

Lorraine followed in an equally simple pink dress. She was carrying a spray of flowers from her garden; blue larkspur and white roses. A wreath of tiny pink roses circled her gray hair.

Gawley and Moss took up places beside the entrance to the gazebo as Marianne and Lorraine stepped inside.

Turnbow took Lorraine's hand.

"Dearly beloved . . ." intoned Fabriano.

Befitting an older couple, the ceremony was traditional.

". . . do you take this woman . . ?"

". . . I do."

". . . and do you take this man . . ?"

". . . I do."

"Is there a ring?"

Wagstaff handed Turnbow a plain gold band. The groom slipped it on Lorraine's finger. Marianne passed Lorraine an identical ring, and she placed it on Turnbow's finger.

"I now pronounce you man and wife. You may kiss the bride."

A tender kiss accompanied by a wave of triumph from Turnbow. Laughter, cheers, and applause from the assembled guests.

Suddenly fireworks erupted from behind the gazebo. Big bangs, bright lights, stunning even in full afternoon sun. Chief Fabriano frowned, but decided not to arrest anyone.

The Tailings lit into Mendelssohn's *Wedding March*, and the newly wedded couple quickstepped back to the house, waving and smiling. The reception was set to take place right there on the lawn, but food wouldn't be served for another hour. Meanwhile, the caterers circulated through the crowd with beer, wine, and hors d'oeuvres.

By the time Turnbow and Lorraine returned to their guests everyone was pleasantly tight. All four of the wedding party had changed clothes, and now wore casual shirts and pants.

Turnbow was carrying golf clubs and a large bucket of golf balls. He took up a position at the edge of the knoll, where he had built himself a proper tee.

"The Tarvolo practice green is a hundred and fifty yards away, right below us. Let's see who can get there." He held up a number four wood.

Wade Gawley stepped forward.

"Yell, 'fore' just before you swing," said Turnbow.

"Fore!" shouted Gawley and took a mighty swing. The ball, which he topped, spun out and down and landed maybe thirty yards away in the rough beside the eighteenth fairway. Cheers and jeers from the rest of the guests.

Chief Fabriano was next. He hooked his shot, and the ball veered to the left, bouncing right into a foursome finishing their round. Distant faces turned upward. Fists were shaken. Turnbow waved cordially, but Fabriano shrank back out of sight. "Fore," he yelled after the fact.

Wagstaff took the club, teed up a ball and cranked a blast to the edge of the practice green. "Not a golfer," he said, excusing himself. The other guests clapped anyway.

Lorraine took a turn. Her ball flew a hundred yards, rolled another forty, and came to a stop ten yards shy of the goal. Angry shouts from below.

Turnbow chuckled as he stepped forward. He was enjoying the chaos they were creating. He smacked a perfect shot that flew high in the air and came down within two feet of one of the practice pins. A man lining up his own putt at the same hole dropped his club in astonishment.

Finally Marianne gave it a try. She had never played golf, except the miniature kind at amusement parks, but she was athletic and competitive. She grounded the club, arched her backswing and — *thwack!* — lofted a shot that soared high over the practice green and dropped onto a table at Rossi's Fine Italian Dining, splattering bolognese sauce and almost causing heart attacks among the startled diners.

The wedding guests, festively immune from ordinary decorum, laughed long and loud.

Now it was time for dinner. Tables were set up on the lawn, chairs were redeployed, and caterers dodged through the group with elegant plates of steak, trout, and chicken. Champagne bubbled into flutes. Wagstaff stood up, clanging a knife against his glass for attention.

"Here's to the bride and groom —"

"Hear, hear!" shouted the guests.

"— may they live long and happily together — long enough to find out if they really enjoy married life!"

This faintly complex sentiment was confusing to some, but the tipsy mood carried the day, and everyone applauded.

Soon light was fading from the sky. Chairs were whisked off the tent floor. The Tailings revved up the old Beatles tune, *Can't Buy Me Love*, and the dancing began.

Turnbow took a blushing Lorraine in his arms and whirled her around. Then they separated, and Lorraine tugged her son onstage. Turnbow grabbed Marianne.

"Happy?" she inquired as she was spun across the boards.

"That I am, Golden Girl, that I am."

"Keep it that way, buster. Lorraine's my best friend, and if you cause her any grief I'm going to put a spell on you."

Turnbow laughed. Marianne kissed him. "Love you both. You guys are great."

▼

Outside, at Tarvolo's main gate, one of the catering trucks was on its way home, mission accomplished. As it passed through the barrier it was forced to drive around an old pickup truck that was waiting to enter. The pickup scooted inside as the gate closed, scraping a fender in the process.

▼

On Turnbow's lawn, the festivities were heating up. Dancing was interrupted as the Tailings rocked out an insane version of the *National Anthem*, which was accompanied by a spectacular barrage of skyrockets, fountains, pinwheels, and salutes orchestrated by professionals from Sacramento.

After the smoke cleared, the dancing resumed. One song ended and another began, this time Lady Antebellum's slow waltz, *If I Knew Then*. Sensing something easy, guests poured onto the floor. Marianne and Wagstaff found each other, embraced, and moved with the crowd to the relaxed tempo.

"If they really enjoy marriage? Really? What kind of toast was that?"

asked Marianne.

"Gotta make sure they're aimed in the right direction. Out loud, from the get-go. My superstition."

"You're not really worried about them."

"No. Not really."

"It's us."

"Hey, come on, we're dancing, Mom just got hitched, don't rain on the parade."

Marianne was silent for a moment, pondering her beau's evasion. Finally, she thought she had a rejoinder and was about to speak when screams and shouts issued from the house.

Suddenly the catering team was running onto the lawn, shrieking and yelling, scared out of their wits.

The driver of their panic was Bo Dingell. He was dressed in a filthy T-shirt and camo hunting pants. He was brandishing a Colt revolver with a long barrel. He advanced across the lawn, searching the crowd for a target. After a surreal pause while time seemed to stop, he noticed Marianne and turned toward her. He leveled his revolver.

"Mari-Annie! The girl for meeeeeee . . !"

Wagstaff vaulted forward and shoved Marianne to the dance floor. He took a step toward the interloper. Turnbow followed right behind.

Blam!

Dingell discharged his revolver. A single shot, but both Wagstaff and Turnbow went down. The rest of the crowd scrambled for the far corners of the property.

Marianne rolled over, yanked her little Beretta from her ankle holster, aimed at the sky, and pulled the trigger.

Pow! Pow! Pow! Pow! Pow!

Dingell blinked, hesitated, advanced again.

Pow! Pow! Pow! Pow! Pow!

Marianne's second volley stopped Dingell short. He seemed to come to his senses. He looked around at the scattered merrymakers peering at him from behind trees, latticework, and guitar amps, blinked vacantly, then turned and ran. After a moment they heard his pickup racing away.

Marianne leaped to her feet and stooped over Wagstaff. "Oh my God, oh my God, oh my God!" she stammered, white with worry. She placed a hand over his ribs, where blood was soaking through his shirt.

But then . . . "Tom's breathing!" she exclaimed.

Lorraine was huddling over her fallen husband. A red patch was spreading over Turnbow's chest. "Help! Howard's bleeding," she sobbed.

Dez Otis, who was shy about dancing, had been hovering in the background until this moment. Now he stepped forward, whipped open his mobile phone, and dialed 9-1-1.

▼

Ambulances arrived from Jackson within fifteen minutes of the attack, practically a world record response time, but enough of a delay for both Marianne and Lorraine to work themselves into a frenzy.

They watched as the EMTs lashed Wagstaff and Turnbow to stretchers and placed them in the vehicles. IV drips were already in place, and the responders were working with calm purpose. Indications were positive, but Marianne was chewing a knuckle. Lorraine was walking back and forth in a catatonic daze.

"Come on, we're done here," advised the senior paramedic. He gestured toward the open doors. Marianne nodded absently, squeezed Lorraine's hand, and got into the first ambulance with Wagstaff. Lorraine joined her husband in the second. Fifty shocked wedding guests watched the two emergency vehicles pull away, yellow lights flashing like another fireworks display.

28

AT SUTTER AMADOR HOSPITAL in Jackson, Wagstaff and Turnbow were lying in adjacent rooms, attached to modern medicine by numerous wires and tubes.

Outside in the hallway, an emergency room doctor explained the situation to Marianne and Lorraine, who were both quivering with anxiety.

"A single bullet wounded both of them, apparently. First, it clipped the young man — Mr. Wagstaff? — bruising the ribs on his left side pretty good, and then hit" — he consulted a note — "Mayor Turnbow is it? — in the chest. Although the wounds are not life-threatening, we have admitted them."

Big sighs of relief from both women.

"They are still unconscious, but vital signs are good. Turnbow has a cracked sternum, but the bullet was deformed by hitting Wagstaff, so it didn't penetrate further. I won't say they were lucky, but it might have been much worse."

"How long . . . how long will they have to be here, in the hospital?" asked Lorraine miserably. "We were supposed to get on a plane for Cancun tomorrow."

"Cancun will have to be postponed, I'm afraid. When they wake up, they're going to be hurting for a while. Not ready for fun on the beach."

Lorraine's eyes were wet. Marianne's too. They hugged each other.

▼

Marianne excused herself and called Deputy Sheriff Al Burns on her mobile phone.

"Al, you there? Talk to me."

After several rings, the man picked up.

"Sarzeau, you okay?"

"Yeah, but my guy Tom and Howard Turnbow are in the hospital."

"I know. Your partner, Officer Otis, he called me."

"Did he give you the perp?"

"No, I don't think he had an ID."

"It was Bo Dingell."

"Don't know the name."

"D-I-N-G-E-L-L, a moronic lunatic. I've arrested him several times. Attempted murder."

"Why would this guy want to shoot the Tri-Town mayor?"

"He didn't. He was looking for me. I was the target."

"Unh-huh, okay. Why?"

"Um, he's got a fixation. He was stalking me. I think the standard formula is, 'I rejected his advances.'"

"Got it."

"Get after him, he's crazy, and he's dangerous."

"Don't worry. We're mustering the troops. Keep your eyes open, just in case."

"Wilco. Listen — I happen to know he works, or has worked, for Golden Harvest Labor, or their sister company, Golden Egg Family Farms."

"How is that?"

"I spotted him on their ranch working the body dump case. Our only ID-able victim was investigating them."

"Duly noted."

Marianne ended the call, walked down the hallway, and slipped into the women's restroom. She faced the mirror, gripped her little acorn tightly, waited for it to feel warm in her hand, and croaked out a name . . .

"Whiskeyjack," she said.

Nothing.

"Come on, come on, I need to talk to you."

Still nothing. She put her other hand around her stony amulet.

"Whiskeyjack! Whiskeyjack! I've said your name three times, for Christ's sake."

A minute went by. Marianne was stamping her feet. Finally a smoky form appeared in the glass. It loomed outward and hovered over her, a feral presence that was at once more real, more fantastic, and more intimidating than her old virtual visitor ever was. She shrank back against the door.

"Marianne . . . I am here." Even though the voice was all in her mind, it rumbled with grave authority.

"Hi, there, Smokey," she said, doing her best to be brave.

"You are troubled. How can I help?"

"Bo Dingell just shot my fiancé and my friend Howard Turnbow. What's going on with this guy — he's some kind of adept, very creepy."

"Your stalker is not himself. He is in thrall to a demon."

"An evil demon."

"Evil? That's a mortal term. Think factions, sides taken, ambitions. But hostile to you . . . oh yes."

"Why? Why in the name of anything?"

"No doubt he is holding your betrothed hostage. I doubt he will ever wake up unless you surrender yourself."

"Surrender?"

"Or fight. That would be my recommendation."

"Fight. How would I ever?"

"You must travel to my world. Be as one of us."

"Oh, ha ha ha, that's good. Become a spirit."

"It is possible. Drugs, incantations. Didn't the Crowfoot woman explain it all?"

"She did."

"Well then. Your choice. But beware, you may not survive. The demon will try to steal your soul. He is very powerful."

Marianne gulped.

"If it will save Tom, I'll do it."

▼

In Wagstaff's hospital room, Marianne leaned over her fiancé. He appeared to be sleeping peacefully. If a demon held him hostage, it was hard to tell. She kissed his cheek.

Lorraine came into the room for a look at her son. She was wringing her hands in grief and frustration.

"How's my boy?"

"Shh. Sleeping."

"He looks okay."

"Whiskeyjack says he's being held hostage. I have to fight a demon to bring him back."

"That's insane. How?"

"In his world, whatever that means. Enter a trance, I suppose."

"Good lord. Don't even think about things like that."

Marianne smoothed Wagstaff's shaggy hair. "It's Tom. He's my guy.

He belongs to me, and no demon is going to have him."

Lorraine was holding back tears. "Howard is restless. He's squirming around, and the nurses have taped his arms down so he won't rip out the IV and the wires."

"I want to see."

Leaving Lorraine to guard her fiancé, Marianne hurried next door, where Turnbow was writhing around in his bed. A nasal cannula was fastened around his nose, delivering oxygen, but he was groaning uncomfortably with every breath.

"Howard?"

Louder moans and groans. His shoulders bucked. His arms rebelled against the restricting tape.

A nurse entered with a syringe. "Excuse me, miss. We need to calm the patient down. Don't worry, he'll be okay."

Next door, Lorraine bent over her son and caressed his cheek.

"Tom . . ."

Wagstaff drew a deep and sleepy breath. His eyes opened wide.

"Mom?"

Lorraine let out a shriek of joy. Marianne came running from Turnbow's side.

"Marianne . . ." he said, slurring the name. "Hello, there, M. How ya doin'?"

"Oh my God, you're awake!"

"Mmm."

"You're going to be okay, going to be fine. You'll be fine."

"There's room for improvement. My left side hurts like hell."

Marianne leaned over and kissed him on the lips. Lorraine held his hand. Tears were falling.

▼

The two women stood watch all night. Lack of sleep and a lot of coffee sobered them both, and by dawn's early light they were too tired to be frantic anymore.

"Tom woke up. Not a hostage after all, no demon to fight," offered Lorraine as early morning sun shot through a distant window at the end of the hall.

"Thank God, or whoever is in charge up there," Marianne replied without any energy.

"Got a funny sense of humor, that guy."

"I'll say. Let's see about your new husband."

They shuffled into Turnbow's room, where the unconscious man was thrashing around in his restraints, evidently in the throes of a vivid dream.

"Why isn't he awake yet?" asked Lorraine.

A nurse was already at his side with a syringe poised at the port on the IV drip, ready to renew the sedation that kept her patient from tearing up his medical attachments.

"Hang on there, nurse," said Marianne. "No more drugs."

"He's going to hurt himself," said the nurse.

Marianne studied her friend and radio boss. His color was good, and he seemed to be struggling to wake up.

"I've seen this kind of condition before," said Marianne. "I'm going to try something, don't be alarmed."

"I'll call the doctor," said the nurse, very much alarmed. She marched away to summon reinforcements.

"What do you think you're doing? Don't you dare hurt this man," said Lorraine.

Marianne stared off into space. She was recalling something from her book of spells. She placed a hand on Turnbow's brow and began to chant in a low voice:

> *Dreamer, lost in drowsy places,*
> *Hear our voices, see our faces.*
> *Turn your mind away from night;*
> *Raise your eyes unto the light.*
> *Thus order I with witch's hand;*
> *Sleep no more at my command!*

Lorraine was dumbfounded by the performance, her first actual encounter with witchy work. "That was a spell?"

"There are a number of *Waking* spells. I picked the one that includes bystanders, I thought you'd like that."

"And you think this beats the nurse's medicine?"

"We'll find out . . ."

Turnbow gradually stopped twisting and turning. His face, previously contorted, smoothed out. But his eyes stayed shut.

"This isn't working. I'll call the nurse."

Marianne grabbed Lorraine's arm to stop her. "Wait, wait, sometimes it takes a while . . ."

The nurse reappeared with a grim-faced doctor in tow.

"What's going on here?" he inquired.

"You'll see," said Marianne, pretending confidence she didn't feel.

Slowly Turnbow's eyes cracked open. They rolled around as he took in the hospital room and the high-tech life support equipment. He turned his head toward the people at his bedside.

"Well, look at you, Mr. Turnbow," said the nurse.

Lorraine leaned over and brushed her lips against his forehead. "Howard, honey? How are you feeling?"

"Unhhh," he said. "Bad dream."

29

GEFU 513914 3, a type 42G1 general purpose shipping container forty feet long and eight feet six inches high, was painted bright blue with *HI-LINE* stenciled along the sides in tall block letters. It was moving north through Mexico along with one hundred and ninety-nine other containers on a train more than a mile long. The cargo manifest claimed it held a collection of Fiat auto parts, and it did — in the first six feet behind the loading doors. The rest of the interior was outfitted like a recreation vehicle, complete with large quantities of bottled water in storage cabinets, a refrigerator full of packaged meals, a microwave to cook them, and a chemical toilet. Twelve reclining seats were arranged in two rows of six. Seven of the seats were occupied. The arrangement was comfortable, but the slow progress of freight travel and the lack of windows made the trip a very boring one.

Simon Hatch and Yannick Brunel, recently noticed by Homeland Security personnel in Mexico City, were riding in the last row. Hatch rummaged around in his duffel and removed a GPS receiver. He stepped to the far corner of the container, racked open a tiny portal, and stuck the GPS antenna through it.

"Here we go — 31.31 degrees . . . 31.33 . . . 31.45. Hey, Yan, we crossed. We're in the states."

Brunel stuck a thumb up. Hatch directed his attention to their five traveling companions, all Mexican nationals.

"Hola, hermanos! We have crossed the border. We're stateside."

Three of the Mexicans were asleep. The other two barely glanced up.

"¡Los Estados Unidos! ¡El Norte!"

One of the men, an older fellow wearing a jacket and loosely fastened tie, raised his eyes from a book and nodded. He didn't seem too excited.

Hatch resumed his seat. "These Mexicans, fooking illegals," he muttered.

"They are unbelievers, Christians, Allah will forget them," said Brunel.

"Not field workers in those clothes. Criminals. And the food they eat. Not *halal,* and it's stinking up the place."

Brunel opened a backpack and brought forth a portable scanner. He tuned the device to 160 megahertz and handed it to Hatch.

"You listen, I cannot hear the fast English."

Hatch returned to the portal, pushed the scanner up against the opening. A long silence followed. Then voices. At least three, having some sort of discussion about subdivisions, tracks, times, and schedules.

"Shit," said Hatch.

He turned off the scanner and dropped back into his seat. "There's a high priority train coming south. That's going to hold us up in Tucson."

"Will Mansour figure it out?"

"He better."

Part FOUR

30

SUMMER SUNSHINE was gleaming through the gauzy curtains in Marianne's apartment where Wagstaff was propped up in bed. His ribs were heavily bandaged. He had Marianne's old laptop open and was reading an article online.

"Hey, M, listen to this . . ."

"Coming . . . hang on." Marianne herself appeared with a tray of orange juice, coffee, scrambled eggs, and waffles. "Breakfast, sir?"

"Wow. Looks great."

She bent over and kissed him. "Don't be too impressed. The waffles came out of a package. I just threw them in the toaster."

"That's okay, I'm hungry."

"Will this information ruin my chance for a tip?" She smiled, pleased to be nursing her fiancé, reinforcing their strained relationship.

"Probably not, someday, when it won't hurt to give you one."

"I can wait."

She sat down beside him, being careful not to bounce around. "What are you reading?"

"Anthropology. All about that name, *Whiskeyjack*. Bird, river, your guardian spirit thing."

"That's not his real name, you know."

"You told me. Says here the origin is a native Algonkian prankster god — a representative of the *Manitou* life force that they believe is everywhere, all around us. Get this, somebody variously called Weesack-kachack, Wisagatcak, Wis-kay-tchach, Wissaketchak, Woesack-ootchacht, Vasaagihdzak, Whiskachon, or Wiskedjak."

"Aren't the Algonquins an eastern tribe?"

"Yes, a bunch, not just one."

"They were having as much trouble pronouncing his name as I do."

"Mmm."

"I don't get it. How did a name like that get out west here?"

"The miners who named the river — and the bird — all came from back east. They probably heard about the Algonkian god."

Wagstaff paused. He closed the laptop and leaned back against the pillows. "You know what I think? If this character, guardian, whatever he is that's haunting you, is real —"

"He's scary real, babe."

"— I think that ordinary people can vaguely sense his presence. Maybe he likes to hang around rivers. Maybe he whispers his name to everyone who will listen."

"You'll make full professor yet."

▼

Marianne took a quick shower and telephoned Al Burns. On the second try she got through.

"Morning, Al. It's Sarzeau. Any news on that crazy guy Dingell?"

"Sorry, Marianne. He has not been seen."

"Did you check on Golden Harvest?"

"We did. They have employed him for several years as a truck driver and welder. He didn't show up for work this week."

"Damn."

"We have other leads."

"Thanks, I'll feel a lot safer when you rope him in."

"Don't you worry your pretty head. We're on it, we're investigating, we'll let you know."

She hung up and glared at the phone. "Sure you will, you lazy bastard."

She had heard Burns' reassuring mantra before . . . and used it herself now and then.

Marianne spent the rest of the morning poring over her spell book while Wagstaff, still propped up in bed, worked on stories for the *Courier*. She was beginning to feel that her only protection against Dingell was Whiskeyjack, and she wanted him to appear beside her on command. She leafed through the pages, looking for a reliable conjuring spell. Mindful of her dangerous errors of a year ago, she was looking for a way to be sure any demon she might conjure would be a friendly one.

▼

By evening Wagstaff had dragged himself out of bed and hobbled onto Marianne's deck. She brought him a beer. They clicked glasses.

"Want to ride somewhere with me?"

"I thought you were off tonight."

"Not on patrol. Little drive, and we can stop somewhere for a bite later."

Wagstaff noted the hint of a smile playing over her lips. "What are you up to?"

"You'll see. Well, maybe, but probably not."

Marianne drove slowly through town and north on Georgetown Road to the South Fork of the American River, being careful to avoid bumps and jolts. Wagstaff was uncomfortable and tense, but game.

At the bridge she turned off the pavement and drove into the China Flat Slate Quarry. Gravel, a product of the river in ancient days, snapped and popped under her little Mini's tires. Sheets of gray stone stood out of the barren hillside facing the water. Not a green plant anywhere within fifty yards.

"Mind telling me what's going on?" groused Wagstaff.

"An experiment."

She opened the trunk, dug through a duffle bag, and hauled out a can of Sterno, which she ignited with a little BiC lighter. She walked away from the car and placed the can on the ground. The pale blue flame was barely visible in the twilight.

"I need a fire, and I don't want to burn down the entire Sierra, so here we are."

"What are you doing?"

"Let's see if Whiskeyjack wants to pay a visit to our little corner of the real world."

She opened a plastic bag containing cat hair and fragments of dried datura blossoms. She pinched a teaspoon's worth between her fingers and threw the mixture into the flame.

Whoosh!

A fiery vortex, bright yellow, spun up out of the canister. She retreated from the heat.

"I don't want to use any blood, that can backfire. But I've made some changes to the magic words. Let's see now . . ."

She began to chant:

> *From searing flame bring forth my guy,*
> *The spirit on whom I rely . . .*

Before she could complete the spell, the vortex whirled up to twice her height. A head-like shape formed. Eyes like smoldering black pits appeared. Fiery arms reached out. Claws snapped.

Marianne leaped backward. Hot fingers raked her forearm, leaving welts. The column of flame became legs. The creature detached itself from the vortex and strode toward her.

"Ogggggg . . ." it bellowed.

Marianne felt dizzy. She lost her balance, collapsed, and vomited into the dirt.

Wagstaff tumbled out of the car, staggered over to the can of Sterno. He bent down, scooped up a handful of sand, and dumped it on the flames.

Sssst!

The fire went out. The creature vanished.

"Jesus Christ Almighty fucking God, M!" he yelped, cradling his injured ribs.

Marianne got to her feet and shook herself. The dizziness was wearing off, but she still felt oddly giddy. She removed a bottle of water from her duffle and gargled noisily.

"You okay? See anything?" she asked, after the wave of nausea passed.

"Fire, smoky blob. It looked alive."

"It was, and — it was not my pal Whiskeyjack."

"Who then?"

"Dingell's guy, most likely. I need a better spell!"

▼

The hour was late when they arrived at Hannah Crowfoot's door in Angels Camp. None of them had eaten, however, so they drove the old woman to the Jumping Frog Café, just around the corner from her house. There, over meatloaf and mashed potatoes, Marianne quizzed the old woman about conjuring spells.

"I never conjured anything worse than a moth," said Ms. Crowfoot.

"But you read, you know all about this stuff."

Ms. Crowfoot consulted a book she had brought with her. "Your demon has a name. Whiskeyjack, is that right?"

"More or less. His real name is a yard long."

"Looks like you need a *named spirit* incantation." She tapped a page. "It says here that such a spell will channel your guardian."

"My book doesn't have anything like that. What's the wording?"

"Doesn't say. Just that you need it to weed out unwanted spirits."

"Great, a spell that doesn't exist."

"You watch yourself, young lady. I've warned you before about conjuring in fire."

"What she said," added Wagstaff.

"I know."

▼

They decided to spend the night in Wagstaff's loft-like home office. When they arrived, Wagstaff immediately tottered off to bed, but Marianne checked her watch and got on the phone. Midnight in America; lunchtime, or close to it, wherever FULTAP was working.

"Ray? That you?" The background noise that always plagued their satellite phone connections was worse than usual.

"Broomhandle?" queried Bagwell. "Can barely hear. Must be a solar flare."

"Thank God you're not getting roasted on Mars."

"Nothing so exotic. Tea at the ambassador's residence. What's up?"

"I need a spell, Ray. To conjure a demon — yup, you heard me — and it has to be the right one. Hannah tells me I can use what she calls a *named spirit* spell, but there's nothing in her books or mine. You're up."

"I'm supposed to be stopping an international spy ring, and you want me to write spook jingles?"

"You're good at it. I'm not."

"The name?"

"Whiskeyjack."

"Call you back."

31

ADI MANSOUR and Irfu Tayeb were parked on the Union Pacific Railroad Access Road in Colton, California, at the end of Marion Way, just west of the Riverside Avenue overcrossing. The scanner in Mansour's moldy old camper truck was running, and occasional bursts of railroad chatter interrupted long stretches of radio silence. Ahead of them dozens of tracks forked into an immense rail yard. Hundreds of cars and dozens of engines were scattered here and there, illuminated by light towers in fading twilight.

The pair were waiting for a train. While they waited, they talked.

"Immigrants. Those fucking Mexicans are swarming all over us. It has to be stopped," opined Mansour.

"And they work for nothing," Tayeb complained.

"Round them up, send them back."

"Arm the fucking border patrol. Shoot the fuckers."

"Inshallah, the country will wake up. Understand what's going on."

"Never happen. We're totally fuckified. And now this." Tayeb waved at the tracks and the long strings of cars there. "They've got the perfect system."

"It's not perfect. Delayed in Tucson." Mansour tapped the scanner. "Hours ago. We heard it. Sometimes you can actually understand this damn thing. And they gotta clear customs in LA."

"What do you think?"

"Another twenty-four hours."

"Shit, trains are slow."

The scanner hissed. A wheezy voice announced something.

"What was that?"

"Didn't catch it."

Tayeb squirmed around in the passenger seat. "This operation, why would anyone work it?"

"Beats running across the desert and dying of thirst."

"I heard the money is Mexican. The labor dude who put the show together has family there."

"Really? He's one of them?"

"Nah. He's Anglo. Valenzuela, on his mother's side."

The scanner hissed again, and the voice made another cryptic announcement.

"Hey, I think this is them."

Mansour got out of the cab and peered eastward down the track.

"Here they come."

A long intermodal train came grinding up the hill from the direction of Palm Springs. Tayeb joined his partner trackside. Five GE diesel electric engines in yellow and gray paint were using eighteen thousand horsepower to tow a mile of shipping containers, two hundred of them, double-stacked in well cars. The ground shook as the immense locomotives rumbled past. Then the sound faded to a steady ticking as the line of cars ran through the yard over multiple switches. It took several minutes for the train to pass their position. Finally the last car swept by and the little red light on the end-of-train device disappeared into the distance.

"And there they go."

Mansour was scowling. "Did you pick up our box?"

Tayeb shook his head. "They all look the same."

"They're supposed to stop when they get to coming back the other way."

"They better. I don't want to sleep anywhere near that shit we've got riding in back."

"We'll tuck the can under the truck. No problem."

"What if I can never have children?"

"Kids tie you down. You don't want kids."

"Ghani might."

32

JERRY PAVLOV returned to his office from a trip to Starbucks. He deposited a decaf latte on Ginger's desk, took a sip of his own, and showed her a photograph on his digital camera.

"The G-H-L part we nailed already. The B and K, no. Want to guess?"

"It's a rendezvous," said Ginger. "Lovers arranging a secret meeting because management frowns on office romances."

"Hmm." Pavlov thought about the idea for a moment, oblivious to any personal significance. "You may be right, you may have hit the button."

"My place at seven?"

"Make it eight, and we'll eat at Steak Street."

"You're buying, buddy."

Pavlov nodded absently, wandered away into his office and sank into his chair.

"Get that cop on the phone, will you?"

"The other woman. Your new friend."

"She's not very friendly, but she's got connections."

His phone rang.

"Here she is."

Pavlov swiveled around to take the call.

"Hey. How you doing up there in, where is it? Placerville?"

"Was that Ginger?" asked Marianne with a sly smile that was audible.

"Um, yes."

"Dating the work force?"

"Tell you what, this was a mistake. Hang on."

He hung up, then re-dialed on his personal mobile phone.

"Sorry about that, I shouldn't be using government equipment when I'm calling you."

"You refer to her as 'government equipment'?"

"I meant the phone."

"Right."

"Here's why I'm calling — the note I found? G-H-L and so on?"

"I remember."

"Now that you nailed the railroad connection, I'm looking at the other words — B-Line and K-M-X. Your take?"

Marianne was silent for a stretch. Then, "The logo on the side of the container I was tracking was B-E-E-LINE in tall block letters."

"K-M-X?"

"Not a clue."

"Mmm."

"But I have a contact that might be able to shed some light."

"I knew it. You've got a better network than Kevin Bacon."

▼

Marianne was sitting on her deck. She held up one of the Union Pacific business cards and dialed the number printed there. A robotic voice announced Union Pacific Customer Service, warned that the call might be monitored, and asked the caller to be ready with a Union Pacific customer ID. Marianne punched many buttons and said the words "agent" and "operator" many times. Finally she reached a human being.

"Customer Service."

"Melissa Caspian?"

"No, sorry."

"I'd like to speak to Melissa Caspian, please."

"May I have your customer ID?"

"I don't have one. I'm a police officer and federal agent investigating a criminal case. I was told specifically to contact Ms. Caspian."

"Name?"

"Marianne Sarzeau."

"Hold, please."

Inane background music filled the phone line. After a couple of long minutes, another voice piped up.

"Accounts, Caspian here."

"Hello. Thanks for taking my call. I got your number from Barney Durham, in Lathrop, CA."

"The intermodal facility."

"That's right. I'm looking at criminal activity involving shipping containers, and he suggested that I call. Can we talk?"

"That depends on what you want to talk about."

"I have some information that I can't decipher. A note. It's short and sweet — BEE-LINE and K-M-X. We think BEE-LINE is a container brand. But K-M-X? What could it mean?"

"Your name again? It sounds French or something, and I missed it."

"Marianne Sarzeau."

"Mary-Ann? One word or two?"

"One, and it is French . . . originally."

"Marianne then. How do I know you're a federal agent?"

"You don't. I will have a letter sent to you that verifies my status."

"I would appreciate that."

"Meanwhile —"

"This is urgent?"

"Yes, ma'am."

"Call me Molly. I don't know what 'B-Line' means — too many brands on containers these days, but K-M-X sounds like part of a train name."

"Trains have names?"

"All of them. The 'K'? It signifies second-tier intermodal. That means containers. The 'MX' could signify origin in Mexico."

"Great. Where do I find this train?"

"Can't tell you that. The name you cite is missing the destination code and the date code."

"What am I missing?"

"Destination code — LA, or LB, or some other city or terminal. And the date code — it gives the day of departure. Without both, I'm not going to be much help."

Marianne wrinkled her nose.

"Well, damn, Molly, I don't have that information."

▼

Pavlov decided to re-visit the Downey safe house for a third time. An unproductive conversation with Marianne convinced him to go over the place yet again. He entered with latex gloves on and a face mask in place, just to be sure he was protected from any residual radioactivity.

The kitchen was still a mess. The remains of a farewell pizza were glued to an open delivery box on the table. Cockroaches were feasting there and were running in and out of the open soda cans on the countertop. Pavlov swallowed hard and continued into the living and bed rooms. He checked the smoke alarm boxes and the ugly shirt again, but found nothing further of interest.

In the garage he studied the work table, where he noticed a pencil stub, to see if anything had been written there. But no.

He was shaking his head and about to leave when he spotted the rubbish and recycling cans in the corner. An ant superhighway was in place there, and traffic was heavy. He lifted the lid of the recycling can and shined the beam of his smartphone flashlight inside. It was empty. Probably never used, he thought. The trash can seemed empty too, except for sticky food scraps, but his light revealed small squares of paper stuck to the bottom. He reached down to pick them up and came away with his hand covered in angry ants.

"Ahhh . . . get . . . off . . . me!"

He shook his hand, throwing ants this way and that. When the pesky little beasts were all brushed off and his heart stopped pounding, he looked around to see where the pieces of paper had flown. It took him the better part of ten minutes to collect them all from the floor, the work table, and the pile of smoke alarm parts.

They proved to be pages from a cheap desk calendar. He leafed through them doubtfully, routinely looking for any kind of clue. One of the dates caught his attention:

July 2
209 h

That date was circled in pencil, and the second number had been scribbled in beside it.

"Hello . . . "

He stepped outside and called Marianne.

▼

"Got something."

Marianne was at the Chevron station, filling up her little Mini when Pavlov's call came in.

"You again."

"A date on a calendar — July 2nd — and a funny number — 209 — with an *h* after it."

"What does that tell us?"

"Might be the departure date for our train. Call UP."

"Oh, man, I'm on duty tonight, I've got to suit up."

But she finished gassing her Mini, drove it around the block, parked, and dialed a number.

"Broomhandle? What time is it?" asked Ray Bagwell through an oceanic hiss. He sounded gruff, probably hungry, working thousands of miles from the comfort of American fast food.

"We're checking on our smoker dudes, and I need some legal heft at Union Pacific. Can you fire off a scary note from FULTAP so the railroad will cooperate?"

"What sort of note?"

"Make it like, I dunno, a federal warrant or subpoena. Address it to Melissa P. Caspian, my UP contact, Harriman Dispatch Center, in Omaha. Your guy Pavlov needs some answers."

She heard Bagwell growl unintelligibly. Their goodbyes were swallowed by the squeals of cosmic rays tickling a satellite high overhead.

She drove home, changed into her uniform, waited five minutes, and dialed another number.

"Accounts, Caspian."

"Hello, Molly, Marianne again. Get a note from the Feds?"

"I do have a dispatch from someone named Major Raymond Bagwell, U.S. Army Intelligence. He's requesting cooperation based on a federal search warrant. You know this man?"

"Very well. We're in the same outfit — we're agents — the military ranks are really just a cover."

"Goodness, it sounds like one of those summer movies. And I'm in it."

"Well, Molly, I wish it was a movie. Here's what I'm looking at. First a date — July 2nd. Could be our container's departure date?"

"Sure, why not? These trains run most days."

"And then, the weird part, another number — 209, with an *h.*"

"Hmm. Intermodals coming across the border on the Mexico Direct program always head for LA. I'm looking at a schedule here, give me a sec . . . and if they're coming all the way from Pantaco in the *Distrito Federal* — Mexico City — the available time is 209 hours at the LA terminal. That's what? Almost nine days."

"So, if the train departed on the 2nd, it should have arrived in LA just about now."

"That's right. And then, customs, unloading, reloading, making up new trains for final U.S. destinations."

"Wow, complicated."

"Welcome to rail freight."

"Tell me if I've got the train name now — K, for second-tier priority . . . MX, for Mexico City . . . LA, for the terminal in California . . . and 2, for the departure date. So, it looks like I'm tracking something like . . . KMXLA-2."

"Pretty good. But look out, if your container is being forwarded to a final destination other than LA, the next train will have another name."

"Oh boy."

▼

When Pavlov heard the news he was thoughtful.

"Nine days. That train must be arriving. My guys have either jumped ship or they're waiting for another ride."

"I suppose so. You've got a lead now — good hunting."

"Listen, men in a container, on a train somewhere. Needle in a haystack situation. Why don't you come on down here and give me a hand?"

"Are you kidding? I'm a cop. I'm on duty right here, right now, in Placerville."

"I know you're psychic, or whatever you call it. Maybe like your dad, you can sense them, help me zero in on their rolling hideout."

"Sorry, I only sense adepts. Dad is the aura guy. I'm not like him."

"Jesus, Sarzeau, you are a pain in the ass."

He abruptly hung up.

▼

The sun rose over Placerville just after 6:00 AM. Tree branches and house tops were glowing in yellow light as Marianne finished her shift. When she arrived back at her apartment, her deck was awash in dappled sunshine. She was tired but happy; the night in Hangtown had been routine. Three speeders, two drunks, and a single instance of property theft; nothing worse than a carton of cigarettes taken from a gas station whose lone attendant left his post to use the bathroom. And, best of all, not a twinge of nausea to mar her vigilant watch over the semi-peaceful territory.

Marianne stripped off her police uniform, noted Wagstaff slumbering in her bed, and tiptoed into the shower.

When she stepped out to dry herself, Wagstaff was standing there, squinting sleepily, telephone in hand.

"Morning, M. Your spook friends are calling." He thrust the phone into her still-wet hand, yawned, and headed back to bed.

"Angel?"

Marianne's heart did a little flip-flop.

"Dad, that you?"

"Ray asked me to call. He worked up a hex for you. Write this down . . ."

"Wait, wait, lemme find a pencil."

She skipped out of the bathroom and dug around in a kitchen drawer.

"Okay, I'm ready. Go."

Her father read off a spell, and Marianne scribbled it down:

> . . .*[name here] . . . burning bright . . .*
> . . .*fight . . .*
> . . . *ignite . . .*
> . . . *light . . .*

"That's it? Just four lines?"

"Ray thinks the name takes care of everything. Give it a try — but you be careful, hear me?"

"Loud and clear."

"Good, we've been through this before. Now, here's something else, it's important —"

"Uh-oh, what now — ?"

"Ray and General Weaver and I want you to go down to LA and help our Homeland contact figure out what's going on with his terror plot."

"Hey, no, no — no can do."

"See, Ray knew you'd say that, so that's why I'm on the phone."

"Earth calling Dad — if you didn't know, here's some news: I'm pregnant. I'm sick every morning. I have enough trouble here in town as it is."

Dad was undeterred. "Something funny is going on at Homeland. They are dodging their responsibilities. FULTAP does not think that is a wise policy."

"You've been talking to that guy Pavlov."

"He called Ray."

"These so-called terrorists. They're playing with smoke detectors. It's a joke."

"Maybe so. But Homeland should be on top of it. Yet they pulled Pavlov off the case. Either we're looking at incompetence . . . or worse, some sort of complicity, a mole. We need to find out which."

"That is just . . . such total bullshit."

"Your FULTAP friends are out of the country, so it's up to you, Angel. Someday, when this is over, you're going to be a wonderful mother."

"Ahhhrrrgh . . !"

▼

Placerville Police Lieutenant Nina Kazmarek, a plus-size woman of forty or so with dark hair and dark eyes, was leaning forward with elbows on her desk and fists propping up her chin. She was studying Marianne, who was squirming around in the facing seat. She doodled on a piece of paper, studied her underling some more.

"Broomhandle . . . . . . that's what they call you, right?"

"My trade name."

"You know, Sarzeau, you are a good cop," she said after another pause. "Conscientious, well-trained, good instincts, sharp. Promising career. Stay with it" — she gestured at the engraved nameplate on her blotter — "and you could make lieutenant someday. Here, or anywhere else."

"Mmm."

"What I don't understand is these sudden departures. Your other job."

"Yeah. Hard to explain."

"I got a call just now from an army officer named Raymond Bagwell. Ring a bell?"

"Oh yeah. Ray. FULTAP. The spook patrol."

"This isn't the first time. You've described your unique, uh, talents — very woo-woo, I must say — and I have to bow to the feds, so you're off and running — again. Lucky for both of us, your partner Dez Otis loves his overtime."

"Thanks for understanding. If it means anything, I'm leaving under protest. This is not my idea, I've been drafted."

"National security. That's a career too."

"So I've been told."

"Your father, right?"

"Yes, he's in it up to his neck."

"Well look, get out of here, go catch the bad guys."

Marianne stood up and turned to leave.

"But listen to me — this can't go on forever. Someday — and soon — you'll have to make a choice."

Marianne nodded unhappily.

▼

Wagstaff had motored down to Applefield to work on the *Courier*. On her way to say goodbye, she stopped off in Tarvolo. Turnbow was sitting in a lawn chair on the back deck of his palatial mansion, dozing, when she arrived.

"How's he doing?" asked Marianne.

"Recovering . . . slowly," said Lorraine, wringing her hands. "Spends a lot of time napping."

"Good, that's good."

"Doctor said not to rush it."

"What about Cancun?"

Lorraine managed a wan smile. "They let me change our dates, given the circumstances. October."

"Weather will be nice."

"I hope so."

"Look, I'm off — off to the races down in LA."

"Broomhandle rides again?"

"'Fraid so. I thought you should know. Don't let your old man get into trouble."

"Enough already."

"Tell him I'll be back in time for my show on Sunday."

"Will do."

They hugged each other.

▼

Marianne appeared in Wagstaff's office with overnight bag in hand. She held it up to indicate her departure. He registered the gesture with a sour nod.

"I don't know how you can do it, babe," he said.

She shrugged.

"Bump starting, our son in there, sick, seizures . . . "

"Quite a list," she said.

He gazed into her eyes, flinty now with professional determination.

"Oh, all right, screw it, I'll drive you down to Sac."

"You don't have to . . . "

"I know."

33

MARIANNE arrived at John Wayne Airport in Orange County not long after 5:00 PM on a nonstop Southwest flight. She exited the jetway and looked around at the crowd waiting to greet incoming passengers. She was frowning. The trip through security and the cramped seating did nothing to improve her sulky attitude toward her new and involuntary mission.

There, over there to her right, was a slim guy in a crumpled linen sports jacket holding up a sign that read: *Sarzeau Over Hear*. He was wearing aviator sunglasses. There was a soul patch under his lower lip. Forty years old or more and ex-military, she judged. She waved.

Pavlov watched the passengers stream off the flight, wondering what his new ally looked like. Then, there she was, waving at him, a curvy young woman with fair hair pulled back in a French twist, dressed in an open flannel shirt over T and jeans. Her frown became a wide smile. Cute, he thought, very cute. Not at all what he expected from a reputed witch with magical powers. But yet, there was something about her eyes, dark and intense, that activated his caution radar.

"Hello, there. Officer Sarzeau?"

"That's me" she said. "Marianne."

"Jerry. Thanks for showing up."

They shook hands. She was grinning now.

"Why the smile? Do I look funny?" he asked.

"You spelled 'here' wrong."

Pavlov looked at his sign. "Shit," he said, and pointed toward the exit.

"Bag?"

She lifted her overnighter. "Carry on."

"Then let's be went."

Pavlov tossed his sign into the nearest trash receptacle. They walked and walked, heading for the parking garage.

"You got my text?" she asked.

"Yes, thanks, good stuff. Using the train name — who knew trains had names? — I contacted UP. Man, they don't want to talk unless you're a customer, but with you signed up we can work under color of FULTAP, so I invoked your authority —"

"Ahh, that's why you dragged my ass down here."

"— and found out that our train is newly arrived at the East Washington Intermodal Facility in Commerce. That's where we're going."

▼

Joe Farrell led the two investigators away from the Union Pacific office at Oak and East Washington and into the maze of containers that stretched across miles of east-west trending track. As they strolled, Marianne could see gantry cranes and side loaders lifting and shifting big boxes. Some of the containers were moving from trains to trucks for local delivery, others from trucks to trains and destinations unknown. The immensity of the operation, the LA smog, and the afternoon heat gave her a headache.

After threading his way through and around row after row of these things, Farrell halted and waved his arms.

"Here's where the vans from your train were grounded. The ones that are local, destined for southern Cal here."

Pavlov was studying the letters and numbers on the nearest doors. "Anything on the road yet?"

"The customs broker has been through, but nothing has actually moved. We're busy, but as you can see, it takes a while."

"Got anything from G-H-L?"

"Well now, you mentioned that company on the phone, so I checked. Nothing."

"Bummer," said Marianne. "Anything with BEE-LINE painted on the side?"

"Wouldn't know that. Our computers use the ISO designation."

"Mind if we check?" asked Pavlov.

"As long as you don't get underfoot. Here's the thing — that train from Mexico? About ninety percent of the cargo was ticketed for Seattle. Our tracks will take it to Portland, and there we'll transfer everything to BNSF. So your Bee-Line box could be on its way north."

Pavlov nodded and ambled away, crooking a finger to bring Marianne with him. "Thanks."

"You can find me at my desk if anything turns up."

They watched Farrell walk back toward his office. When they were alone, Pavlov took off his glasses and fixed a pair of piercing green eyes on her. "Any idea? Can you sense anything?"

Marianne surveyed the pleated steel that surrounded them. "No," she said.

"Damn. I was hoping for serious witchcraft."

"I think Ray might have oversold me. But if it will make you happy, I'm going to try something."

She stepped into the shadows cast by a pair of long hi-cube units. There she got out her BiC lighter and snapped the sparkwheel. A small yellow flame appeared.

"What are you doing?"

"Conjuring a spirit. Stick around, maybe you'll get an eyeful." She closed her eyes and chanted:

> *Whiskeyjack, Whiskeyjack, burning bright,*
> *Join me here prepared to fight;*
> *Let your powers now ignite;*
> *Find me where I bear this light!*

The flame doubled in size. A flickering form arose, the size and shape of a burly ape. Marianne eyed it uneasily. One moment it was hot and fiery, the next invisible, then just points of light.

"Whiskeyjack?"

"*Marianne . . . I . . . frrr . . . can't see.*"

"I'm having the same problem. What about it? Can you sense anyone? Anyone hiding nearby? I sure can't."

"*. . . not sense . . . harm . . . bzzt . . . far away.*"

The form exploded. Sparks drifted down onto the concrete pavement. Pavlov stared at Marianne, dumbfounded by her performance.

"Yes? See anything?" she asked, hoping to get past the usual doubts.

"Fireworks. Do you also do card tricks?"

"Very funny. Contact is bad, I'm doing something wrong. But our targets are not here. They're on that train."

34

ADI MANSOUR and Irfu Tayeb were still hanging around the outskirts of San Bernardino. They had relocated their dingy camper from the Union Pacific yard to a narrow canyon carved into a long line of mountains thrust up by plate tectonics. There, four parallel tracks wound up into the Cajon Pass, which, at 3800 feet above sea level, was the low point in a formidable stone wall dividing southern and northern California. Almost all rail traffic running north-south routes was scheduled through there, a hundred and fifty trains a day, grinding slowly up and down grades that were among the steepest in North America.

A mobile phone call and scanner chatter had informed the pair that a Union Pacific intermodal train, KLAPT-12, was now rolling eastward on its way to the pass. Their train.

But it was still two hours away. They were bored. Mansour checked his watch.

"They're supposed to stop for traffic coming downhill, and then we make the handover. Crap, by the time they get here, the radioactivity will be gone, like bubbles in soda water."

"Don't be such a jerk. That stuff lasts four hundred years, man. Four hundred years scorching our balls."

"Who cares? Jihad, brother!"

"I care. Who knows? I might need the seed."

"What? Still on about Ghani? She's my sister, and I'm telling you, she's a bitch. Doesn't wear the veil, goes to the movies with her girlfriends, can't cook a thing."

"She cooks pizza. *Inshallah,* we're going to open a pizza place. There's a storefront in Culver City, right near the bus stop. Up for lease. Ghani read about this used optical oven for sale. The pizza cooks in thirty seconds."

"If someone is selling that oven, their business failed. Ever think of that?"

"Ghani says no, the old man who owned it is retiring. It's a bargain."

"You're not really going to marry her?"

"Why not? This is America, land of the free."

"That's a fine fucking thought."

Mansour's mobile phone rang. He looked at the number and answered the call.

"Bag One here."

Pause.

"Good news, way to go."

Pause.

"G-E-F, not G-H-L, got it."

Pause.

"Right, H not B, blue not red, I'm with you. Eyes open."

Pause.

"Halfway down, right."

Pause.

"Oh shit. Where, then?"

Pause.

"Crew change?"

Pause.

"Waiting. Another train. Side track. Where?"

Pause.

"Unh-huh, writing it down."

He jotted letters on his forearm with a ballpoint pen.

"Inshallah, we will meet you there."

Mansour pressed a button to end the call.

Tayeb was following the conversation with great interest. "What was that?"

Mansour turned the key in the camper's ignition. He pumped the accelerator. The starter motor whined, the engine coughed and sputtered to life.

"That was Hatch. They have cleared customs. But, the new train is not going to stop here in Berdoo. The train they were supposed to meet, to wait for, is delayed somewhere way up north in the Big Valley."

"Shit."

"And the container isn't G-H-L, it's G-E-F."

"Who?"

"General Enterprise Freight. That guy Muñoz has different companies he uses."

"We'll never spot those numbers on the damn doors."

"Of course not. Verification, double check. And we're not looking for

Bee-Line anymore. It's *Hi-Line* on the side."

"The train will be a mile long. A hundred cars. How will we find the damn thing? How long will they stop for?"

"Won't matter. The car is right in the middle."

"How do we know?"

"Hatch knows. He told me."

35

"ARE WE AHEAD of our train?" asked Pavlov.

He and Marianne were traveling east on California Route 60, otherwise known as the Pomona Freeway, and although the evening rush hour was winding down and traffic was thinning, an army of commuters was still toiling homeward. Pavlov's Crown Vic was not moving fast.

Marianne had a paper map open on her lap. "Your guess is as good as mine," she said. She looked out the window at the arid landscape rolling by. A green sign was visible a quarter mile away.

"Next exit, let's jump off."

Pavlov swerved down the exit ramp.

"North on Phillips Ranch Road," she advised.

Pavlov turned north. The street was actually moving faster than the freeway.

"Right on Rio Ranch."

"Where are you taking us?" asked Pavlov, scowling at her over his sunglasses.

"UP tracks. It's a ways — hey, right here, right now, this is it!"

Pavlov veered onto Rio Ranch.

"Okay, now left on South Garey when we get there."

"How far?"

"Two miles or so. Then north, another two."

Pavlov nodded, drove on in silence. Marianne was impressed by the endless supply of palm trees lining every street. After a couple of miles of tedious progress along traffic-clogged South Garey, Pavlov was getting anxious.

"Now what?"

"East on Mission, north on Towne, that's where we'll cross the tracks."

But when they neared the tracks on Towne they found themselves in an underpass. The invisible tracks were above their heads.

"Whoops."

"Okay, okay, go east on First."

Pavlov spun the car around the underpass support pillars, annoying several drivers who leaned on their horns in outrage, and turned onto East 1st Street.

A long block's travel brought them to San Antonio Avenue, and a merciful grade crossing. Pavlov drove across the tracks and parked in the gravel. He checked his watch.

"Think we beat them?"

"I dunno. Who's on that train? Your smoke alarm jokers?"

"No. Those morons are American citizens. Can't be sure — maybe just a bunch of illegals."

"Undocumented, remember?"

"What are you, some kind of bleeding heart save the whales tree hugger?"

"Just staying neutral. Doing my duty, not judging."

"Unh-huh, what they teach you in cop school?"

"That's right."

"Well, okay, any *undocumented* riders with enough money to pay their way first class? That means they are criminals."

"Makes sense."

"Listen to you. Now then, our assets in Mexico City spotted a pair of European terrorists, serious bazookas, who have since vanished. We have knowledge that my alarmists and these two belong to the same loose Al-Qaeda group, AQ-4."

"And you think they're trying to hook up?"

"That's the picture I'm painting."

"Homeland knows all about this. Why would they pull you?"

"The orders came down the pipe from on high. I barely understand how my office works, and Washington is a fucking 'riddle, wrapped in a mystery, inside an enigma.' Political, somehow. They just don't see the threat."

"That's why you need FULTAP," said Marianne.

"Gives us authority."

"Great, I'm a technicality. Unless we need a potion or something."

Pavlov pushed his sunglasses up onto his forehead. He made a face.

"I spoke to Major Bagwell. He thinks you're quite an asset, however things play out."

Marianne looked glum, but she was secretly flattered. She opened her door and stepped out beside the tracks.

"Hang on, I'm going to use my authority."

She dialed a number on her smartphone.

"American TV & Appliance. How may I direct your call?"

"Uh, this is Agent Broomhandle. I'm on assignment here in Southern California."

Pause.

"FULTAP gig. Major Raymond Bagwell's unit."

Pause.

"All right, then, here goes — I need a telephone location, device belonging to Ghani Mansour."

Pause.

"That was then, and my question is, where now?"

Pause.

"Thanks. I don't have a perfectly encrypted phone, but call this number."

While she was talking, she became aware of a deep rumble coming from the direction of Los Angeles.

"Hear that?" she called.

She peered westward down the line. A train was approaching, moving at a measured pace. The lights on the lead locomotive were getting closer and brighter.

Pavlov got out of the car. He leaned over the hood, staring at the tracks. In less than a minute the engines were rolling by, four of them, a mix of GE and EMD road switchers. The deep thrum of the diesels beat against Marianne's chest, advertising tremendous power. Following the units was a long line of well cars loaded with double-stacked containers. The cars clanked and groaned as they passed.

"Look for Bee-Line," she yelled, firing up her BiC lighter. She recited her *named spirit* spell:

> *"Whiskeyjack, Whiskeyjack . . !"*

She could hardly hear herself over the noise of the train. The same anemic form that appeared in the LA intermodal yard flickered in and out of existence atop her little torch.

"Marianne . . . meaning of . . . summons?"

"I want to know if you can sense anybody on this train here. People looking for trouble."

The containers moved past in a kaleidoscope of colors. Red, green, blue, gray, white, beige. The names made little sense to Marianne: APL, Cosco, EMP, Evergreen, Hanjin, Hapag-Lloyd, K-Line, Maersk, half a dozen others.

"Your skill equals mine . . . . . . your sense?"

"Nothing. Just a suspicion. Vaguely red."

"I suspect also . . . nothing more."

Whiskeyjack flickered in and out of existence for a few more seconds, and then Marianne's BiC ran out of fuel. Her spirit vanished. Soon thereafter the last car trundled by.

"Bee-Line?" queried Marianne.

Pavlov shook his head. "I counted one hundred and seventeen cars. But I did not spot our target."

"Shit. And my guy from Whereverland did not pick up any bad thoughts. On the other hand, this stupid lighter isn't working like I hoped, and he was only here part time."

"We need to figure out where the train will stop. The forces of evil aren't going to hook up while the thing is moving."

"I still think this is the train."

"Gotta be. It was on the northside track here. The other one over there leads to Arizona."

They were getting back into Pavlov's Crown Vic when Marianne's smartphone buzzed.

"Broomhandle here."

Pause.

"Got it. Thanks for the big ears."

Pavlov raised his eyebrows.

"That was American TV & Appliance, FULTAP liaison, calling back. They recorded a call today from Ghani Mansour's phone in San Bernardino, presumably in the possession of her brother Adi. I have the address."

36

IN WASHINGTON, in the Homeland home office, Dylan Roche, assistant to Assistant Deputy Director Sizemore, was holding down the fort, working late, when the call came in. Like FULTAP, his group had access to telephone traffic that might impact national security, and like Marianne, he was very interested in the progress of what he was starting to think of as the Smoke Bombers.

"This is Roche. What can you tell me?"

Pause.

"Say again, please, I'm not sure I understand."

"Oh, Mansour. AQ-4. Now I get it. Location?"

Pause.

"Unh-huh, stateside. California. You had both ends of the call?"

Pause.

"Then our targets are here. Thanks, good to know."

He stood up from his desk, started gathering his things, and pressed an intercom button.

"Ruby, you there?"

Like her associate, Ruby Judson was also working late.

"Here I am."

"Jim is on the town tonight. Some event. What is it? Where is he?"

"He's at that gathering for the Guatemalan foreign minister. At the John Hancock Hotel, I think. They've got that big ballroom."

"Thanks."

"He won't want to be disturbed, Dyl."

"Yeah, but he should hear the latest."

▼

The John Hancock was within walking distance, and Roche made it there in less than ten minutes. There was a delay while security checked his identification, and another when the event monitors tried to force a necktie on him for appearance's sake.

Inside the ballroom lights were dim. Two figures stood behind lecterns under spotlights on a little stage; the Guatemalan foreign minister, and a slender woman who was translating his remarks. The minister was speaking in Spanish, even though, thirty years ago, he graduated from Yale.

". . . and I look forward to the day," said the woman, "when, bound by our common interests in democracy, a strong economy will ease the sometimes vexing issue of immigration, and the people of my country, happy at home, will see the people of your country embracing your southern neighbors in mutual friendship . . ."

General applause greeted these unimpeachable platitudes.

Roche dodged between tables until he was near the stage, where Jameson Sizemore, on his own tonight, was seated with Secretary Quincy, Senator Daggett, and their young trophy wives. The men wore dinner jackets and black ties. The women were gowned like goddesses.

"Sir, a word . . ."

Sizemore frowned, lifted a finger to excuse himself, and quietly stood. Roche led him away to the rear of the hall.

"What the fuck, Dylan?" exploded Sizemore, when they were out of the crowd.

"Smoke alarms, sir. Early this evening our sources recorded a telephone exchange between known members of the AQ-4 group. Hatch and probably Brunel on one end, Mansour and his pal on the other."

"Summarize?"

"Sir, both ends of the call originated in California."

"Meaning?"

"Meaning, ahh, that Hatch and Brunel are in the United States. They've crossed the border, dodged customs, and are on a freight train heading inland."

"Hoboes?"

"Apparently they are riding in a shipping container."

"You're kidding."

"No sir, I'm not. We have seen people come all the way from China in those things."

Sizemore impatiently squared his shoulders.

"Lucky for you, Roche, it's the foreign minister of fucking Guacamole that's got me here tonight propping my eyelids open. If it had been the British ambassador . . ."

"I know, sir, sorry, sir. But these men are a known threat."

"Not a very big one."

"The question is, do we want to act? Given that we have determined their approximate location."

"No we do not."

Roche hesitated to voice his real worry, but he had walked a long way and decided to press ahead. "Think about it — there might be repercussions, here in the Department, were we to neglect the problem."

"We're not neglecting a thing," insisted Sizemore stoutly. "We are biding our time to obtain further information. Jesus, Roche, go home, get some sleep."

"Yes, sir."

"Glad you're alert, that's good, good attitude. But next time I'm swooning at some diplomatic soirée, stand in the back and call my cell instead of dragging me away in full view of the Secretary, for Christ's sake."

Sizemore returned to his seat. Secretary Quincy leaned over and whispered in his ear.

"What was that all about?"

"A case just caught fire. My assistant has standing orders to keep me informed at all times."

"Glad to hear it. Staying on your toes. Doing a fine job, Jim."

37

"I DON'T CARRY any kind of FULTAP ID card, in case you're wondering, or if railroad security doesn't like to see us nosing around," said Marianne. "To most of the world, I'm just local fuzz. You're on Homeland's dime here."

"Yeah, fine, I don't care."

Pavlov's Crown Vic was parked on Railroad Access Road in Colton underneath the Riverside Avenue overcrossing. Almost exactly where Mansour and Tayeb had been waiting a few hours earlier, and almost exactly where the suspects' last known telephone communication had occurred. The sun was down. Twilight was fading.

The two agents were meandering through the Union Pacific's vast train yard, crisscrossing the fan of rails, wondering when and on which track their quarry would approach.

Pavlov was particularly interested in a westbound train sitting on a siding one track over from what he took to be the main line. Three huge locomotives fronting a hundred box cars, lumber cars, tank cars, and coil cars, were humming quietly in anticipation. Air brake valves were popping noisily every few seconds. Two figures were visible in the lead cab. Pavlov waved. The conductor waved back.

"Maybe there's a meet scheduled. These guys are waiting to roll. If our train stops and waits, I'm betting our targets will make a move."

"Our targets," mused Marianne. "Where are they?"

"Yeah, where?"

"And what kind of move? If you don't mind telling me, what's your theory?"

"I thought you were psychic."

"Ooooh. Any more jokes like that and I'm going to put a *respect* spell on you."

Pavlov grinned. "Sorry," he said. He was pleased to discover that his young colleague was not a timid soul. *"My* theory? I think our radioactivity boys are going to hand the serious dudes on the train enough dangerous shit to cause a lot of trouble."

"If it stops."

"Right, if."

They didn't have long to wait. A deep rumble rose up from the west, and a distant headlight appeared. They hopped across the tracks to line it up.

"It's moving."

"Not that fast."

"Trains take miles to stop."

"It's slowing down."

"I don't see that."

"You wait."

"I don't see our targets either."

Two GE locomotives, then a pair of EMDs, then one hundred and seventeen well cars double-stacked with colorful containers thundered past under a thin veil of odorous black smoke. The rails bent visibly under each set of wheels. The ground trembled. Up close, Marianne thought the effect was like standing next to an elephant herd, or a buffalo stampede, or a ship passing.

"Not stopping."

The train disappeared into the lights of San Berdoo.

"Shit on a stick," said Pavlov.

Marianne was walking a circle around a railroad signal pole, kicking at the gravel underfoot. "Hang on, let's think. We saw no evidence of the smoke alarm guys. They probably knew the train wasn't going to stop. That means they got the word somehow and are heading . . . somewhere."

"We're not really sure if that was our train. I looked again, but I failed to see any Bee-Line logo."

"Lemme check." She punched a number on her smartphone.

"Molly Caspian, please."

The male voice on the other end of the call was apologetic. "Molly's shift is over. This is Ralph Gorman. I'm in her seat tonight. Who am I speaking to?"

"Hello, Mr. Gorman. My name is Marianne Sarzeau. I'm a federal agent. Maybe Molly left a note on her desk there."

"Uhh . . . looking . . . uhh, don't see anything. Wait, FULTAP? Is that you?"

"Yes it is. We're an intelligence-gathering branch of the Defense Department."

"Another one? Never heard of you."

"No you haven't. We're a secret operation that kicks in when the others poop out."

"Poop out? Is that a military term?"

"Mr. Gorman — I am standing in the West Colton yard out here in California. A train we're targeting is due or just went through. Can you tell me if KLAPT-12 just passed me?"

"Secret operation, huh? Who you after, spies?"

Marianne rolled her eyes at Pavlov.

"Terrorists, Mr. Gorman. With bombs."

"On a train of mine?"

"Maybe, we're not sure."

"That doesn't sound good. So, what have we got? I'm looking at the board here . . . and yes, the train you named just passed through Colton on its way north."

"Thank you very much. Second question: do you have some info on when and where it will stop."

"It's scheduled for Portland, Oregon. Block transfer there to BNSF and on to Seattle."

"No, no, I mean — before then, waiting for another train, or whatever might cause a delay."

"Unh-huh, gotcha. Here, it looks like a hotshot is coming down the Big Valley, and your K-wagons will have to go in the hole. In Tehachapi. Then, the crew will be dead on the law by Bakersfield. I'm showing a new one coming aboard there."

"Tehachapi. Bakersfield."

"That's right."

"How long before the train arrives in Tehachapi?"

"Five hours."

"Wow, that's slow. No wonder railroads are failing."

"Our railroad is doing just fine, miss. That slow train you're talking about is worth two hundred and fifty trucks on the road. You get after those evildoers."

"Thanks, Mr. Gorman. Tell Molly hello."

She put her phone away. Pavlov cupped a questioning hand behind his ear.

"That was train control in Omaha," said Marianne. "I've heard they call it the Bunker. The train we just saw — hey! — ours! — will be stopping to wait for another train in Tehachapi, wherever that is."

Pavlov snapped his fingers. "That's where the smokers will be." He strode across the yard to his Crown Vic.

"Come on, Sarzeau. Gotta hump. It's more than a hundred miles."

38

NIGHTFALL in Tehachapi.

Mansour and Tayeb were leaning against the front bumper of their moldy old truck, which was wedged in between construction vehicles in an unfinished shopping center. They had been there for hours, watching the sun set, choking down vegetarian Subway sandwiches, drinking a lot of lemonade. They were now entertaining themselves with their radio scanner, which was hanging out of the passenger side window. Mansour was smoking a cigarette.

"When?"

"When the squawk box squawks."

"All that shit in the back, and here we sit."

"You're such a moron. It's harmless, dude."

"Yeah? Then why do our friends want it, huh? Why? Answer me that."

Mansour thought about the question, mulling their improbable situation. Finally he voiced his conclusion: "Propaganda."

"Oh yeah? Who's the moron? Who?"

Mansour turned to a map he had laid out across the camper's fender.

"They'll be coming up through the pass. Two hours or so, if we're lucky. Trains fucking creep up those grades you can't even see with the naked eye."

"And the scanner will warn us."

"Or we'll see the new engineer arrive in some damn Jeep. Supposed to be a crew change, whatever that is."

"The capitalist railroad bastards hate to pay overtime."

"True. They are bastards."

"Okay. The train stops. Our friends are here. Where? The train will be a mile long. What if it stops for ten minutes only? We will never find them."

"Our GPS unit. They will call us with their position. It's in the middle somewhere, that we know. Our receiver will show us exactly where to look."

"Exactamundo. Anywhere, as long as we get rid of the radioactivity."

Mansour folded up his map.

"Everything is packed?"

"You know it. For sure."

"Check list — your gun?"

"Check."

"Loaded?"

"Check."

"The gunpowder?"

"Check."

"The tubes?"

"Check."

"Gorilla tape?"

"Check."

"Telephones?"

"Check."

"Igniters?"

"Check."

"Smoke alarm dust?"

"It's hot enough to check itself."

"We are ready."

"Inshallah."

39

PAVLOV AND MARIANNE arrived in town in the dark. They were both hungry. After driving back and forth along Tehachapi Boulevard they settled on Kathy's Kountry Kitchen for a late dinner.

"At least it's not Denny's," said Marianne, over a hot cup of coffee. "My last road trip, whew, it was every other meal."

"Denny's by any other name, you ask me," Pavlov replied with a skeptical eye on the menu.

Marianne glanced at her watch. "My UP contact said five hours from Berdoo. We've still got time to kill. We can tell each other our life stories."

"If you insist."

"You first. Ex-military, right?"

"Easy guess."

"That posture, those steely eyes when they're not hidden behind your glasses. How'd you wind up working for Homeland?"

"Army intelligence. I was in Iraq, junior officer."

"Combat?"

"I was rarely out of the green zone. I studied maps. I read interrogation reports, scanned the local newspapers."

"You speak Arabic?"

"Not well, but I can read a little. My team, we were tasked to hunt down Hussein. Operation *Red Dawn.*"

"And you got him."

"Months after I rotated out. We had him in the Tikrit area, but I was already stateside when they dug him out of his hole."

They paused to order. A steak medium-rare for Pavlov, chicken tenders for Marianne. More coffee.

"You call yourself 'Jerry,' but your real name is what, 'Jaromir'?"

"Dad came over from Czechoslovakia."

"An immigrant."

"He's a citizen. Loves this country."

"And here you are trying to stop immigration."

"Just the illegals — excuse me, *undocumented.* We've got to stop the flow," he declared. "Toss 'em back."

Marianne cringed. "Whew — they just want better lives."

"The ones who work to get here? I admire their energy."

"But ..?"

"They should stay home, use that energy to force their damn third-world countries to provide better lives."

"Think that'll work?"

"Probably not. But I hold out hope."

Marianne sipped her coffee.

"Married?"

"Back in the day, I was."

"Uh-oh. Kids?"

"No."

"What happened?"

"I was young, a jerk, no idea how to handle life. Peggy got tired of the mess I made."

"Then Homeland called."

Pavlov nodded. "Astute, Ms. Sarzeau. Yes, a career path opened up. Salvation. Here's to government work."

He clinked his cup against hers.

"What about Ginger?"

Pavlov scowled. He didn't reply right away. Their food arrived, and he bent over his steak, slicing it into many pieces.

"Come on, who would I tell?"

"Neither one of us wants to be cruising the bars," he said at last. "The neighbors don't look attractive . . . but . . . ." He shrugged.

Marianne sensed an intuition blooming. She reached across the table and placed her hand over his.

"What .. ?"

"I just got a funny feeling. Touching you, now I know."

"Huh? Know what?"

"Something you apparently don't. You are going to marry Ginger."

"Oh really."

"Really. You can't wait."

"Is that so? You're a fortune teller?"

"You heard about my weird talents. They come and go, but now and then I hit a home run."

"Or whiff. You're nuts."

Marianne made a fist and struck the table. "The only thing holding you two back is the office romance problem. You both think the way you hooked up is . . . skanky. You feel guilty. Well, don't."

Pavlov pulled his hand away, startled by Marianne's insight. He thought for a while. "Our sad story," he finally admitted. "She's a nice gal."

"Gal?"

"I know, we don't use that term nowadays — woman."

Marianne stirred a french fry around in a little cup of ketchup.

"I'm getting married," she announced.

"Good for you."

"At least we're scheduled. August, a month from now."

Pavlov studied his unfamiliar dinner companion, dreading a confession of some sort he wouldn't know how to address.

"You don't sound like you're sold on the idea."

"No, but I'm already pregnant."

"Really? I couldn't tell."

"You will if I throw up. Fair warning — I'm sick almost every day, so it could happen."

"I'll look the other way."

Marianne was in a mood to brood, feeling reckless. "I'm worried we'll get to fighting, and our marriage will go right down the toilet," she said.

"So that's why you're quizzing me. See what the afterlife looks like."

"Yeah. How to pick up the pieces."

Pavlov put down his fork.

"You'll be a single mother. Child care costs a fortune."

"Mmm."

"And visitation rights. You'll be negotiating."

"Mmm."

"You'll call it a friendly split, but then your ex will dodge child support when you don't let him see his kid, and you'll wind up hating each other."

"Mmm."

"How's that sound?"

Marianne shook her head and pinched her nose to prevent clouds from forming.

"You love the guy?" He was pretty sure he knew the answer, but wanted to hear it.

"What does that have to do with anything?" she pouted.

Pavlov shrugged. "All the songs say it's kind of important."

"Love me tender . . ?" she sniffled.

"See, this is why your stout-hearted men resent women on the force, for Christ's sake. I thought witches couldn't cry."

"You must have been watching that old movie, *Bell, Book and Candle.*"

Pavlov handed her a clean napkin. "Here, use this."

Marianne dabbed at her eyes.

"You are not military — obviously — although your dad is," he noted. What's the story on that?"

"Seizures when I was a kid. Four-F. Still get them now and then. A side effect of my so-called powers." Her lips twisted into an ironic grin. "I'm a *high-functioning* witch."

"The people I get mixed up with."

They agreed to share a bowl of ice cream with strawberries. While they nibbled, Marianne got out her smartphone and called Omaha.

"Where's our train?"

Pause.

"Twenty minutes, unh-huh."

Pause.

"Long siding, right here in town . . . okay, we're on it."

The Union Pacific train named KLAPT-12 worked its way up the Tehachapi pass from the desert side. The locomotives, roaring like lions, crested the summit on the east end of town. The containers followed. Pretty soon half the train was over the top. Cooling fans atop the engines howled as the dynamic brakes took hold on the downhill side.

Pavlov and Marianne were parked at the Chevron gas station. They were unaware that the summit was right in front of them, owing to the subtle change in grade. They watched the cars go by, listened to them clanking and banging. Brake shoes were squealing as the train slowed.

"See our box?"

"K-Line . . . another one . . . Hanjin . . . Seaco . . . here's a Hi-Line . . . no Bee-Line yet."

"Maybe the bad guys use different names. Maybe we're hosed."

"Train is stopping. Let's go, see if we can detect our smokers."

Pavlov maneuvered the Crown Vic out of the gas station, and he and Marianne raced west along the frontage road.

"They're in an old camper truck," said Pavlov, slowing down. "This is their chance. See anything?"

Marianne was glued to the window. "Nothing."

Pavlov drove to the end of the road, turned up Mill Street, and cruised back along F.

"What if they're on the other side of the tracks?"

▼

The train came to a gradual halt right in the middle of town. A series of metallic *booms* rattled the length of the consist as the cars slammed together.

The scanner in Mansour's camper truck squawked.

"Shit, it's not a crew change like we thought. There's another train going the other way."

His phone rang.

"Bag One."

"We have arrived."

"We're here too. We see the train."

"Got our ordnance?"

"Oh yeah, we do, affirmative."

"Write this down — GPS — 35.1318141 north, 118.4411779 west. Use the west number, that will be more sensitive," came the instructions in a distinctly British accent.

Mansour nodded to Tayeb, who was scribbling on his sleeve with a Sharpie.

"Read it back," commanded the British voice.

Tayeb read the numbers off.

"Find us. We expect the train we are forced to wait for in five to ten minutes."

"Sit tight."

The camper truck emerged from the camouflage of manlifters and backhoes, turned onto Green Street, and proceeded south to the tracks, where the grade crossing was blocked by well cars. Mansour drove east on H Street for three blocks, then parked in a wide gravel turnout.

"Which way from here?" asked Mansour, glancing both ways at the seemingly endless line of cars. Tayeb consulted his GPS receiver.

"East, we go east. That way." He pointed.

They donned backpacks and set off down the track with their eyes on the container logos. Tayeb called out the changing GPS readout.

"4426021," said Tayeb.

"Shit, where are they?"

"4423737 . . ."

"Fucking run. Run, bro!"

They jogged along the train.

"4413576 . . ."

"Man, I am not made for this crap."

"4411779 . . . we're here!"

They halted. They were both winded. Mansour leaned over with hands on his knees, panting. When he finally caught his breath, he glanced up at the train. The bottom container was freshly painted bright blue. The logo on the side read *HI-LINE* in large white letters. He stumbled to the end of the car to check the ID.

"GEFU 513914. This is them," he wheezed.

Tayeb marveled at the sight. "You would never know. Where is the door on this damn thing?"

"It'll show."

Tayeb had a thought. "What if they shoot us?"

"What? Are you nuts?"

"We could tell on them."

"Don't even worry about it."

"Once I hand over my pack, they'll have my popper."

"Shit, Irf, sometimes I wonder."

Mansour reached up and pounded on the steel wall.

Wham! Wham! Wham!

Pause.

Wham! Wham! Wham!

A portal cut to exactly fit the *H* in the container logo swung open above the top edge of the well car. Tayeb backed away.

A head appeared, and a British voice spoke: "Bag One?"

Mansour nodded vigorously. "Got a handle?"

"Panic Demo. Who else could it be?"

"Homeland, that's who," said Mansour.

A chain-link ladder clattered down. Tayeb warily climbed up, handed over his backpack. Mansour followed, did likewise.

"Thanks, gentlemen. Now get out of here. Stay low, keep your fooking mouths shut, and tune in the evening news."

Mansour gave a little salute, and the two messengers moved away from the train.

▼

Pavlov's Homeland Crown Vic was parked at the grade crossing on the south side of Green Street. Pavlov himself was trackside, pacing back and forth. He ran a hand through his well-clipped hair.

"They're on the other side. Gotta be."

Marianne was leaning against the car door.

"We don't know that. Maybe they haven't shown up."

"I'm going to check."

"Go ahead. I'll stick, just in case."

"Don't screw around with these guys if you see 'em, they are probably armed."

"Most likely."

Pavlov marched along the train until he found a little platform on the end of a car. Marianne watched him laboriously climb up and over the couplers to the far side.

Minutes passed. Then she heard shouts and curses.

▼

Inside the smugglers' container, Hatch and Brunel were performing a supply check.

"Everything's here. The bagmen have performed."

"Smoke alarm dust?"

"Plastic kitchen jar, wrapped in a plastic baggie. Looks like it got mixed with baking soda or some sort of white powder. Don't worry, it is sealed *très bien,*" affirmed Brunel.

Hatch reached into the open backpack and withdrew the 9-millimeter CZ. He checked the clip, worked the slide to load a round, then turned his attention to the Mexican passengers.

"You five. Out!"

The older man put down his paperback book, fingered his necktie, and folded his arms. "No, no, *señor,* we go to San Joaquin Valley. Long way. Then bus to Chicago."

"Sorry, *viejo,* out! O-U-T, right fooking now!"

"Long way to go still," said the man. His companions were starting to pay close attention to the discussion, even though they could not understand the English.

Hatch showed off his pistol. "Hear me? *¡Ándale! — ¡Ándale! — Vamos,* you bloody sods!"

The Mexicans reluctantly got to their feet. Hatch waved them toward the portal. Slowly, with sullen and fearful expressions, they filed out and down the ladder.

"We have paid the way to San Joaquin Valley!" yelled the older man from the relative safety of the roadbed.

"Get out of here!" yelled Hatch.

"Señor Muñoz will hear of this. The cartel will know. You will have *remordimientos,* I tell you, and *muchos problemas."*

Hatch pulled the trigger.

Pop!

Stones and sand exploded from the ground at the Mexicans' feet. The men rushed away from the train in five different directions.

Marianne barely heard the shot. Another train was bearing down on her, coming from the western side of the pass, evidently the reason for KLAPT-12's layover. As it approached the grade crossing where she was standing the lead engine emitted a long wail on its air horn, a shattering blast at close range. Marianne clapped hands over her ears as the locomotives rolled by, moving at a deliberate pace. A long string of box cars, lumber cars, hoppers, and reefers followed. When the engines were well down the line, and the noise of their passage had faded, she thought she could hear cursing and pleading over the click-clack of steel wheels.

"What?" she asked herself. Then, fearing the worst, she ran along the right of way in the direction Pavlov had taken. But she was prevented from dodging between the cars, as he had done, because of the priority train clanking past on the nearer track.

More yelling and cursing.

"Shit, shit, shit," she muttered. She yanked her little Beretta out of its ankle holster and peered anxiously back westward, hoping to spot the last car. No such luck. It looked like the train would go on forever.

"Mom, that gun, it's not enough. You need help."

"Hey, kid, not now, I'm busy."

"You're risking both of us."

"I know. Now shut up."

"Just saying . . ."

Finally the last southbound car trundled past. She ran along the stalled northbound train, found a platform, and clambered up. She was teetering across when — *bang bang bang bang bang* — the locomotives reversed, compressing the stalled cars together, preparing to restart a mile of containers, one at a time. She grabbed the brake to keep from pitching over the hand rail. Then, with a deep roar, the locomotives began moving forward. The car she was standing on lurched, and Marianne tumbled to the ground.

"Unnhh . . ."

It took a few seconds to gather her wits and decide that a banged-up knee and scraped forearm were the worst of her problems. Beside her, the train was moving now, picking up speed. The Hi-Line container rolled by, all buttoned up again.

From her new position she could see a decrepit camper truck a couple of blocks away, silhouetted by streetlights. Three men were on the ground beside it. Two of them were holding down the third. Fists were rising in the air. Punches were landing hard.

"Oh my God!"

Marianne got to her feet and advanced cautiously. Then she stopped, fished her BiC lighter from a pocket, and thumbed the sparkwheel. It sparked all right, but no flame appeared.

"Goddammit!"

She threw the thing to the ground. Desperate rummaging through her pockets turned up a small LED flashlight. She aimed it skyward and pressed the switch. A surprisingly powerful beam of light shot out.

"Not much, but please . . ."

"Whiskeyjack, Whiskeyjack . . ."

She recited the incantation in breathless haste. At first, nothing happened.

"Come on, come on . . ."

A vaporous ball of pinkish light formed just above the flashlight's lens.

"Whiskeyjack?"

"*Urrrrh . . .*" said the ball.

Marianne tipped the flashlight down toward the camper. The ball wobbled away along the beam. Marianne broke into an awkward run and followed.

"Who do you work for?" shouted Mansour. His face was contorted in fear and anger. Pavlov, down on his back underneath the soldiers of jihad, winced as another fist came down on his chest.

"Ugh," he grunted.

"We will kill you!" insisted Mansour. "Who? FBI?"

Punch.

"CIA?"

Punch.

"DEA?"

Punch.

"Homeland?"

Punch.

Pavlov's mouth was bleeding. One eye was closed.

Mansour raised his arm for another blow and paused mid-move. A translucent pink blob was floating toward him. Little fingers of static electricity were jetting out of it.

Mansour stood up. The blob pushed against him.

Zazzz!

A static charge crackled. He staggered and fell over backward.

Tayeb let go of Pavlov. He stood up and windmilled his arms at the apparition, breaking it into little cloudlets. Pavlov rolled aside and started to crawl away.

"No you don't, fucker!" said Tayeb, making a grab for the Homeland agent.

"Oh yes he does," said Marianne. She was now ten feet away, and her Beretta was trained on the bad guys.

Tayeb forgot all about Pavlov. He reached down and yanked Mansour to his feet.

"Run!" he said.

The two of them fled to their camper. Marianne bent over Pavlov.

"Jesus, Jerry, you are a mess."

The camper truck kicked up a wake of sand and gravel as it departed for parts unknown.

Part FIVE

40

IN THE EMPLOYEE bathroom of Tehachapi's only pharmacy, Pavlov sat patiently on the toilet seat while Marianne applied a variety of lotions, poultices, and bandages to his wounds.

"Ahhh . . ." he said, as medicinal alcohol touched a laceration.

"We could have gone to the emergency room down the street, you know," said she.

"And wait for hours while they triage the shit out of us."

"How are those ribs?"

"They hurt."

Marianne placed a hand on his torso and gently pushed. Pavlov groaned.

"I don't think they're cracked or broken. How did those morons get the jump, anyway, Mr. Special Agent?"

"I was watching our container. When the guys aboard pulled up their ladder and closed the door they made, you couldn't tell it was all fake. Impressive work."

"And a lot of it was done by a lunatic who's been stalking me back home, believe it or not."

"Really."

"Yeah, he took a shot at me, but hit my fiancé and the local mayor."

"They okay?"

"Tom's fine, thank God, and the mayor is recovering."

"Nailed the perp?"

"Not yet, but everyone's out there looking. Attempted murder stirs the blood."

"I thought your biggest problems would be drunks and traffic tickets."

"Most of the time."

Pavlov squinted at her. "How's that arm?"

"I'm okay. Hey, your eye is open. Sort of."

▼

The famous Tehachapi Loop, where trains circle under and over themselves to negotiate the steep grade between the Big Valley and the pass above, was just visible from the main highway on California Route 58. The two agents stopped there for a few minutes, hoping to catch sight of their train, but bushes and hills impeded the view. Pavlov gave up and drove three miles further west and downhill to Tweedy Creek, where the track curved over next to the main road. There they parked and waited.

"What about those thugs in the camper truck? Are we going to let them get away?"

"For now. I can't make an official arrest. We know their names. Mansour has a sister, and we have her address. We'll twist her arm when the time comes. Forget about them, they're a sideshow."

"A sideshow with fists. Did you see anything?" asked Marianne in an innocent tone.

"I think the train went through already."

"I mean when those two had you on the ground. Why they took off?"

Pavlov's brow furrowed. "I was pretty busy getting knocked senseless by those peace-loving Muslims."

Marianne ignored the slur. "That all?"

Pavlov thought back. "I did see a funny cloud out of the corner of my good eye."

"What color?"

"Uhh . . . pinkish."

Marianne was pleased about any manifestation visible to other mortals.

"I knew it! That was my so-called guardian spirit," she said with pride.

"You're joking."

Her face fell.

"Absolutely not. I conjured a demon. And you saw it. That's what stopped those dopes."

"And here I thought you were the Lone Ranger in a skirt."

"Hang around, Tonto, hang around. Skirt, sheesh."

A long silence followed, interrupted by Pavlov clearing his throat. "Let me get this straight — that's what FULTAP is all about? Magic tricks? Is your dad a nut like you?"

"He can sense people's auras, understand their intentions. I can't. But I can conjure, and he can't do that. Now and then we team up."

"Your Major Bagwell never explained any of this."

"Ray plays his cards close to the vest."

Pavlov drummed his fingers on the steering wheel.

"Let's move on. Find me another spot where we can see the tracks."

He pulled the Crown Vic back onto the highway. They drove downhill for fifteen miles. Marianne was studying her smartphone.

"Exit at Bealville Road."

They turned off to the north. The road pitched steeply downward into open country. Scattered oak trees loomed in their headlights.

"Watch out for jackalopes."

A mile later they were crossing the tracks in the hamlet of Bealville. They parked beside the crossing gate. The heat of the day was still rising from the pavement. With the engine off, the car was stifling. Pavlov rolled their windows down. Outside, the night was quiet. Not the faintest sign of a train. Frogs and crickets were chirping in the weeds.

"Late again," complained Pavlov. "It's the Mexican national pastime."

"Why do we bother? You think they'll pop out like jack-in-the boxes in the middle of nowhere?"

"They might know of a slow spot, might have more accomplices waiting."

"Whew. You've got more of an imagination than I have."

Pavlov ignored her critique. "You pulled a gun back there," he noted. "A little Beretta, looked like."

"My backup piece."

"Ever let loose in the line of duty?"

"Yes."

Pavlov whistled. "Interesting. Not too many locals ever do."

"So I'm told."

"Hit anything?"

"Nope. I'm a terrible shot."

"I'll do my best to stay out of your way."

All of a sudden a bell on the crossing signal began to toll. The gate arm swung down to block the road.

"Hey!"

Now the headlights of a big GE locomotive glared in the passenger side rear view mirror. Their beams reflected into the agents' car, whitewashing both their faces.

"Whoa, I'm wrong again," said Pavlov.

He limped onto the pavement and stood by the crossbuck as the locomotives slowly cruised past, dynamic brake fans howling. The line of double-stacked containers rattled along behind.

"Catch our car?"

"It's coming down, halfway along."

"There, *Hi-Line!*"

"Think our terrorists are still aboard?"

"Gotta be. I saw them pull their heads in while they were stopped back in town."

Marianne punched a number on her smartphone. It rang several times before a telephone robot picked up. She thumbed her way through the choices until a real human voice offered a greeting.

"Hello, Mr. Gorman? Sarzeau again. Right, the secret agent. I'm looking at our train rolling downhill toward the Big Valley. We're, um, west of Tehachapi somewhere."

Pause.

"I need to confirm when this thing will stop again."

Pause.

"Bakersfield. Crew change."

Pause.

"Thanks, you're a big help."

The train disappeared around a brush-covered hillside. The little red light on the end-of-train device winked out. The crossing gate rotated up and out of the way.

"Come on, Jerry, they're going to change crews in Bakersfield. Next stop. Next chance for our boys to bolt. So says the horse's mouth. We don't need to follow the tracks."

Pavlov grunted agreement. "All right. You drive for a while."

Marianne trotted around the car and got behind the wheel. Pavlov slid into the passenger seat. She performed an expert one-point turnaround and pointed the Crown Vic back toward the main highway.

41

ON BOARD the train, Hatch and Brunel were checking their inventory again, sorting through the materials of their plot against America.

"Tubes?"

"Got 'em."

"They okay?"

"Thinner than we'd like. Paper towel tubes."

"We can tape 'em. We do have tape?"

"Gorilla Tape."

"Good. But look at the explosives. Only half is powder, and the rest is still inside the fireworks."

"Our bagmen were in a hurry."

"Or stupid."

"Or both. Start peeling."

"*Eh bien.* We will have enough to cause big bang."

"And the gun. A fooking Czech spanner."

"It worked."

"Once. We may need it again."

"And the Americium?"

"Got it, all bagged up."

"Where's the tester?"

"Here is what they have supplied — the cheapest possible." He sniffed contempt. "Surplus from the cold war."

"What do we think?"

"We'd be lucky if it could detect a hydrogen bomb."

Brunel stuck the sensor plug into a jack, flipped three little switches. He held the sensor head against the plastic enclosure. Lights flashed. A series of urgent beeps emerged from a tiny loudspeaker.

"Oh-ho! Listen to that!"

"*Allah Akbar!* The American infidels will have cause to weep!"

They bumped fists and slapped high fives.

"You know, Yan, our delivery sods were seen by an American agent. We have been discovered," said Hatch, sobering up.

"I know this."

"Somehow, they were followed."

"The messengers were not careful."

"Not trained. So let's decide — bail out at the next stop, or stay with the plan?"

Brunel considered. "We have defeated American customs. An important victory."

"But we may not survive the mission."

Brunel nodded. He held up the bag of Americium powder. "This meets the test. So must we."

"Right you are, brother!" said Hatch.

They clasped hands.

42

PAVLOV'S TURN with smartphone maps routed Marianne through the streets of Bakersfield to D and 16th, where she parked their car right beside the tracks on the edge of a vast railroad classification yard.

"Crew change coming up."

"Think our terrorists will jump off here?"

"No idea what they're up to, what their intended target is. But I don't see any suspicious vehicles around. Just us."

"Man, I'm whipped. What time is it?"

"After midnight."

"Be right back."

Marianne dragged herself out of the car and walked a block to Mercy Hospital, where she dispensed coffee from a vending machine outside the closed cafeteria. Back at the car she handed a cup to Pavlov.

"Long night."

"When is that damn train due?" he grumbled.

"Omaha said" — she checked her watch — "damn, just about right now."

"Do you see a train?"

"I do not."

Marianne strolled out into the train yard, sipping her coffee, stepping over the steel rails, peering to the east, where she expected to spot headlights. But the main line was empty.

She returned to the car and leaned over the passenger windowsill.

"Hey, Jerry, got any road flares?"

"In the trunk, why?"

"My lighter and flashlight are not the greatest ways to conjure a power spirit. And a bonfire is not only impractical, but dangerous, as I have learned the hard way."

"You are very strange, Ms. Sarzeau."

"Pop it for me?"

Pavlov leaned over and pulled a lever. The Crown Vic trunk lid tilted up. Marianne dug around in the police gear stowed there. Rubber boots, gloves, a flak jacket, hi-vis safety vest, first aid kit, fire extinguisher, jumper cables, a Tyvek bunny suit. Finally she discovered a package of road flares.

She tore it open and carried one of them back toward the tracks.

"What are you doing?" asked Pavlov.

"Watch and learn, pal."

She scraped the top of the flare against the bottom, and a jet of smoky red flame shot out. She held it up and recited her mantra:

"Whiskeyjack, Whiskeyjack . . ."

Within seconds the smoke billowed up into a thick cloud. A smoky head appeared. Crude arms ballooned outward. A pair of bright eyes, like white-hot coals, opened. They turned their gaze toward Marianne. She shivered.

"Hello, there, Mr. W."

"Marianne, far from home." The voice in her head jarred her, as always. She teetered backward, then caught herself.

"Wow, this works better than my flashlight."

"The puny candle was hard to see. The path was hard to find."

"I need some help, big guy. I'm waiting for a train. There are terrorists on board, plotting some kind of bomb attack. Because they hold hateful thoughts . . . I thought, maybe, you could sense them."

"I sense no one."

"Maybe they're not close enough yet."

"Those who would harm you are far away. You are safe."

"Really."

"I will come when you need me."

The cloud of smoke rose above Marianne's head and dissipated into the night air. She jammed the flare into the ground and snuffed the fire.

Pavlov was watching her performance from his seat in their car. "What was that?"

Marianne grinned. "What did you see?"

"A lot of smoke. Smoke with sparkles."

"That was my guardian from the other side."

"Jesus, how *do* you do it? Stay on the force, being so obviously mental?"

Marianne placed hands on hips. "Mental, huh? You have no idea."

She cranked open the driver's door and dropped into the seat.

"That train, if you want to know, is nowhere near here."

"And you figured this out . . . how?"

"I showed you how. My guardian."

"Good Christ."

She handed him her smartphone. "Your turn, smart guy. Call Omaha."

Pavlov fumbled with the phone, looking for the right contact.

"Oh crap, I'll do it." She snatched the phone back and punched a key. The number rang and rang, but no one picked up.

"Either my good friends in the Bunker are gone for the night or having a midnight lunch."

"Then we wait."

An hour went by in sullen silence. Pavlov was nodding off, but Marianne could hardly sit still. She got out of the car and checked the tracks again. Railcars were collected on sidings here and there, but nothing was moving. No headlights appeared in the distance in either direction.

After pacing back and forth for a few minutes in frustration, she ignited another road flare, appealed again to the spirit world, and again found herself staring at a smoky bearlike apparition floating above the red spout of flame.

"Marianne again. The reason for disturbing me?"

"Same problem. No train. Any ideas?"

"I know nothing. Your train is far from here."

"Hmm. It should have arrived."

"But I do bring news."

"Oh?"

"Trouble in Applefield."

"Tom? Lorraine? That maniac Dingell?"

"Your friend Howard. He is slow to recover. Lorraine is in distress."

"The demon . . ?"

"I fear so. You must go home soon."

"I will, but first, I'm on the job — a case — orders."

"Your tenacity impresses. Don't wait forever."

The smoky form evaporated. Marianne extinguished the flare.

"Good God," she said, marshaling her smartphone for an update. This time when she punched the Omaha number, the call connected. After jumping through the inevitable telephone hoops, Ralph Gorman came on the line.

"Sarzeau? Late for you, what?"

"Hey, Mr. Gorman. I'm in Bakersfield, waiting for our train — KLAPT-12, right? — supposed to be a crew change here, and I don't see anything."

"You're in the yard?"

"Affirm."

"Well now, let me see — whoa, Nelly, that crew change occurred just about one hour ago."

"Impossible! We've been here longer than that."

"Your train is already moving again. You say you're in Bakersfield, right there in the yard?"

"Yes, sir. Lots of tracks, lines of cars everywhere."

"Unh-huh." Gorman was silent for a moment, apparently lost in thought.

"Mr. Gorman?"

"Now I'm wondering — see any units where you are?"

"Pardon me?"

"Units, locomotives, big diesel engines?"

Marianne looked over the tracks. At some distance, partly concealed behind a cluster of tank cars, was a locomotive. It was unoccupied, all lights off.

"Uhh, I think so. Way over on the other side."

"Right. Tell me, what color is it?"

"Pretty dark here, but . . . orange, I guess."

"Orange! Honk! You are in the BNSF yard, my dear. UP is two miles east of you. Both railroads run through Bakersfield, in case you didn't know."

"I didn't."

"Look for yellow engines. Yellow, that's us, the Union Pacific, building America."

Marianne was crestfallen. "Tell me the next stop."

"I'm looking at the board here. It's quite a run, but, okay, I do see a meet in Gridley. Your train will go in the hole again, while a hotshot barrels south."

"Gridley? I never heard of it. Where the hell is Gridley?"

"Up between Yuba City and Chico. It's all single track north of Sacramento, but there's a long siding in Gridley."

"No stops along the way?"

"Nothing on the board. That train is rolling."

"Got it. Gridley it is. Gridley, Gridley, Gridley."

▼

It took some shaking to wake Pavlov, but he snapped to attention when he heard about their mistake.

"Your mistake, Jerry. You had the map."

"My fucking luck," he grumped.

"The question is — do you want to check the UP yard, or just hustle after that train?"

"This all happened an hour ago? If our bombers got off, they'll be miles away." He expelled a weary sigh. "But, just to cover our sorry butts, we should take a look."

Look they did. To anyone unfamiliar with railroads, the UP yard looked just like the BNSF operation. Tracks forking every which way. Cars seemingly set out at random. Engines (yellow ones) idling here and there, purpose unknown. Nothing to arouse suspicion.

"Let's go. It's 350 miles to where is it? Gridley? Nothing till then?"

"What the man said."

▼

They stopped for gasoline in Elk Grove and again, for coffee and pie, on the outskirts of Sacramento. Fuel for the long night ahead.

Back on the road, Pavlov took over driving duties, and Marianne fell asleep beside him after a careful briefing with her smartphone maps.

They were traveling on U.S. Route 99, in order to stay near the tracks. Pavlov's stint at the wheel didn't last too long. His injuries cramped and ached, the long straight highway was hypnotic, and within an hour his eyes were drooping. He turned into a rest area outside Olivehurst, and nudged Marianne.

"R and R, Sarzeau. Then you drive, I'm sore as hell."

"Where are we?" she said, barely cracking an eye at the brightly lit facilities.

"I dunno. North pole? I have never been this far north."

"Come on."

"Ever."

Marianne stumbled out of the car, wobbled to the women's rest room, and then walked around under the oaks to wake up. Suddenly she didn't feel at all well. She bent over and vomited into the grass.

"Ohhh, crap . . ."

She returned to the rest room and washed her face.

"Sorry, Mom. That was me this time."

"Well, stop doing it, kid. Gahhh, not fun."

"It's the way things work. You want a healthy baby, right?"

"Of course I do. I want to be healthy too, however. Got it?"

"It will be over soon. Another week max."

"Wait till you're spitting up Pablum, we'll see how you like it."

43

ON BOARD KLAPT-12, Hatch was checking his GPS receiver.

"37.622 something, 120.99 plus," he said, munching corn chips from a bag.

Brunel examined a paper map. "I make that Modesto. We are close."

"Let's hope Golden Harvest knows what to do."

"Or we will end up in Canada."

"If we don't starve first. Fooking Doritos. Our contacts say they've done this before. Many times. I'm told they were briefed on our stop. Supposed to meet us."

"With a car."

"Right, with a car." He shrugged. "We are a trusting lot."

Brunel held up the lightweight cardboard tubes they received from Mansour and Tayeb.

"We have enough explosive to fill three of these tubes."

"That's all?"

"I have been measuring. Question — do we want three bombs, two bigger ones, or" — he spread his hands apart — "one that is *vraiment très grosse?*"

Hatch thought about the problem.

"If we are careful to blow one big bomb in the sight of a crowd, that would get their serious attention. Yeah?"

"D'accord. We will make a splash."

"Literally."

Brunel put away his tubes and braced himself as the train swayed and rattled over a rough set of switches.

"Golden Harvest will be looking for payment when we arrive."

Hatch removed a wad of bills from his backpack. He peeled the rubber band holding the notes together and idly flipped through them.

"We have the cash."

"Enough? We are sure?"

"Here, count it, if you're worried. I'm not."

Brunel took the money and nervously started counting.

"We must not let money ruin our plan."

"Hey, Yan, man up. We will pay — pay in full."

44

PAVLOV'S company Crown Vic was parked in front of the Nutcracker Café in the Big Valley town of Gridley, California, facing a walnut grove and the Union Pacific railroad tracks running beside it. A mile and a half long siding paralleled the main line, the only place where two trains could meet and pass each other for a hundred miles in either direction. Marianne and Pavlov were asleep in their seats, worn out by five hours of night driving that seemed endless to both.

Dawn was breaking. Shadows still shrouded the valley, but clouds above the Sierra foothills to the east were already glowing in golden yellow light.

Marianne's head was tilted back against the seat. Her mouth was open and, in a most unladylike manner, she was snoring.

The noise woke Pavlov. One eye was glued shut as a result of the night's adventures. His good eye opened and rolled around. No trains were in evidence, but he did notice a silver Hyundai SUV parked across the lot, with a man sitting behind the wheel.

"Hey, Sarzeau, wake up."

He pried his other eye open and nudged his companion. She jolted awake.

"Whahh?"

"Morning, officer. Take a look over there — think the driver is waiting for our bombers?"

Marianne attempted to shake the sleep out of her brain. "No idea," she mumbled. "Gotta pee, gotta eat, gotta get some coffee."

She opened the car door, almost fell out, then recovered and marched across the asphalt to the café, an establishment that promised to serve *Breakfast 24 Hours.*

Pavlov followed her in. They took up seats in a booth overlooking the tracks. A young waitress appeared to take their order. Marianne could not help noticing her prominent bump.

"When?" she asked, after they had ordered eggs and pancakes.

"Four more months."

"I've got seven to go, plus or minus. You get sick anymore?"

"Nope. The big thing is weight gain. I'm a blimp." She looked at her order pad. "Sure you want pancakes?"

Marianne grimaced. "Got to chance it. Blood sugar has dropped through the floor."

"Tell me about it."

While the moms-to-be discussed their conditions, Pavlov's attention drifted around the room. The lunch counter was granite. The seats were leather. A flock of taxidermy geese was flying above fancy ceiling fans. A brass model train was strung out on a wooden track suspended above the kitchen.

"Nice place," he said.

The waitress smiled. "Why thank you."

"Up here in Nowhereville," he continued, with no sense of tact.

Marianne winced, but the waitress chuckled. "I know what you mean. I'm from Sacramento, and we're on the moon."

"Who pays for this?" he asked, glancing at the menu and its prices.

"Farm wealth. You'd be surprised. Walnuts everywhere, and we're the plum capital of California." Her face lengthened. "But first the recession hit, and now the drought. We're just hoping to hang on till duck season."

She scooted off for the agents' food.

The two were debating train schedules, and Marianne was about to dial up Omaha, when the waitress returned.

"It's no mystery," she said, when she overheard their concerns. "Train from the south rolls up and stops right outside every morning" — she glanced at her watch — "just about twenty minutes from now."

"Really."

"Like clockwork. Eat up."

They ate in silence. Pavlov watched Marianne scarf down her pancakes. "If you hurl in my car . . ." He let the ugly thought hang. He twiddled his fork, drummed his fingers, slowly becoming agitated. Finally he threw some money on the table and stood up.

"Gotta boogie, Psycho. Finish your coffee and hit the john. Duty calls."

Outside, Pavlov led the way across the road and onto the tracks. Looking south they could see the lights of an engine, still far away, but already too bright to stare at in early morning half-light.

They waited as the train drew closer. Pretty soon they could hear the diesels thrumming, then brakes grabbing. By the time the lead locomotive reached them it was gliding past at a walking pace. Marianne involuntarily stepped back from the rails, reacting to the rumble of all the horsepower seething under yellow paint.

"See our target?"

"Not yet."

It seemed to take forever for the long string of cars to come to a complete stop. But suddenly, a succession of rattling *bangs* rippled down the line, and the train was standing still. Off to the north the motive power was humming and hissing, but the well cars and their containers, bound for Portland, Seattle, and Canada, were inert and silent.

The train stretched half a mile in each direction from the agents' position. Pavlov was uncertain where to find their quarry. He pointed.

"You go that way, I'll go this. *Hi-Line!*"

"Hi-Line," repeated Marianne, with a big thumbs up.

"Don't sprain your ankle on this damn gravel," he called out as he jogged south.

Marianne hiked toward the engines with an eye on the silver SUV waiting in the Nutcracker parking lot. It occurred to her that she didn't know which side of the train the Hi-Line container's secret door was on. What if their terrorists popped out on the far side and retreated into the nearest walnut grove until the coast was clear?

"Oh, man," she said.

She hauled herself up onto the end platform of the nearest well car and was preparing to cross over when the roar of southbound locomotives froze her in place. She felt her heart thumping as the giant GE units blew past right in front of her face, followed by an array of refrigerator cars full of fruits and vegetables, lumber cars loaded up with plywood, and automobile cars full of Asian imports, all heading south to market.

When the last car was safely past, she climbed down to the far side of the stalled train. A good look up and down the consist revealed no open portals.

"Where are those guys?" she griped. The gravel was tugging at her ankles. She quickly discovered it was easier to move by walking on the crossties of the now empty southbound track. She was making good progress when a series of concussions echoed along the standing cars, and the lower-priority train began to move again. She stopped and watched the containers roll northward, picking up speed.

"Hi-Line, Hi-Line, Hi-Line," she repeated hopefully.

It took a couple of long minutes for the train to clear out. When the final car went by, there was Pavlov on the other side of the track, looking as confused as she was.

"Did you clock it?"

"No."

Marianne shrugged defeat. They turned their attention to the Nutcracker and the mysterious SUV parked there. While they were staring at it a figure emerged from the diner: their waitress, leaving work after a long night shift. She was juggling a bag, a sweater, and work shoes as she crossed to the vehicle and climbed inside. The headlights came on, and the SUV moved out of the parking lot, crossed the tracks, and disappeared into a forest of walnut trees.

"We are eff-ing eff-ed. Any smarter and we'd be stupid."

The pair trudged morosely back to their car. Marianne decided to console herself with another tall cup of coffee, and returned to the café. On her way inside she glanced at yesterday's newspapers. One of the headlines caught her eye, and she plucked a copy off the rack.

45

AS WAS HIS HABIT, Jameson Sizemore arrived early in his Washington office. On this bright summer morn, Dylan Roche was there to brief him on overnight developments.

"What's cooking, Dyl?"

"My concern revolves around the smoke bombers we discussed."

Sizemore plunked himself down in his chair and started plowing through email messages while his assistant talked.

"That . . ."

"Yes sir. We have a license number for the vehicle used to deliver the radioactive material to our suspects. We have an address."

"Good, that's good."

"Should we make an arrest?"

"Not yet. Let's not tip off anyone we don't have to."

"Right. We have also been tracking a suspect telephone. For several hours it was moving north — we picked it off registering with a long line of cell towers — presumably on the train we have previously identified. But it's no longer moving along that trajectory."

"Where then?"

"Not anywhere really. It seems to be sitting in Stockton, California. The AQ-4 operatives may have left the train. Their target may be nearby."

"Mmm. What could they hit?"

"Hard to tell. Stockton is a port city. The Defense Department runs a depot there. Fruit crops . . ."

"Don't tell me your crazy terrorists are going to blow up the nation's almond supply."

"I don't know what they're going to do. Don't you think it's time to stop them? Before harm is done?"

Sizemore crossed his arms. "No, I don't. Any harm will be minimal at worst. I want to get a sense of their goal. What do these jokers think can be accomplished with a teaspoon full of radioactive whatever the fuck?"

"Americium."

"Right, a fool's errand."

"If you say so, sir."

"I do. Look at the big picture. We're in a battle here."

"Of course. Al Qaeda and the Islamic State are continuing threats."

"Oh for God's sake, kid. Grow up. Those ragheads are on the run. I'm talking about the U.S. military. Budget fight."

Roche swallowed. Talk like this made him very uncomfortable. "So what if something happens?"

"We get newspaper coverage, and Congress gets to realize we need more money, not less, to intercept all the zany little plots our enemies come up with. *Comprende?*"

Roche nodded unhappily. "I'll get back to my desk. Keep you posted."

"Attaboy. Stay on it. I can't wait to see how this plays out."

46

IN THE EARLY morning hours at Golden Egg Family Farms, Alejandro Muñoz was down by the corrals feeding ostriches, as he sometimes did. He was very fond of his livestock, especially an older female who was eating out of his open palm. Luther Handy drove up in the farm's ancient Jeep Cherokee, got out, and watched the performance with bemused detachment.

"See, Luther — Sandy Top, she's my girl."

"She certainly is, boss."

"Is there some gas in that four-by?"

"I filled it up."

"Good."

"I dunno about this idea. Long way down the hill, and I'm not sure the old jalopy will get there in one piece."

"It's part of the deal. I agreed to supply transportation, and I'm sure as hell not going to hand over my Lexus."

"Of course not. I was just wondering."

"Or your Honda. This whole thing is all about money. Different kind of operation."

"Are we talking about cash?"

"Always."

"More than usual?"

Muñoz pointed toward the sky. He cackled cheerfully. "For high-value passengers, the price goes up. Valenzuela made a down payment. But they owe us twenty-five thousand upon delivery. That's this morning. Don Diego assured me his riders have it with them."

"We're going to collect the twenty-five? You and me?"

"Yes we are."

"I dunno, boss, could get sticky."

"I doubt it. We're settling accounts, repatriating some money without Fed scrutiny here. No one wants to see our system go down."

"Sure you want to be there . . ?"

"Who would we send? That idiot Dingell? A painter? One of the ranch hands?"

"Guess not."

"And if there's any problem . . ." Muñoz pointed his finger and cocked his thumb. Handy removed a Ruger SR9 handgun from his belt, dropped the clip to check the loads, and slammed it home again.

"That's right, my friend," said Muñoz. "We kill them."

47

IN GRIDLEY, Marianne marched back and forth through the Nutcracker parking lot, pressing buttons on her mobile phone, negotiating the telephone robot at Union Pacific train control in Omaha.

"Hello, Molly?"

"Good morning, Officer Sarzeau. Marianne, right?"

"That's me. You're back."

"Another day, another dollar."

"Here's my problem. The train I've been tracking — it just went through Gridley, right?"

"Tell me the name again?"

"Uhh, KLAPT-12, I think it's called."

"Gridley? Gridley, California?"

"Yes, right, wherever I am. It was waiting for another train, and then it took off again."

"I'm looking, looking. All right, I do see your train, it's on its way to Klamath Falls, Oregon. Must have passed you in the last half hour or so."

Marianne smacked the side of her head.

"Here's the thing. My colleague and I are looking for a container. It's got the name 'Hi-Line' painted on the side. We walked the train and couldn't find it."

"I don't see anything by brand name, we use the ISO ID. The letters and numbers on the door. You might see 'em on the side marking panels too."

"Shit — whoops, sorry — we don't have any ID."

"Then I can't help you." Ms. Caspian fell silent.

"Molly?"

"Well, here's something. A little 'clue' for you detectives, heh heh. A three-car consist was dropped in Lathrop. Six containers in all, looks like."

"Lathrop, the cargo yard. Near Stockton."

"Very good."

"I've been there."

"I do see a diversion order for a box that was previously destined for Seattle. GEFU 513914 3. Grounded this AM. Does that help?"

"It was diverted?"

"That means an order came through once the train was underway from LA."

"Holy crap."

"Could be your van?"

Marianne threw up her hands, accidentally tossing her phone. She grabbed desperately and snatched it out of the air.

"Could be."

▼

Pavlov had the Crown Vic speeding down U.S. 99 at twenty over the limit.

"Jesus, Jerry, slow down," said Marianne. "If we get pulled over we'll spend all day with the CHP."

Pavlov reached under the dash, pulled out a fireball, rolled down his window and squished its big rubber suction cup onto the roof. He flipped a switch, and a red light began flashing. Then he grudgingly knocked five miles off the clock.

"Lathrop. Where is Lathrop?"

"Stockton suburb. South of Sac. Long way."

"Our bombers jumped off there?"

"Looks that way."

"And we have no idea where they are now or what they're going to hit."

"Maybe we do. Look at this —" The newspaper she had found was open on her lap. She showed him one of the headlines:

WATER FIGHT OVER FLUORIDE

"Yeah? What about it?"

"Lemme read you something . . ."

> Portland, Oregon, residents are up in arms over a new proposal to fluoridate Multnomah County water. Protesters against this contentious issue crowded the steps of City Hall yesterday, where passions were high. Fistfights broke out and police were forced to intervene. The mayor blamed the fracas on "mass hysteria." Asked about the issue, one opponent declared, "This is big. We will never drink contaminated water."

"Your point, officer?"

"I quote — *hysteria* and *never drink contaminated water.*"

"What? You lost me there."

"I figured it out," she declared with certain pride.

"Figured what, for the love of justice?"

"I know what our bombers are going to bomb."

"Oh really? Want to let me in on the secret . . ?"

"A water supply."

"Marianne . . ."

"No joke. A water supply for a city."

"With some dust from a smoke alarm?"

"It's a stunt. They're hoping for headlines. Chernobyl, Fukushima, people are terrified of anything radioactive. They're terrified of the damn word. The radioactivity we're talking about won't really poison anyone, but hey — hysteria! — contaminated water! — that stuff will scare the pants off all their customers. Bottled water will fly off the supermarket shelves. There will be shortages . . . people will panic."

Pavlov stared hard at Marianne, trying to gauge her theory, trying to absorb the idea.

"Hey, eyes on the road," she said, feeling very self-conscious.

"So they blow up a reservoir. Or a canal. California has a lot of reservoirs. And we know jack shit."

Marianne nodded. "I thought about that. One — the actual damage is minimal. They need publicity, news coverage."

"So you say."

"Two — they want to scare as many people as possible. So, it's got to be Big City water. Either Hetch Hetchy, for San Francisco, or Folsom Lake, for Sacramento. And Hetch Hetchy is in Yosemite, in the middle of nowhere."

"Terrorist responsibility claim," argued Pavlov. "They could send a note to all the TV stations."

"I think they want to make as big a splash as possible. Literally. Touch off their bomb in public. Folsom Lake is right in town, a recreation area with lots of visitors."

Pavlov drove in silence for several miles. "You'd make a pretty good analyst," he allowed at last. "Where to — Yosemite, or Folsom?"

"This is on me?" she asked, shrinking into the seat.

"What's your vote?"

Marianne wasn't all that sure of herself or any of her bright ideas. She thought about the situation. "Hang on a sec." She tapped a contact on her phone.

"Tom?"

"Morning, M. Where are you?"

"Rolling down 99, on our way to Sacramento. Need a favor."

"What can I do that witchery can't?"

"No teasing, I've been up all night."

"Sorry."

"You can call the newspapers, the *Bee*, *Channel Four News*. See if anyone there has received a tip about any kind of bombing."

"Is that what you're after?"

"Bombers, yes, terrorists."

"Do you have your bulletproof vest with you?"

"No . . ."

"Jesus. Better find one, hear me? No kidding, M, stay out of trouble."

"Doing my damnedest."

"How's our kid?"

"Still in there. Make the calls. If you hear anything, call me back."

Pavlov raised his eyebrows. "That your fiancé?"

She nodded. "He's a journalist, knows the right people. If nothing turns up . . . I vote Folsom."

Pavlov flexed his fingers on the steering wheel. He stared at the road that stretched ahead of them, wide and straight.

"If I call Home," he speculated, "and maybe I should — they're going to hand me my walking papers."

48

IN THE UNION PACIFIC Intermodal Facility in Lathrop, fifty miles south of Sacramento and eighty-five miles south of Pavlov and Marianne, a gantry crane lifted the bright blue shipping container designated GEFU 513914 3 with *HI-LINE* painted on the side, and deposited it on a skeleton trailer. A tractor hauled it away and parked it among a thousand other similar boxes.

Inside, the sudden move pitched Hatch over a seat. Brunel rolled across the floor, and terror supplies rolled with him.

When the floor stopped heaving, Hatch staggered to his feet, opened the tiny portal cut into an upper corner of the container wall, stuck an antenna through, and checked the GPS readout.

"37.84, 121.26 — This is the number we were given, give or take some decimal points. We have arrived."

"Where is our ride?" asked Brunel, gathering up his materials.

"They'll be here. Let's get the mix down," said Hatch, cracking open the side portal and risking a peek.

"Anybody out there?" asked Brunel, full of anxiety.

"Not a soul, mate. I see daylight. Somewhere on the other side, the sun must be up."

They both donned facemasks and goggles. Brunel slowly and carefully poured the Americium powder — a tiny amount bulked up with baking soda — into the considerable store of gunpowder he had already collected. Using a plastic rod, he stirred the mixture very slowly. Hatch then held the cardboard tubes while Brunel filled each one. When the operation was complete, Hatch covered the open ends with a plastic bag.

"We should wire it up."

"Not yet. We're supposed to blow the Americans to kingdom come, not us."

Brunel nodded. *"Inshallah."* He sealed the bag with rubber bands and tape.

Hatch's phone rang. He dug it out of his backpack. Brunel tore off his facemask and waved frantically. "Don't answer, the people who saw us in Tehachapi will trace the call."

"Never in time. And if I don't answer, our friends can't find us."

"Merde!" said Brunel.

"Panic Demo here."

Pause.

"That's us. Find us at lat 2301, long 8677."

Pause.

"Those numbers are just the seconds. Last four digits, all you need, chum."

Pause.

"Of course we have the money."

Pause.

"Yeah, Valenzuela gave us the lecture too. Car?"

Pause.

"A jeep? Better yet, we're waiting."

▼

Outside, Handy drove the Jeep Cherokee, on its oversize farm tires, into the facility at a slow walking pace. He was on the phone with his boss, trailing behind in a white Lexus. He hadn't gone far when Muñoz barked.

"Far enough. We will leave the cars out of sight."

Muñoz parked and strode forward to the Cherokee.

"Think they'll go for this old piece of shit?" asked Handy, looking very doubtful.

"It runs, it got you here. But, in case they turn up their noses, we show them only the keys until the transaction is complete."

"Right."

"Got that Ruger ready?"

"You bet."

"Then *ándale.*"

Handy thumbed a GPS app on his smartphone. He checked the notepad where he had scribbled the numbers supplied by Hatch against his readout.

"This way."

He led Muñoz along the row of containers, angled diagonally away from the truck lane for compact storage. Thirty units from their starting point the men arrived at a bright blue box.

"Here we are," said Handy.

"You sure?"

Handy double-checked his GPS. "Yup, our GEF unit." He pointed at the end doors. "See the numbers? She looks good, not too banged up."

"Let's say hello."

Handy eased up to the container and rapped his knuckles on the pleated steel side.

Wham! Wham! Wham!

Pause.

Wham! Wham! Wham!

The secret door concealed within the large white *H* swung open. Brunel appeared, blinking, looking fearful.

"Welcome to California, gentlemen," said Muñoz affably. "Got our money?"

"Qu'est-ce que c'est?"

"Our fee — train fare."

"What? What is that?"

Now Hatch appeared in the open portal, half-concealed behind his comrade. "What money are we talking about?" he inquired.

Muñoz and Handy glanced at each other.

"The twenty-five thousand dollars we agreed upon. Due on delivery, and here you are."

"Muñoz? That you? How do we know?"

Muñoz made a little bow.

"I am Alejandro Muñoz. Perhaps your contact in Mexico mentioned my name?"

"But you could be a fooking Fed, right? Trying to fook us."

"We are who we say we are. We built the container you're riding in. Who else would know about it?"

Hatch nodded. "Okay, okay, mate, I believe you."

"And, excuse me, where are your Mexican traveling companions? Five of them, I believe."

"Oh them. They got off back in Tee-what's-its-name."

"Really? That's funny, I have their bus tickets."

"They changed their minds. Not sure why. Don't speak Spanish."

Munoz nodded to Handy, who let a hand inch under his jacket.

"At least you two made it all the way, that's something."

"Do you have the jeep ready?" asked Hatch.

Muñoz dangled the keys.

"Pay up, and it's yours."

"Here, we have the money, we're ready to pay."

Hatch stepped out from behind Brunel. He had the CZ 75 in his hand.

Pop!

The bullet caught Muñoz just below his right eye. He staggered backward and collapsed. Handy leaped sideways and jerked the SR9 from under his jacket. Not in time.

Pop!

The second shot took Handy in the chest. He teetered, dropped to his knees, fell over on his face, hit before he could take aim.

Both men were dead.

The chain ladder rattled down the side of the container. Hatch and Brunel climbed to the ground. They searched the bodies, being careful not to touch the blood seeping onto the concrete, found the Jeep keys, bus tickets, and Handy's Ruger.

"You did not tell me you were going to shoot," Brunel whined.

"No turning back now, eh, comrade? Look on the bright side — we've got pocket money and tickets to ride."

Working hard, they heaved the two bodies up to the open portal and dumped them inside. Then, exhausted from the effort, they wandered off to find the Jeep.

49

MARIANNE AND PAVLOV were taking a break at the Feather River rest stop on Route 99. They had moved away from the Crown Vic to a picnic area overlooking the water, where they were holding a debate.

"I say, go for the lake. It's the obvious target," insisted Marianne.

"Man, the river . . ." said Pavlov, gazing at exposed gravel beds between the banks. ". . . is it always this low?"

"Drought, Jerry. We're in a drought. You vetoing the lake?"

"No . . ."

"Well what, then? What do you want to do?"

"Well, I'm off the reservation, but I'm still part of Homeland enforcement. I think we need to look at the smugglers' operation. Before someone hauls it all away."

"That will cost us two hours, at least."

An ironic grin creased his face. "I feel a professional urge."

Marianne threw up her hands. "It's your car, you're driving."

Pavlov winced. In their twenty-plus hours together he had come to respect, if not exactly trust, her oddball ideas.

"Look, call your guy, see if anyone in the news game has received threats. If the Sacramento outlets are worried, we hit the lake. If not, we check that container."

"Okay, I'm calling. But what if our bombers have decided not to make threats?"

"They want publicity? They have to make threats."

Marianne held her smartphone high and punched in a number from her contact list, conceding the point with sullen fury.

"Yo, Tom — what do you hear?"

"Oh hi, M — you'll love this, I'm in the car, I saw it was you, I picked up. I'm talking while driving. You could pull me over."

"Consider yourself busted. Meanwhile, what about it?"

"Sorry, no one has heard a thing. They'll call if they do."

"Great, put down the phone before you cause an accident."

She lowered her phone. Her shoulders sagged.

Pavlov cocked his head. "Yea or nay?"

"No joy . . . so . . . we check out the smugglers operation."

"Here we go." Pavlov led the way back toward the car. Marianne followed, then came to a halt.

"Wait a minute. I'm nervous about my stalker. He's tied up in this." She keyed a different number into her phone.

"Hi, Al --- what's the scoop on Dingell? Nailed his ass yet?"

"Sorry, Marianne. The alerts are out. But so far, no tips, no traces."

"Call me, please, if and when. On the loose, he worries me."

"I will do so."

"Good hunting."

"Be safe."

Marianne walked to the rear of the Crown Vic. "Pop the trunk."

Pavlov pulled a lever and the trunk lid lifted. Marianne reached into the pile of gear to extract Pavlov's bulletproof flak jacket and a road flare. She hooked the jacket over one arm, took a few steps, and fired up the flare.

"What now?" grumbled Pavlov.

Marianne held up a hand to forestall chatter. She walked around in a little circle, chanting softly:

"Whiskeyjack! Whiskeyjack . . ."

The flame on the road flare remained steady, a bright red spike. In morning light the smoke was almost invisible, and the flame itself was pale and unimpressive. No power spirit of any description offered to show itself.

Marianne repeated the chant several times without success.

"Goddammit!"

She reared back and heaved the flare toward the water. It arced high over the bank and came to rest among dry river stones, where it continued to burn.

Pavlov looked to be sure Marianne wasn't starting a brush fire. "If I may ask . . ?" said he.

"I was hoping to conjure my pal Whiskeyjack." She registered the doubtful look on his face. "I know, I know. But the guy, or thing, whatever he is, is not responding. I don't think my tricks work in daylight." She thought about the problem for a moment, then removed her little acorn from a pocket. She rolled it around in her fingers.

"There's another way. Come on."

She led Pavlov into the women's rest room.

"Everything is gender-free now?" he asked nervously.

Marianne pointed at the mirror, a stainless steel panel etched with graffiti. Their reflections were a dull blur.

"I'm going to do something. You may or may not see anything."

"I can't even see us."

She reached into her blouse for her stony amulet. She held the acorn in her free hand.

"Here goes — Whiskeyjack! *Hey you!*"

Marianne was used to the indefinite delay that usually accompanied her little séances, but after a minute she was getting fidgety. In another minute she was bouncing up and down.

"Come on!"

"I've seen magicians in Vegas," said Pavlov. "They know how to put on a show. Why don't I just go wait in the car?"

"Shh!" said Marianne.

A billowing smoky presence was forming in the mirror. All at once it seemed to bulge out of the panel and hover above the agents.

"Marianne . . . moving . . . hard to find today . . ."

"Yeah, I'm on assignment. This is my partner on the case, Jerry Pavlov."

"He can't see me, you know."

"No? I was hoping."

"Does he disparage your powers?"

"No, not really, but it's always a stretch with regular people."

"As it should be. Bring me forth at night — I'll set him on fire."

"Oh no you won't. We're on the same side. Now listen, what about my stalker, Bo Dingell? Where is he? Why haven't they caught him?"

"They try, but he is elusive. His guardian protects him."

"Bad news for me."

"That is true. I am watching, but I make no guarantees. Be careful. Be alert."

▼

Pavlov was silent all the way through Sacramento, debating with himself. Finally, as he and Marianne motored into Stockton, he spoke up.

"Back there, you saw something in the mirror? No kidding?"

Marianne nodded. "Affirmative. A power spirit."

"I couldn't see what you saw, so I'm taking you on faith." He eyed her speculatively. "That's a big leap."

"For sure."

"Like over the Grand Canyon — on a motorcycle — with no wings — and no fucking helmet."

"Right. Don't worry, I won't turn you into a frog."

"Christ, I hope not."

"But you're out in the wind, hanging your professional butt off a cliff. Your Homeland superiors might do the job."

"I've thought about it. I could be running security at a mall next week."

"And yet, here we are checking on smugglers."

"I love my work."

Marianne punched his shoulder. "Me too."

Arriving in Lathrop, Pavlov turned into the Union Pacific Intermodal Facility at the Roth Road entrance. They cruised slowly along between endless rows of containers.

"The numbers are too small, they're going by too fast. Stop! We need to walk," protested Marianne.

Pavlov parked the Crown Vic and they continued on foot. Marianne shrugged into the flak jacket she had discovered and zipped it up tight.

"Body armor? Sure you'll need that?" Pavlov scorned the idea.

"Tom made me promise." She leaned over and pulled out her Beretta. "Maybe our boys are still here. Maybe they have guns."

"Doubt it, but . . ." Pavlov patted his armpit to locate his own weapon.

They checked the numbers on the containers as they walked. Suddenly Marianne stumbled. The Beretta flew out of her hand and skittered across the asphalt. Pavlov grabbed her by the shoulders and helped her up.

"You okay?"

She nodded bleakly. "Yes." She dropped to her hands and knees, retching uncontrollably "I mean, no. Ughhh . . ."

"Morning sickness?" asked Pavlov, thoroughly unnerved by female biology.

"Or something. Ohhhh . . ."

Pavlov had become cubist, all angles and colored edges. Marianne was having a seizure. A surreal landscape opened before her eyes; little gray hills dotted with skeletal trees under hazy orange light. The vision gave her a queasy feeling. She understood, with sickening certainty, that she was glimpsing something real, an alien world. A grim world. A world in which a monster was stirring. She stared at the ground until the impression faded. When everything seemed normal again, she became aware of a faint reddish impression in a quiet corner of her mind.

She wiped her mouth on her sleeve and scrambled across the pavement to retrieve her gun. Then she slowly stood, all of her senses quivering.

"Jerry . . . I sense an aura."

Pavlov gave her a quizzical scowl. "What?"

"I can sense adepts. Sort of like they have halos. In color. This one is red."

"And . . ."

"Red belongs to a hostile person. The only one I've seen anywhere in northern California is Bo Dingell."

"Your stalker–shooter perp."

"That's right. He's here. He's close."

"Marianne . . . this hocus-pocus stuff is hard to take."

"Over this way." She pointed across the facility. "He's employed by the smugglers. I'll bet he's here to collect the container that brought our terrorists into the country."

She motioned Pavlov forward and led the way between big steel boxes to another traffic lane and more rows of containers. He followed along without much concern.

"Jerry! Your gun. Present arms! Finger on the guard, partner!"

Pavlov dutifully obeyed and drew his pistol.

As they moved, the reddish glow Marianne felt became stronger and stronger. After passing by dozens of containers, they came upon a bright blue one with *GEFU 513914 3* stenciled on the doors.

"Here we are."

The box was sitting on a skeleton semi-trailer ready to haul, and on the far end a truck tractor was backing into position to hook it up.

Marianne ran along the side, Beretta pointed at the cab. She jumped on the running board and hammered on the driver's door. The truck slammed to a stop. The door opened and Bo Dingell peered out.

"Marianne!"

"Get down here, Bo, you're under arrest."

"I never killed nobody, never did, never my intent, but I could start on you." He poked his Colt revolver out the door and fired off a round without bothering to take aim.

Ka-twang!

The bullet zinged off the side of the neighboring container. Marianne dropped to the ground and rolled under the trailer. Pavlov, further back, ducked around behind it.

Dingell slammed his cab door shut, ground the truck gears into first, and pulled away, forgetting all about the trailer he was attempting to transport.

Once he was rolling, Marianne crawled out from underneath and watched him go. Pavlov walked forward just in time to see the truck turn east on Roth Road.

"That was Dingell?"

"Mmm. Still the loyal employee. But he's possessed by the devil, or something a lot like him."

"You and your spooky friends."

"Wonder where he's off to?"

"He can wait. Let's have a look at our chariot, shall we?"

Pavlov gazed up at the *HI-LINE* logo painted on the side. The opening was hard to see. He reached up and touched the bottom of the **H.** The concealed portal cracked open a few inches.

"Hey!"

Pavlov crooked a finger to draw Marianne over. He stooped and cupped his hands to make a stirrup.

"Here, I'll boost you up."

Marianne put a foot in Pavlov's little cradle, got a hand under the edge of the portal and tugged it open. Then she hauled herself up and inside.

"Holy crap," came her voice, echoing from within.

"What?"

The chain ladder tumbled out and down.

"Get up here," she commanded.

Pavlov climbed up and peered inside. Marianne was standing near one of the seats. She pointed at the floor, where two bodies were sprawled, one on top of the other. Her face was pale. She had blood on her hands.

"Whoa," said Pavlov. "Surprise."

Marianne covered her mouth. She was feeling sick again. "I, um, I know who they are."

Pavlov stared at the bodies. "How's that?"

"I met them both. The older one here is Alejandro Muñoz, he owns Golden Harvest. He's the smuggler. The other guy is his ranch foreman. I think the name is Luther Handy."

"Think that guy Dingell smoked them?"

Marianne shook her head. "Bo is crazy, and he's in the thrall of a demon, but I don't see it."

"Then it was Hatch and Brunel."

Pavlov hurried back to the Crown Vic and returned with his little radiation detector. Marianne was already back down on the ground, waiting. There was a smear of blood across her upper lip. She was holding her hands away from her body to prevent any more of a mess.

Pavlov climbed the ladder, activated the detector and pointed the sensor wand into the gloomy interior. At long intervals a tiny light flashed and a *click* sounded, reporting a very faint residue of radioactive material.

"I'm getting a reading. They were here."

They hiked across the facility to the operations center. Marianne was on the phone to the Amador County Sheriff's office as they threaded their way between and around the long lines of grounded containers. She was holding the phone delicately between two fingers to avoid getting blood on it. Pavlov trailed behind, looking morose.

"Al, it's me, Marianne. I'm down here at Union Pacific in Lathrop, where I have discovered the bodies of Alejandro Muñoz and his foreman, Luther Handy. They've been shot."

Pause.

"That's right. Not your jurisdiction, but Muñoz is — was — the owner of Golden Egg Family Farms, outside of Jackson, your territory."

Pause.

"Right. I'm notifying the locals. But get this, the container involved was being used in a smuggling operation."

Pause.

"A shipping container. Big steel box. Up from Mexico on rails. They were converting these things right there at Golden Egg. First class accommodations. You should see it."

Pause.

"That's enough, right? But it's *not* all. I had a run-in with my stalker and fugitive suspect, Bo Dingell, who was attempting to tow the container away."

Pause.

"He worked for Muñoz. I doubt he killed the guy."

Pause.

"Sorry, he drove away in his truck. Who knows where?"

▼

The Lathrop police station was located just a few blocks south of the intermodal facility, and officers arrived in minutes, following the UP supervisor's call. They took control of the crime scene from a dozen railroad employees who were gathered around the Hi-Line container, uncertain how to behave, but filled with morbid curiosity. Soon Stockton police joined them, followed by two CHP highway patrolmen.

After Marianne cleaned herself up in the operations center bathroom, she and Pavlov looked on as a police photographer documented the scene. When the local medical examiner appeared, they decided they'd had enough.

"The lake?"

Pavlov nodded absently. He looked very unhappy. "I need to make a call."

Marianne noted his reluctance. "Hey, call Ginger. Have her forward the information as an anonymous tip. You can still be doing surveillance on your fraudulent dentist."

Pavlov considered the idea for a moment, then flicked a hand to dismiss it.

"Then, when they find out, they'll fire Ginger too."

"Don't be like that. You're a hero."

He grimaced.

"Piece of advice, Sarzeau. Avoid working for bureaucrats."

50

RUBY JUDSON knocked politely on Jameson Sizemore's door, and stuck her head in.

"Sir? Got a minute?"

Sizemore turned away from his window and his view of the capitol dome.

"Whatcha got, Rube?"

"More on the AQ-4 penetration we've been tracking."

"Ho hum."

"Sir, police officers have discovered the shipping container that carried Hatch and Brunel into the country in Lathrop, California. Our targets have left the immediate area."

"Where the hell is Lathrop?"

"Big Valley, near Sacramento. Union Pacific has a cargo handling facility there."

"And the bad news I'm going to hear is . . ?"

"Radioactivity was detected, proving that these men are in possession of the Americium we discussed."

She fidgeted with her badge.

"And two bodies were found in the container. They had been shot. The situation is now a murder case."

"Somebody killed our terrorists?" Sizemore sounded displeased.

"No sir, the victims appear to be the men behind the smuggling ring. There was a dispute of some kind, apparently."

"Honor and thieves, huh?"

"Our targets are obviously planning some sort of violent demonstration. Our Long Beach office — which is where my information comes from — is suggesting an attack on Folsom Lake."

"Really, where'd they come up with that?"

"I don't know. But that lake is Sacramento's water supply. If it is poisoned with radioactive material, it could cause panic. Shouldn't we call in the troops and start a manhunt?"

"Panic? How big is Sacramento?"

"About half a million people drink that water."

"Really? That's a pretty good number. Any threats?"

"Not so far."

"Then we don't know for sure. But I like the odds."

"Sir?"

Sizemore noticed her expression of disapproval.

"All right, Ruby, take it easy. We do need to react. Tell you what, call the nearest office out there and get someone to monitor the Sacramento news outlets, check on any terrorist manifestos, jihadist warnings, etc., etc."

"That's all?"

"That's enough. If people go into a tizzy because someone dropped a teensy weensy scoop of harmless smoke shit into their water . . . think of the publicity."

"Yes, all of it bad, we'll be accused of negligence."

Sizemore rubbed his hands. "And our defense will be budget shortfalls."

Part SIX

51

FOLSOM LAKE was seventy miles from Lathrop. Pavlov got them to the Folsom Point boat launch in fifty minutes by driving up Route 99 at say-your-prayers speeds and by taking bold chances on narrow Grant Line Road. Marianne, an aggressive driver herself, was tight-lipped and white-knuckled for the whole trip.

"You are scarier than Dingell," she declared after Pavlov put wheels over the double line to skirt a school bus, barely avoiding a head-on collision with a truck full of tomatoes.

They parked in the boat launch lot and sat there to await events.

"Lake is low this year," she said.

"Unh-huh. Where are they?" he wondered.

Marianne was antsy. Soon she could no longer sit still. She hopped out of the car and crossed to the public restroom to relieve herself. She was even less certain of the situation on the way back.

"Maybe they're off to Hetch Hetchy after all," she muttered.

"Calm down, Sarzeau. You were right the first time — that other reservoir is in the middle of nowhere. There's a what? A hundred miles and more of aqueduct to San Francisco. Even paranoids will figure out that the threat is washed out by the time the water gets there."

"Then we're still in the wrong place. Look around" — the parking lot was nearly empty — "there's no one here, no witnesses."

Pavlov thought about it. "Where else?"

"There's a picnic area on the other side of the dam. Lots of people. We used to get drunk there."

Pavlov cocked an eyebrow. "Oh?"

She blushed. "In my younger days."

Her phone rang; Wagstaff calling. "Hi, Tom, got something?"

"Okay, here you go — *Channel Four News* and the *Bee* both have received anonymous threats."

"And . . ."

"You know," he said, "'Sacramento lives are hostage to the Truth of Allah, blah blah blah. Until the Middle East is free, water will not slake your thirst, but kill you and your children unto the seventh generation.' I'm paraphrasing, but that's the gist. You get the idea."

"Where? Where will this happen?"

"The threats came as text messages. No target was specified."

"Shit."

"Don't you dare risk the life of our son, M. I'm serious."

"I know."

She killed the call.

"Hey, Jer, it's official — threats have been made."

"What's the target?"

"No target, but they were addressing Sacramento. Water was mentioned. They're here somewhere."

▼

They drove around the western end of the lake, past the dam, and into the Beals Point picnic area.

The parking lot was dotted with cars, pickups, minivans, and SUVs. Families were gathered around tables and tailgates. Barbecues were smoking. Children were wandering along the shoreline. Bicyclists were coming and going on the paved bike trail.

"See anything?"

"How would we ever?" Marianne gestured dismissively toward the cars and crowd. "This looks pretty All-American to me."

"I dunno, a suspicious car, odd clothing."

"Do we even know if they have a car?"

"No, but they must."

"Maybe they stole one."

"We would have heard from the railroad guys if that happened."

"We could call the cops, see if anyone reported a theft."

"People report thefts all day and all night."

"You're right," admitted Marianne. "That's true even up in my little town."

Pavlov opened his door. "Let's have a look around. Maybe we'll spot something."

Marianne didn't move. She was thinking. "Forget it, Jerry. We're never going to find them in time."

"No? We don't even know they're going to attack today. It could be next week."

This possibility did not comfort Marianne. "They must know someone is on their trail. They aren't going to fool around after issuing threats." She pushed a wisp of hair away from her eyes and got out of the car.

"Here's my idea — those telephone numbers I sent you. Got 'em?"

"With me?"

"Where else?"

"You emailed them. They're on my computer, back in LA."

"So dig out your smartphone and look at your mail," she ordered.

Pavlov seemed perplexed, but lit up his phone. After tapping on several different icons he managed to start his mail program. He scanned through a pile of messages until he found the one from Marianne.

"Okay, here's your list. Seven numbers. What's the point?"

"You'll see." She touched an icon on her own phone. Then, grumbling and muttering, she tapped her way through a litany of robotic challenges until a real person came on the line.

"American TV & Appliance. How may I direct your call?"

"This is Agent Broomhandle. FULTAP. Ray Bagwell's outfit? I have a list of telephone numbers for you. Seven in all, connected to a terrorist plot I'm tracking. Can you locate them for me?"

"Sorry, I'm new on this desk. I need to verify your identity. Count from one to ten, please."

"Are you kidding? Okay, okay — one, two, three, four, five, six, seven, eight, nine, ten."

"Now please say, 'pack my box with five dozen liquor jugs.'"

Marianne made a face for Pavlov's benefit. "Pack my box with five dozen liquor jugs."

"Now say, 'Mary had a little lamb.'"

"Screw Mary's little lamb, I need some information here."

"Just a moment, please." Bland orchestral music swelled while Marianne's call went on hold. It took several seconds for her to identify the music as the lazy rendition of an old Beatles tune, *Norwegian Wood.* Then, abruptly, the call resumed. "All right, I see a good voice match. Read your numbers."

Marianne turned to Pavlov, snapping her fingers. "Give me that." She grabbed his phone and read off the numbers she saw there.

"This may take a while," said the man from TV & App.

"Call me back."

The two agents meandered down to the lake shore and commenced to skip rocks out over the water.

"That's three!" said Marianne, trying to distract herself from the job at hand.

Pavlov leaned over, sidearmed a nice flat river stone and watched it skip five times.

"Not really my thing," she growled, kicking the pebbles at her feet. "And anyway, where is my callback?"

A half hour later they were eating ice cream from the concession stand when the call from TV & App came in.

"Broomhandle? We have found one of your telephone numbers. It is currently registered to a tower in Roseville, California. The owner is Valley Mobility LLC, tower designated Q-C12-84-0, located at 38.748917 north, 121.262083 west on your GPS dial."

"Fantastic, but that's an earful. Can you give me a street address?"

"My map puts it in an office complex east of Sunrise and south of Lead Hill. Does that help?"

"Does it! You are my hero!"

"Owen's the name — recommend me to Bagwell, if you will."

"Done."

Marianne was jumping up and down. "Hey, Jerry, got a hit — Roseville! — our smoke bombers are in Roseville."

Pavlov leaned into the car and pulled a road map from his glove box.

"How far?"

"Ten miles or so. Next town over."

"What have we got anywhere near that tower?" muttered Pavlov, tracing over the map with an uncertain finger.

Marianne brought up a map on her smartphone. She panned around Roseville and stopped on a parking lot. She shoved the phone at Pavlov.

"Look — two big shopping centers within a quarter mile. And over here" — she slewed the map sideways — "we have an office complex, a clinic, a post office. Basically, a dozen parking lots. They could be sitting there, waiting to hear their stupid threats on the radio."

Pavlov took a look. "Or," he said, "they could be having lunch. Look, there's a Subway in that shopping center."

"Let's get after them," said Marianne.

Pavlov opened the Crown Vic's door and dropped into the driver's seat. Marianne threw the remains of her ice cream cone into the trash and slid in beside him. He backed out of the parking spot and turned toward the exit. Then it hit her.

"Whoa, boss. That's still a big search area. And we don't know how long our targets will stay put. Or even if the one phone we traced is a decoy."

Pavlov brought the car to a halt.

"What are you saying?"

"Our list shows them with what, seven phones? Throwaways? Why would our smoke bomber dudes want them?"

Pavlov sighed.

"In Iraq, a lot of the IEDs were detonated with cell phones. The igniters of choice."

"We don't need to eyeball them."

"No?"

"No. We call them."

▼

Pavlov's guess was a good one. Hatch and Brunel were, in fact, eating lunch in the Grand Slam Sports Bar on Douglas Avenue, where a San Francisco Giants baseball game was in progress on a large flat TV screen. They had been watching America's favorite pastime for a while, bored and confused by the impossibly alien sport, nursing iced tea and lemonade. Now, as they finished their sandwiches and onion rings, their patience was rewarded.

A red banner appeared at the bottom of the screen. *BREAKING NEWS BREAKING NEWS BREAKING NEWS* marched across the stripe in bold white letters. Then the picture switched to an announcer from the *Channel Four News* team.

"We interrupt our sports programming to bring you an important bulletin. This morning our newsroom received a warning from would-be terrorists threatening to plant a bomb of some sort here in Sacramento."

Hatch and Brunel sat up straight in their booth.

"We contacted the *Bee* and learned that they have also received a threat. No target was specified, so we don't have that information for you. The threat did appear to be directed against water, however, and we may be looking at an attempt to disrupt recreational activities on any of our streams or lakes. Yes, we could be reporting a hoax, but our editorial staff has decided that, on balance, it is prudent to warn our viewers to be on the alert. We'll be following this story until we have all the facts. Stay tuned."

The announcer disappeared, baseball coverage resumed, and the Giants went down swinging in the second inning. Hatch and Brunel paid with their wad of cash and left the restaurant.

"Let's get on it, Yan," said Hatch as they hiked across the street to the shopping center parking lot and Golden Egg's ancient Jeep Cherokee.

There Brunel took up a position in the rear seat and laid out the pair's bomb materials in the wayback. Hatch brought forth the throwaway telephones from his backpack and handed them over.

Using a small screwdriver, Brunel removed the cases. Hatch handed him a small voltmeter. Brunel found the ringer on the first receiver, an HTC flip phone, and clipped the leads in place.

"Call me," he said.

Hatch turned on Ghani Mansour's phone and dialed a number. The HTC unit rang, and the readout on the voltmeter registered a value.

"Kill it. Not enough *énergie.*"

Hatch ended the call. They repeated the procedure with an LG feature phone. Another voltmeter readout, a bigger one.

"Better. What else do we have?" Brunel looked over the pile of equipment and selected an unlocked Samsung Android handset. He attached the voltmeter leads, and Hatch dialed the number. The readout spiked.

"Aha, *mon petit ami,* you are the chosen one," said Brunel.

Hatch handed him a small square of blond plastic attached to a pair of wires: an explosive igniter. Brunel carefully shut down the Samsung and attached the wires to the ringer.

"Where's that Gorilla tape? Tear me off a piece."

Hatch handed him a length of black tape. Brunel draped it over the connection he had fashioned and mashed it down tight.

Hatch removed the plastic baggie from the top of the three cardboard tubes that, taped together, constituted their bomb. Brunel lowered the little plastic square into the gunpowder. He crimped the top edges of the tubes and sealed them with Gorilla tape. He forced the wires down along the tubes and taped them in place. Finally he switched on the phone and taped that to the tubes as well.

"Okay, *mon frère,* we are hot. Got the big bag?"

Hatch handed him a large plastic bag. Brunel pushed the bomb inside and taped the plastic down tight.

"The tighter the better, if we want a real explosion, eh?"

"And waterproof. We float this, we will have ourselves a terrific geyser for the infidel bystanders to notice."

"In fooking shock and awe."

▼

Back at Beals Point, Marianne and Pavlov discussed their options.

"If we do this, and there's an explosion, it could hurt civilians," said Pavlov.

"That's true. But if the bad guys reach the lake, it's going to be worse. A lot of people hurt, plus the panic they're after."

Pavlov compressed his lips, furrowed his brow, and proceeded to give it some thought.

"Well?"

Pavlov gave her a guarded thumbs up.

"Okay then," she said, returning the gesture, "here goes . . ." She read off a sequence of telephone numbers, carefully pronouncing each digit. Pavlov dialed them, one after the other.

"Unable to connect. That's three, all cold."

"Unh-huh, keep going . . ."

She read off another number.

▼

Brunel was packing up his improvised work area when the HTC handset rang, issuing the standard musical chime.

Bling-a-ling.

Brunel automatically picked it up and shut it off.

"Who would know to call us?" wondered Hatch.

"No one," said Brunel, then *"Merde."* The color drained from his face. He tore at the tape sealing their bomb.

The LG unit rang.

Bling-a-ling.

Hatch threw himself down onto the floorboards. Brunel scraped away, tearing madly at the plastic baggie covering the detonator with his fingernails

"No, no, no . . ."

The Samsung unit rang.

BOOM!

All four doors on the Cherokee blew open. Dense white smoke exploded outward. Tongues of flame erupted. Brunel was ejected by the blast. He skidded across the asphalt and slammed against a Buick SUV. Hatch rolled out of the passenger door, kicking and screaming. His hair and clothes were on fire.

The driver of the Buick came running with a picnic blanket and smothered the flames.

▼

Marianne was going through the phone numbers on their list and directing Pavlov through another round of calls.

"That's funny," said Pavlov. "When I repeated the last number, it said, 'unable to connect.' First it rang, and now it doesn't."

They worked through the list a third time.

"None of them are ringing."

Marianne sucked air through clenched teeth. "Holy crap, we might have scored."

"If one of those phones was hooked up . . ." mused Pavlov. "Especially if they're not professional bomb-makers and didn't take all the precautions."

"We had rings from three numbers."

"We did."

Marianne felt a cold tickle of guilty suspicion in the pit of her stomach. "We probably ought to get over there."

"Unh-huh." He dialed 9-1-1. "You tell 'em, I'm still undercover or something." He handed the phone to Marianne.

"Oh boy."

She did her best to compose herself.

"Hello, this is Marianne Sarzeau. I'm a Placerville police officer and a federal agent. I'm currently tracking a possible terrorist plot centered on Folsom Lake."

Pause.

"That's right, Sarzeau, Placerville, FULTAP."

Pause.

"Listen to me — the men I'm after have issued threats against the Sacramento water supply. I have reason to believe they have accidentally ignited the detonator of their bomb prematurely, or possibly even the bomb itself —"

Pause.

"Hang on, I have details. They are located somewhere near the cell tower between Sunrise, Lead Hill, and Douglas in Roseville. Their bomb contains radioactive material. Take a look — and wear your bunny suits."

Pause.

"Absolutely serious, ma'am. I'm on my way as well."

▼

By the time Marianne and Pavlov wound their way through the Sacramento suburbs, from the lake in Folsom to Douglas Boulevard in Roseville, the location of the unfortunate terrorists was obvious. Smoke was still rising from the parking lot of the Valley River Mall. A fleet of ambulances, fire trucks, police cars, and hazmat units were on the scene. Red, blue, and yellow lights were flashing. Dozens of shoppers were gathered behind yellow crime scene tape, gawking at the dazzling display.

Channel Four News was already there as well. Mila Jansky, the station's young roving reporter, was holding forth in front of the camera.

". . . this burned-out hulk is all that's left of the SUV in what we are told is a failed terrorist plot. The two men responsible have been taken to Kaiser hospital, just down the street. Both were alive following an apparent explosion, but one was badly burned, and the other has sustained internal injuries. When we learn the details of their medical condition, we'll bring you that news. Meanwhile, we are still awaiting an explanation from officials here. All we know is this — although the incident is a big surprise to those of us in the capital corridor, some law enforcement agencies were aware of the two men's activities and may have played a role in thwarting their attack."

The Channel Four cameraman twirled a finger over his head. The reporter took the cue to wind up her gig.

"Looks like we dodged a bullet, folks. Mila Jansky in Roseville, back to you, Bob."

Marianne and Pavlov presented their credentials to the officer in charge of the cleanup. The man, who was wearing a Tyvek hazmat suit, handed them surgical face masks, which they were quick to don.

"What's all this I hear about radioactivity? It's hot in these fucking bags."

Pavlov handed over his AN/PDR-60 alpha probe. "Americium. Try this, and you'll see. What you have here was an attempt to plant a dirty bomb."

"No shit."

"I'd move your civilians further away, if I were you," said Marianne.

The man turned away and made to rearrange his troops with big and urgent gestures.

▼

After a while, the situation cooled. The news truck retracted its microwave antenna and drove away. Half the police cars moved on to other business. A tow truck arrived to haul away the blackened Cherokee hulk.

The hazmat team had laid down a layer of foam over the surrounding area, and was busy vacuuming and bagging debris. One of the team members was going over the ground with Pavlov's specialized radiation detector, motioning the rest of the crew to remaining hot spots.

Marianne and Pavlov stayed in the background, still wearing their face masks, fascinated by the operation.

While they watched, a black Ford Taurus drove up and parked. A large African-American man wearing a suit and tie got out and ambled over.

"Agent Pavlov?" he inquired, showing his badge.

Pavlov removed his mask. "That's me."

"Terrell Boone, ICE, HSI, San Francisco."

"Homeland?" asked Marianne, unsure of the acronyms.

"Yes, ma'am." He watched the tow truck operator winch the Cherokee onto a flatbed trailer.

"Mmm, this is some mess. You found these jokers and tracked them down, Pavlov?"

"I did, with some help from the lady here."

"Unh-huh. Is it true the parking lot is all covered over with radioactive shit?"

"If you can call smoke detectors radioactive, yup. I wouldn't get too close and breath any dust."

Boone took a backward step. "All right, then. Looks like the team has everything under control. Man, I'd hate to wear those hazmat suits on a day like this." He paused. "You ready? I've got a charter to fetch you back to our office. Debriefing . . . you understand."

Pavlov nodded. "Let's go."

The two men started toward the Taurus. Marianne ran after them.

"Hey, hey, hey, wait a minute, buster."

Pavlov stopped and faced her. "It's okay, Sarzeau. I knew this was coming."

Marianne threw her arms around him.

"You're a bigot, you know that? But you're the nicest bigot I've met."

"And you're a witch, but not a bitch. Say hello to your ghosts for me . . ." He waved as he got into Boone's car.

Marianne watched them drive away.

"Nice going, Mom, we're still alive."

"My unborn son . . . talking . . . again."

"You did a good job today."

"Well, thank you."

"I know you were worried about doing the wrong thing."

"Just . . . business as usual."

"I need you to be confident. It's important not to be conflicted."

"Conflicted? Where did you ever hear a word like that?"

"You read it in a magazine. I want you to be strong. I want a strong, confident mother."

"You want? Sheesh. Here's what I want — a respectful son."

"Don't be mad. Kids need a healthy ego to survive."

"Tell you what, let's do a trade — confidence for you, no more tummy trouble for me."

"That's easy — morning sickness should be gone by now. If you throw up again, be wary, it won't be me."

"I'll make a note. Now shut up, I have to call your father."

She hoisted her smartphone and thumbed a call.

"Wagstaff here."

"Hi, Tom, it's me."

"M? You okay? Where are you? Everybody's talking about these threats."

"It's over. Long couple of days. You don't happen to be down at State by any chance?"

"As a matter of fact. Class just let out."

"I'm just up the road in Roseville. Pick me up?"

"Don't move."

52

IN WASHINGTON, late in the day, Sizemore was prowling his office, stomping back and forth, waving his hands in extreme agitation. Dylan Roche and Ruby Judson, recent telexes from California in hand, were standing by, mute and troubled.

"Pavlov! What is he, a field agent out there in Long Beach?"

"That's right, sir," said Judson. "Showing a lot of initiative."

"That bastard. He was told to back off. Our pals the terror-istas are within ten miles of their target and, boom, they miss, thanks to him. Fucking initiative."

"A Subway, an Applebee's, a Kohl's department store, they're all closed until safety can be assured, sir, along with other businesses in that Roseville mall. It's pretty dramatic," said Roche.

"Not to mention half the parking lot quarantined. There's a hazmat unit still working the area," added Judson.

"We're on TV," continued Roche. "Any more publicity would be a major disaster for us."

Sizemore's lip curled. "So what? So thirty people will be having lunch at the McDonald's across town for a month and buy their underwear down in Sacramento. I wanted half a million people to be too damned scared to drink their water. I wanted Congress to sit up and take notice. No one will even cancel a golf date over this."

"No, sir."

"Did we arrest the accomplices?"

"Mansour and Tayeb? Yes, we did," said Judson. "They are in custody in Los Angeles."

"I don't know whether to fire Pavlov's ass, give him a medal, or what."

"Give him a medal and then fire his ass, sir?" suggested Roche.

The office phone rang. Assistant Deputy Sizemore was staring out his window. He made no move to answer. After the third ring, Judson picked up. She chatted briefly with someone on the other end and held the handset out toward her supervisor.

"Secretary Quincy is on the line for you. Careful, sir, he's got a bee in his bonnet."

53

IT WAS A QUIET RIDE up through the hills to the Tri-Town Area. Marianne, in comfortably familiar company again, allowed herself to be as grumpy as she felt. After a few terse words, she dozed through most of the trip. When Wagstaff pulled into Applefield her eyes fluttered open. He glanced at his passenger, hoping to start a conversation.

"You look tired."

Marianne stared straight ahead. "I am whipped."

"Sick? Seizures?"

"Yes, both. Gone now."

"At least you're all in one piece. Or two pieces, including our son in there."

Marianne didn't react. Wagstaff took a breath and tried again.

"Everything okay? I heard on the news that your bomb was diverted."

Marianne stretched and straightened up. "Everything is not okay. Two people are dead, the terrorists are in critical condition, a shopping mall is radioactive, and five undocumented Mexican nationals, criminals probably, are on the loose."

"Unh-huh."

"To say nothing about the guy who shot you. He was working for the smugglers. From what I heard of his garbled chatter, I'm betting he's the one who ran those bodies down to the Whiskeyjack."

"I've been keeping an eye on the Dingell situation," said Wagstaff. "Nothing from Otis or your friend in the sheriff's office. What's-his-name, Al Burns."

"Not surprised."

"But here's the thing —you gotta talk to Mom. She is having a fit."

Wagstaff's big yellow Toyota rolled into the circular drive of Howard Turnbow's fancy Tarvolo mansion, and Lorraine rushed from the front door to greet it.

Marianne stepped out and was immediately engulfed in her future mother-in-law's arms. Big hug.

"You're back!" Lorraine held Marianne at arms' length. "You look healthy, no wounds that I can see. We were so worried."

"Just pooped. I'll sleep for a week."

Lorraine turned to her son.

"No hugs, Mom, I'm still sore."

She kissed him lightly on the cheek. "I know. Howard too. Come have a look."

She led them through the house to the back lawn. Turnbow was sitting in a wooden deck chair overlooking the golf course. He had a wide plantation hat pulled down over his face. His right arm was hooked up to a portable heart monitor perched on a tray next to the chair. A glass of lemonade stood untouched beside it.

Lorraine tapped his shoulder. "Howard, honey?"

The man stirred.

"Look who's here."

A hand came up and tilted the hat back. Vacant eyes stared at Marianne.

"Hey, Howard. How ya doin'?" said she, trying for an upbeat tone.

He seemed puzzled by the visitor.

"Hey, it's me. Your Golden Girl."

A hand extended toward her. Marianne took hold and gave it a solid shake.

"Nice to meetcha, young lady. You say your name is . . ?"

"Marianne. Marianne Sarzeau."

"Sarzeau. That's a funny name."

Lorraine gestured and led Marianne across the lawn to the little gazebo built for her wedding. She ran a nervous hand through her gray hair.

"He's been like this since the shooting. Awake, healing just fine. Theoretically recuperating, but . . . vacant. It's Howard's body, but he's not in there anymore."

"Oh God, Lorraine."

Lorraine bobbed her head up and down, looking for the words to make a request.

"I remember how your whatcha-ma-call-it, spirit guardian, wanted you to battle the demon who had Tom trapped," she began. "And you said you would do it."

"Anything, I would have done anything."

"But Tom is fine, and, and, it's Howard who got trapped."

"Maybe . . . we don't know for sure, do we?"

"He's a zombie. What else could it be?"

Marianne was starting to feel pressure. "I don't know, no one knows," she insisted.

Lorraine smoothed her dress, fidgeted with her necklace. She braced herself. "This is hard to say. I don't know how to say it. You . . . this, this terrible situation . . . it all happened because of you. The thing that has Howard was after you."

"Yeah?"

"That's what you told me. That's what I heard."

"It's true. Whiskeyjack warned me."

"And you said you would do anything to save Tom . . ."

Marianne nodded slowly. "You want me to do some magic I don't understand, go to some place *no one* understands, and rescue Howard, your husband."

Lorraine exhaled. "If you could, if you could. Your weird tricks, powers, whatever they are, I don't know how they work, but I believe in you. I trust you."

"I don't trust myself, though. I've seen the other world. Part of it, anyway. A little peek while I was throwing up. Oh, Lorraine, it scares me. I could get killed. My son could get killed."

Lorraine hung her head. She was twisting her hands together. Her eyes were wet. "I know. Forgive me, I shouldn't have asked. It's just that . . . now that I have Howard — a year ago, who knew? — I hate to lose him."

Marianne put her arms around her best friend. "Let me think. I need to think."

She returned to Turnbow, leaned down, and looked closely at his smooth untroubled face. "Howard? Hey in there, say hello to your best disc jockey."

The eyes stared at her without recognition.

"Come on, it's me — Marianne. I work for you."

A hand rose, flailed around, and gripped hers.

"Nice to meetcha."

▼

Marianne tried to raise her guardian spirit in one of Turnbow's downstairs bathrooms. When that didn't work, Wagstaff drove her into

Applefield, where she tried to make contact at the prospector statue in the town park. Whiskeyjack failed to show up in that location either. Fatigue was setting in, so she called off any further attempts.

Wagstaff then drove her to his office, where she flopped onto his couch and nodded off. She slumbered late into the evening, got up once to relieve herself, and went right back to sleep. Around midnight Wagstaff snuggled down beside her. She did not object.

▼

"Hey, I'm not sick," Marianne announced when morning finally rolled around.

"That's great," said a still sleepy Wagstaff. The sun was already high in the sky.

"He told me the morning blahs were over," she continued. "Back there in Roseville. He was right."

"Told you? Our baby?"

"He still talks to me. I know you think I'm crazy."

Wagstaff tottered off to the bathroom. He came back shaking his finger. "This talking stuff, a kid in the womb . . . you . . . ."

Marianne was ready for a fight. "Yeah?"

Wagstaff shrugged. "I . . . I'm going to give you the benefit of the doubt on this one. Someday you'll wonder about me, and you can pay me back."

She gave him a quick kiss. "I'm sure you'll remind me."

"You bet I will."

Marianne found a clean pair of jeans among her clothes in Wagstaff's walk-in closet and pulled them on.

"Your mom wants me to disappear into Neverland to find Howard."

"She's desperate, who can blame her? But I woke up okay, and I bet Howard will recover on his own."

"Right. Instead, as soon as I brush my teeth, you're going to help me find Bo Dingell."

"Isn't that a job for law enforcement?"

"As you may remember, I *am* law enforcement. And unlike my lazy colleagues, I'm the target of a madman. We need to corral that guy."

▼

Wagstaff drove Marianne south out of town to County Road 520, followed that for five miles, then turned east along Forest Road N621, paralleling the north bank of the Whiskeyjack River. They missed the steep approach to the river itself and continued for another mile before they realized their mistake. They were then forced to drive another half mile before Wagstaff found a spot wide enough to turn his SUV around. They backtracked slowly, searching for the ancient mining road that led from the bluff they were on down into the river canyon. Finally Marianne spotted a gap in the trees. Wagstaff backed and filled several times to line up, snicked his machine into four-wheel drive, and they cautiously bumped and pitched down the narrow track cut into the steep canyon wall. At the bottom the trees opened onto a wide gravel expanse on the outside of a sharp bend in the river. They were at the site of the body dump they had previously discovered. That trip, which started innocently in pursuit of Wagstaff's gold-panning hobby, seemed part of the distant past, although it had only been a couple of weeks.

"What are we doing?" said Wagstaff, looking uneasy. "Want to tell me? The cops cleaned everything out,"

Marianne stood stock still and lifted her chin into the faint breeze blowing down the canyon. "I'm trying to pick up an aura. Dingell has one. It's red and hostile. I think he knows all about this place. If he's still around, I will sense him."

"He has a gun."

"I know."

"He shot me with it."

"I know that too. But he's too crazy to act with any sense of purpose."

She drew her Beretta just in case, then moved into the brush where the bodies once were.

"Well, well, look at this . . ."

Tucked into the hollow of the rock face was evidence of a campfire. Ashes and blackened tree branches were scattered in and around a ring of stones. Marianne picked up an empty can of Dinty Moore's beef stew lying nearby.

"Someone was here," she declared.

"Yeah, and look how he started his fires . . ." Wagstaff fished a charred shred of newspaper out of the ashes. The word *Courier* on the masthead was still legible.

"Read me the date."

"It's last week's edition. That article about fish dying in Upper Bar Lake on account of the low water . . . I recognize a couple of words from the headline, see?"

Marianne looked at the paper scrap. "Someone was here all right, and not too long ago. Good supporting evidence."

She walked back and forth around the area. At the river's edge an indentation in the sand allowed a little pool of slack water to form. Marianne looked, and saw her reflection staring back at her.

"All right, you . . ."

She dug out her little acorn, curled her fingers around the amulet under her blouse, and summoned her guardian spirit.

"Hello, Whiskeyjack, wherever you are. If you're not too busy in some other galaxy, how about a little help here?"

The river rolled on, her reflection remained steady in its little pool, but her connection to the spirit world did not appear. Instead . . .

Weeahh!

A familiar-looking jay flew into view and landed on Marianne's head. It nipped playfully at her hair. Then it flew over and landed near the abandoned campsite. There it hammered noisily on the empty beef stew can.

"Great," said Marianne. "Charades again."

The jay flew up on top of Wagstaff's SUV. It ran back and forth along the roof rack, flew up in a little circle, landed back on the roof itself, and pecked at the sheet metal.

"You see that?" asked Marianne.

"Of course, it's a real live bird. I think Lassie is trying to tell us something."

"But what? I'm stumped."

Weeahh!

The jay suddenly took off and flew away up the lane leading out of the canyon.

"Here's what I think," said Wagstaff. "Dingell, if he was our thoughtless camper, ran out of food here and headed back to civilization for supplies."

"Probably . . . we don't really know."

Marianne scanned the cliff face behind the fire pit. There she discovered an odd picture, sketched in charcoal, apparently with a burned stick. She pointed it out to Wagstaff, suddenly filled with excitement.

"Wait a minute — this might as well be Bo's signature." She spread her arms wide as if to embrace the image. "A man possessed . . . It shows me that Dingell is our so-far-unidentified body dumper. I doubt he killed those men, but he is accessory after the fact, I swear. Al Burns and his team should have checked. They would have had him in custody."

A scraggly figure had been scratched onto the rock. The hands were upraised in fear or warning. What looked like a lightning bolt was blasting into its oversized head, out of which radiated short lines, like a child's idea of sunbeams.

"Shazam," said Wagstaff.

54

MARIANNE met with Lieutenant Kazmarek to announce her return from FULTAP duty. She received perfunctory congratulations and an assignment to night patrol as a reward. On her third day back she was gearing up, pulling her hair into a workaday ponytail, when a smoky image formed unbidden in her bathroom mirror.

"Whiskeyjack?"

"Hello, Marianne."

"Where have you been, I called and called."

"Other duties. I have many."

"So you're not just, like, everywhere all at once?"

"No being is so blessed."

"What about Howard and crazy Bo Dingell?"

"As I feared — the demon who holds Dingell in thrall has taken your friend hostage."

"We have to get him back. Lorraine is beside herself."

"That will not be easy. It's you he wants. He is proposing a trade — his spirit for yours."

"Let's pretend to agree, get Howard, and I'll dodge the evil one."

"Impossible. If you willingly submit, it will mean your death."

Marianne sagged against the wash basin. "No, no, no."

"Oh yes."

"There's got to be a way."

"There is. But it is difficult and dangerous. You will be risking yourself and your son."

"Tell me."

"You must journey to my world and do battle."

"How on Earth?"

"Find Dingell. Engage the demon. You will see."

"Everybody is looking for that guy. Where is he?"

"I do not know, but I have made a suggestion to someone who can help. He doesn't see me or hear me, but the thought has been planted."

"Who?"

"The answer is approaching."

"How do I know you're not in on this? The demon's best pal?"

Whiskeyjack did not replay. His smoky image shrank into a tiny blur in the mirror and vanished.

Marianne stood there, shivering, staring at herself, marveling at how pale her complexion had become.

While she was fretting, a truck rumbled to a halt outside. Brakes squeaked. Wheels squelched noisily on rough pavement. A door slammed.

The sounds jolted Marianne out of her reverie. She hurried outside. there below her apartment was an Army Humvee in full camouflage. Standing beside it, looking this way and that, was a small wiry man in army fatigues. He had a duffle bag under one arm.

"Dad — ?"

The man looked up at her. He waved.

"Angel."

She ran down the stairs and jumped into his arms.

▼

"How did you find me? You've never seen my apartment before."

Marianne and her father were standing in front of his Humvee on the slopes below Placerville's water tank. He had changed into jeans and a cotton work shirt.

"I sensed you, of course. That's what I'm good at."

"Right. Are you sensing Mr. Dingell?"

"Not yet. How's your pregnancy coming along? You look okay."

"Fine. Creepy but fine."

"Oh?"

"The little guy talks to me."

"Really? I never heard of that."

"Hannah says it's not unusual. He's quite an earful."

"And your fella? How's that going?"

"We're maintaining."

"Maintaining? That's your formula for married bliss?"

"I don't know anymore. Tom's worried about every little thing. We hardly speak."

"He's marrying a cop who's a witch. Cut him some slack, why don't you?"

"Yeah, slack. Cut, cut, cut."

"You know better than me. Imogen sends her love, by the way."

"That's nice."

Dad stiffened. He turned slowly in a complete circle with his hands raised.

"I do sense something."

"What? Where?"

He pointed tentatively toward the southwest.

"The aura is right out at the edge of detection. It's powerful, or I couldn't see it. That way, somewhere out in the valley."

Marianne squinted into the afternoon sunlight. The distant Big Valley landscape was shimmering on the horizon, almost lost in the hazy summer air.

"Whiskeyjack said you could find him."

"Whiskeyjack?"

"Long story."

▼

Marianne knocked on Lieutenant Kazmarek's office in the Placerville police station.

"Come in."

Marianne led Sergeant Sarzo into her supervisor's presence.

"Nina, I'd like you to meet my father."

"How do you do?" said the lieutenant, standing up from her desk.

"I think we have figured out where Bo Dingell, our suspect in attempted murder, is hiding out."

"Good for you. Call Al Burns."

"Will do. But Al has had several chances to nab this guy, and I'd like some authority behind any information I turn over and requests I might make."

"Bureaucratic authority," said Kazmarek. "You want me to call."

"Kind of. I want to organize a posse. The last time I was involved in a manhunt I was on my own. Never again. It's got to be all hands on deck."

Kazmarek dropped back into her chair. "How do you know the suspect's location?"

"Dad spotted him."

"Spotted?"

"He's FULTAP's main asset."

Sergeant Sarzo stuck his hands in his pockets. "I'm a sensor, ma'am. People have auras, and I can often see them, see their owner's intentions."

"Where exactly do you have the man?"

"Out in the valley."

Marianne was quick to fill in the details. "Southwest, about twenty miles. That can only mean Golden Egg Family Farms, where Dingell is an employee."

"I know you have a special interest. This is sheriff's work."

"But he was targeting me, a Placerville police officer. We have a stake in this."

Lieutenant Kazmarek snorted.

"You're asking me to light a fire under Amador County's butt on the basis of . . . what? . . . witchcraft?"

Father and daughter looked at each other.

"That's about the size of it," said Marianne.

55

AT SAINT PATRICK'S Catholic Church, halfway up the hill leading out of town, Sergeant Sarzo elected to wait in the Humvee when Marianne insisted on making a stopover.

"What's this all about?"

She gave her father a vague shrug. "Enlist the Commander in Chief's blessing. Can't hurt."

"What makes you think your peculiar talent has anything to do with the Almighty?"

"The fact that I'm tapping the supernatural, what else?"

"What if the things we're aware of are just nudges from another part of the universe? As natural as we are, just . . . different?"

"I can't prove a thing. But the crazy stuff I've been through has turned me into a churchgoer."

Inside the warm wooden interior, she found a pew, kneeled, crossed herself, and took a seat. Late on a weekday afternoon, she was the only soul in the building. She let her thoughts drift for a while, hoping for some insight or guidance; she really couldn't say what she wanted. When nothing inspirational whirled her into a decisive mood, she bent her head and prayed, conscious that she was not reciting one of her spells.

"Almighty Father, hear my plea — my friend Howard has not recovered. His wound was light, he's healed over, so he should be okay. But he's not. I've been told his spirit is being held hostage by a demon. If you're listening, please make him well. I'm ready to help you do the job, but I'm hopeless all by myself. So I would appreciate some, you know, divine assistance. Please show me how to rescue my friend . . . and . . . and keep me safe while I'm doing it, for Tom's sake, and for our son."

She looked up at the altar and glanced quickly around the room, suddenly aware that she was muttering aloud. No one, except possibly the prayer's addressee, was there to hear her appeal.

"Amen," she said.

▼

The sun was already down when Marianne and Sergeant Sarzo arrived at Golden Egg Family Farms. Marianne was in her police blues, and Dad was back in military dress. A number of other law enforcement officers were already assembled at the main gate. Dez Otis from Placerville was there. Wade Gawley and Ricky Moss came down from the Tri-Town Area. Al Burns, representing the Amador County Sheriff's Department, was the man in charge.

Marianne joined the group, to skeptical nods and salutes.

"Evening, Marianne," said Burns. "I have a warrant for this little drill, but I've got to tell you, we've already looked the place over on two different occasions."

Marianne nodded to concede the obvious doubts and banish the frowns. "Hey, guys, meet my father, Sergeant Emile Sarzo. He's how we spotted Dingell."

"You saw him here?"

"In a way," said Dad. "I sensed his aura."

Murmurs of doubt rippled through the officers.

"Dad is an intelligence agent with the Army's *Full Spectrum Threat Assessment Program,*" explained Marianne. "FULTAP. No kidding, paranormal sensing is what we do."

"Jesus, Squeek," piped Otis. "You brought us out here to watch you ride your broomstick?"

Before the grumbling could escalate further, a middle-aged man and woman emerged from the nearby ranch house to confront the group. They looked confused and frightened by the police presence.

"Hello, there," said the man. "What's the problem?"

Burns handed over his warrant. "We have reason" — he rolled his eyes toward Marianne — "to believe that a fugitive from justice is hiding on this property. And, uh, since we know the owner is recently deceased, who might you be, if you don't mind my asking?"

The woman took a hesitant step forward. "Alejandro Muñoz was my uncle, and this man is my husband. This is a working ranch. There are ninety-five ostriches here, and they need daily care. When we received the very sad news about . . . you know . . . we came around to help."

"Have you seen our man? Bo Dingell?"

"No. No one. The only people here are workers during the day." She paused to consider the matter. "They have Hispanic names."

"Undocumented?" asked Otis.

The woman turned pale. "I don't dare ask."

Burns tapped the warrant. "Please excuse us, then, while we get on with a look-around, according to the terms of the paper here."

▼

While the conversation at the main gate was proceeding, ostriches in the farthest corral suddenly exploded away from the little shed where their feeding trough and water supply were located. In a panic, they bolted to the far corners of their enclosure. Dust rose from the dirt under their feet. Feathers drifted down through the night air. The shed door creaked open, and a man peeked out. He was wearing a dirty T-shirt over ragged jeans, and he was covered with straw and sawdust. He listened to the voices for a moment, then stole across the corral, gripped the fence with one hand, and vaulted over the top with an uncanny display of superhuman strength. He was looking over his shoulder at the flashing police lights as he jogged away into a dark stand of oak trees.

▼

Marianne led the way down the driveway.

"He's not in the main house," she declared.

"Big building. How do you know?" asked Moss.

"My sixth sense," said she.

"Oh, that," he replied with heavy irony.

"Dad?"

Sergeant Sarzo shook his head. "She's right. I sense his presence, but it's farther away."

The group moved on to the pre-fab shop where Dingell was helping rig containers and cautiously slipped inside. Burns found a switch, flipped it, and overhead lights blazed. Gasps issued from astonished cops as they gazed upon the unfinished box. Otis unholstered his pistol and cautiously peeked into the open portal. Seats and cabinets were already installed.

"Nice," he said. "First class ticket to ride — but no Bo."

"You tracked down the jihadis in one of these?" asked Gawley in a tone that suggested admiration.

"Almost identical," said Marianne with considerable pride.

Whistles of appreciation echoed through the shop interior. Her colleagues had never seen anything like it.

Back outside they checked the derelict motorhomes whose interiors had been stripped for the smuggling operation.

"He's not here either."

The cops were now at the edge of the developed property. Stretching away before them, a wide field had been carved out of the woods. And there, set out at intervals, were stacks of timber slash ready for burning. Evidently Muñoz had been planning to expand his ranch facilities.

"He's somewhere out here," said Marianne. "I can sense him."

As they all started into the field, Sergeant Sarzo took his daughter aside.

"Listen, Angel, I don't think the aura we're sensing belongs to your stalker."

"No?"

"I sense two auras. A weak one, fluctuating yellow-red-green, and on top of that a powerful red one."

"I only see the red one."

"I know. What are we getting into here?"

"My guardian spirit told me that Dingell is possessed by a demon. I think the weaker aura belongs to him, and the strong one is . . . whoever."

"You're up to something."

"I want to stop Dingell and save my friend Howard."

"Let's be damned careful about this, understood?"

She nodded.

Dez Otis was not satisfied with their situation. "We've got like two thousand oak trees up front. Our toad is armed, right? Which one is he hiding behind?"

"Spread out, men," ordered Burns.

Marianne was aware of a growing red impression off to her left. She pointed.

"He's that way. Dad?"

Sergeant Sarzo nodded agreement, aimed a finger in the same direction.

Moss stared at the dense foliage. "I'm not going in there," he said. "We need to flush that boy out."

Marianne reached behind her back and pulled a road flare out from under her belt.

"Here goes."

She snapped the cap off and scraped the striking pad against the flare tip. A bright red flame spouted forth. She marched over to the nearest slash pile and shoved the flare into the twigs and bark. The dry wood crackled and popped as flames spread through the pile.

"Christ, Sarzeau, have you lost your mind? It's mid-fucking-summer, you'll burn the foothills flat," said Burns.

"Get a couple of fire extinguishers if you're worried."

"Marianne . . ?" quizzed Dad, eyebrows raised to his hairline.

"Demons love fire. Ready?"

▼

Thirty feet up in an oak tree, Bo Dingell observed the fire start and take hold. He swayed, caught himself.

"Ahhhh . . ."

The flames were soon a raging bonfire. Moving mechanically, he let himself down through the branches. On the ground he stumbled out into the field and lurched toward the police officers, as heedless of danger as if hypnotized by the flickering light.

▼

"Here he is," announced Marianne.

Sure enough, Dingell stepped out of the darkness and stood beside the bonfire. He was grinning. His eyes were glazed.

The officers drew their weapons.

"Bo Dingell? You're under arrest for attempted murder," decreed Burns.

"Ha ha ha ha ha ha . . ." cackled the fugitive.

His defiant indifference sent shivers up police spines.

"Don't shoot! Don't shoot!" commanded Marianne. She had a pair of handcuffs ready.

"Come on, Bo, turn around, hold out your hands. Gotta cuff you."

She took a step toward him.

"No thanks, I won't need them," he muttered.

"Bo . . ."

Dingell abruptly turned toward the fire and pushed himself into the flames. Then he turned back toward the assembled cops. His clothes were burning. His hair was alight. Horrified shouts of warning as he staggered toward Marianne.

"Mareeeee-Anneeeee!" he shrieked.

Marianne backed away, chanting her mantra:

Whiskeyjack, Whiskeyjack . . .

But before she could complete the spell, Dingell was upon her. He cocked a flaming arm, swung it around, and knocked her to the ground.

▼

Marianne sat up and looked around. Gone were Dingell, her fellow police officers, the bonfire, the land, the trees, the night sky.

Hazy orange light illuminated a hummocky gray field that stretched to the horizon, dotted with fibrous gray trees that looked like translucent umbrellas or spidery mushrooms. She thought of Alice dropping through the rabbit hole.

"Hi, Mom. It's me, your son. Got a minute?"

Marianne was completely confused. "Sure, why not? That wouldn't be the strangest thing right now. Where are we, anyway?"

"I don't know. But trouble isn't far away."

"What a shock."

"Anyway, that's not what I want to talk about. I decided on a name."

"Oh really. Isn't that your parents' job?"

"You need guidance. So here it is — Gabriel."

"Gabriel?"

"It's a good name."

"I'll discuss it with your father."

She stood up and looked herself over, surprised and appalled to discover that her body was no longer her own. Instead of womanly curves, she saw a smoky mass. She raised a hand and saw paws. When she flexed them, blue sparks shot forth.

"Holy crap," she breathed.

She clapped her paws together. A fireball bloomed and drifted away across the landscape.

"Good God."

She peered around, looking for any detail, trying to make sense of her situation. In the middle distance she spied a little hillock. On that hillock was a chair. And in that chair sat a man, slumped over, with a wide plantation hat pulled down over his eyes.

"Howard?"

Marianne started toward him. She marveled at the speed her strides produced. Before she knew it, she was standing at his side.

"Howard? That you? Talk to me."

The man reached up and tilted his hat back. His eyes sparkled.

"Hello, Marianne. What a nightmare. Help me out of this awful place."

She was pleased to find her friend alert and well, but she suppressed a shudder . . . he wasn't quite completely opaque.

"The man is thine when thou art mine."

Commanding tones reverberated in Marianne's head. She turned to find the source of the telepathic voice. Appearing from out of nowhere was a smoky giant, with a lump above broad shoulders she took for a head, because a pair of eyes, like deep black pits, were staring at her. She could see through the creature.

"Who . . ?"

"I am Oggaloggattahagalogg."

"Ogg . . ."

"Good enough. Thou and I must needs be joined. Our spirits' powers double when they be intertwined."

"Not a chance."

"I insist."

The demon heaved toward her, bent down over her. Marianne backed away. The demon stuck out a huge hand to grab her. Marianne reared back and swatted. Her paw slammed against the demon's arm, throwing sparks, jolting him. She swung her other arm, connecting with his diaphanous body.

Bash!

More sparks, another jolt. Marianne was astonished. She herself had become a monster. The demon quickly recovered and threw a punch of his own. Marianne ducked, and the smoky fist sailed over her head. She smacked the thing again, causing it to stagger back in a flash of light. Then she turned and ran, bounding across the rippling terrain with long powerful strides.

The demon followed, floating effortlessly through the dank air. Marianne turned and there he was, flying toward her. He released a crackling sphere of electrical energy. She raised her paws to block it, but even so . . .

Krazzz!

. . . tendrils of static charge enveloped her. She felt numb. Then a fist landed on her shapeless chest.

Wham!

The blow catapulted her high into the air. She came down on top of one of the skeletal trees, crushing it to the ground. She tried to move, found she couldn't rise. The demon advanced, hit her again.

Slap!

She tumbled backwards, end over end, and fetched up against another tree. Her vision blurred. The demon coming for her was now a shadowy cloud, sliding between the slender tree trunks, rolling over the gloomy little hills and dales.

"Don't worry, Mom, Whiskeyjack will protect us."

"Oh yes please! Where is that guy?" She coaxed her unfamiliar body around behind the tree, mumbling his name:

Whiskeyjack, Whiskeyjack, Whiskeyjack . . .

Suddenly a new figure appeared. Smoky, like the demon Ogg, and almost as tall, but edged with a purple aura that pulsed with terrible intensity. It took up a position between Marianne and her pursuer.

"Away with you! The sorceress belongs to me!" roared Ogg.

"You are denied. She and her circle shall ever be free," replied the mysterious figure.

Marianne squinted to study the creature's details.

"Whiskeyjack?"

The thing's head turned toward her briefly. Flaming blue eyes glanced her way. A huge hand rose and saluted. White fire danced on the fingertips.

"Be at peace, Marianne. I will deal with your tormentor."

The demon floated forward, challenging the blockade. Marianne's guardian opened his arms wide and clasped the horrible Ogg in a hard embrace. They wrestled, gyrating back and forth in a titanic struggle. A blazing red plasma danced around their interlocked shapes. Marianne closed her eyes against the sight, and still she could see them twisting and turning.

As the two otherworldly creatures struggled, Whiskeyjack appeared to be getting the worst of it. Ogg threw him to the ground. Whiskeyjack rebounded, grappled, was thrown again.

Marianne was whimpering with terror. She could see that her rescuer was losing the battle. She rocked back and forth, gathering her courage. Whimpers turned into a low growl. Fear turned to uncontrollable rage.

With an almighty roar that surprised herself, she rose from her hiding place, charged forward, and landed a tremendous blow against the demon's foggy face.

Smack!

Ogg flew backward. She clapped her paws and bolts of lightning crackled from her claws.

Zapp!

They rippled through the monster's translucent body. Then Whiskeyjack renewed his attack, once again clutching the demon in a deadly grip. Flames erupted. Sparks flew. Smoke billowed. Then . . .

Spung!

The two apparitions vanished in a blinding explosion. Marianne was knocked flat. She lay on her back for what seemed like forever with her vision seared. When she finally made the effort to sit up, she blinked and scowled to clear the explosion's afterimage. The blast slowly faded from view, and she gradually became aware that her fragile human body was restored, with aches and pains from top to bottom. She groaned.

"Here, take my hand," said someone.

Marianne blinked, blinked again.

"Howard?"

She grasped his outstretched hand.

"Up-see-daisy, here we go." He pulled her upright.

She made an effort to brush herself off.

"Let's get out of here."

She looked around at the gray world, its flimsy trees, its undulating terrain, the cloudy orange illumination.

"Weird place," she said.

Turnbow nodded. "And you never saw the little people."

Now that the spectacular pyrotechnics were gone, she discerned a dull red glow in the distance. Wisps of smoke were drifting above it.

"Come on," she said, hiking toward its location.

They came over a little rise, and there in the shelter of a hollow was her road flare, still burning.

"What do you say we head on home?" she asked.

"Bless you," said Turnbow.

Marianne picked up the road flare and buried the burning tip in the soft gray soil.

Hiss!

The flame went out and the world went dark.

Tom Wagstaff got wind of Marianne's expedition from Lieutenant Kazmarek and roared down Old Sacramento Road to Golden Egg Family Farms at breakneck speed, sick with a premonition of disaster. He registered the flashing code three lights in the main driveway with a sudden pang and slammed to a stop behind the police cars. He hurried through the yard toward a distant fire and raised voices.

Marianne lay on her back in the grass where Bo Dingell had flattened her. She opened her eyes to find Wade Gawley and Ricky Moss bending near.

"Marianne! Hey, there, you okay?"

"I dunno . . ." She squirmed around experimentally. "Ooh, I am one sore sister."

Dingell himself was a charred corpse lying nearby, dead from burns and three bullets from Dez Otis' Glock. Otis was examining the body with distaste.

"Fucking counseling, here I come," said he.

Wagstaff arrived in their midst just as Gawley and Moss were lifting a very groggy Marianne to her feet. He rushed forward to take her in his arms.

"Oh my God, M, look at you."

"Mmm."

He turned to Al Burns, who was attempting to douse the bonfire by kicking dirt on it. "How long was she out?"

Burns shrugged. "Less than a minute. It all went down just now."

Marianne heard the timing. She spun around to object. "That can't be right. I was over there for an hour at least."

Burns and Wagstaff looked puzzled.

"Over where?" asked Burns.

"On the other side with Dingell's demon. Whiskeyjack destroyed him."

She felt around in her pocket for her talismanic acorn, but found only shards. She opened her palm to display the pieces. "Look, my nut got smashed." She shook her head to unscramble her thoughts. "Whiskey-jack's gone too."

Burns was beginning to worry about a concussion. Otis came over for a close inspection. He held up his hand. "How many fingers?"

"Six."

"Don't joke, Squeek. Get her to the hospital, Tom. She was assaulted in the line of duty, and she needs to be checked out."

"Will do."

Wagstaff steered Marianne away from the fire and back to his SUV. They reached the ranch driveway just as the fire brigade and the medical examiner were arriving.

Marianne dug in her heels. "I should wait and be debriefed."

"Later, babe."

▼

Wagstaff's yellow Toyota pulled into the hospital parking lot in Jackson with Wade Gawley right behind. The Tri-Town cop insisted on being Marianne's official escort.

"Otherwise," he explained, "they'll think Tom beat you up."

In the emergency room a nurse practitioner gave the woozy officer a good going-over.

"You led a manhunt tonight while two months pregnant?" The woman was incredulous.

Marianne nodded weakly.

"You're not concussed," she concluded. "Just banged up. How many times did that guy hit you?"

"Just the once, I think."

"Seems like more, you've got bruises all over."

"Ouch."

"Let's have a listen." The nurse applied a stethoscope to Marianne's belly.

Wagstaff frowned affectionately at his adventurous fiancée. "The little guy will have some tale to tell."

"He's already been telling it. While I was lying over there, our kid was talking to me again."

Wagstaff studied her, trying to convince himself that his betrothed still had all her marbles. "Whoa, babe. I've had enough for one night."

"No, listen. He's picked out a name."

"He picked?"

"Yup. He told me. I kind of like it, and I hope you will too."

Wagstaff bristled, wary of being rushed into anything.

"Let's hear it."

"He wants to be called 'Gabriel'."

"Gabriel . . . Gabriel . . . " Wagstaff savored the possibility. "I don't know, M . . . *Gabriel?"*

The nurse, sensing an impending lovers' quarrel, quickly wrapped up her examination. "I hear a tiny heartbeat. Your baby is alive and well." She patted Marianne on the shoulder. "And bruises aside, you'll be okay. Take some Advil."

56

IN THE MORNING Sergeant Sarzo drove Marianne down to Tarvolo in his Humvee. She called on the intercom attached to the main gate, and a husky voice buzzed father and daughter into the exclusive enclave. They parked in the circular drive of the Turnbow mansion, where Lorraine was waiting for them.

"Meet Dad."

The new Mrs. Turnbow took Sergeant Sarzo's hand in hers.

"The mind reader," she said.

"Lorraine — !" hissed Marianne.

Dad just smiled. "Don't worry, ma'am, I can't read minds. Just some auras, and the stuff that goes with them."

"How about me?"

"Well now, you're blue, relieved to see us. Looks like we're dispelling some of your, uhh, anxiety. How's that?"

"Pretty good, you're pretty good. Come and meet my husband . . ."

She led the way across the wide back yard to Turnbow, who was snoozing in his lawn chair. A doctor and nurse stood awkwardly beside him, faces creased with deep concern.

"Howard? Look who's here," said Lorraine.

Turnbow tilted his plantation hat up and stared at his visitors.

"Nice to meetcha, folks," he said. "Nice day."

Marianne winced. Sergeant Sarzo tugged at her elbow and tilted his head to draw the group aside.

"I thought he'd be raring to go by now," he said.

Marianne pressed her lips together. "Me too. I went through hell to bring him around."

Lorraine was pale with worry. "No change since the incident. He's still missing in action."

"That's very strange, because on the other side he was walking and talking. His old self," affirmed Marianne.

"What do the doctors say?" asked Sergeant Sarzo.

Lorraine threw up her hands. "Psychic trauma. Things will improve with time."

"This has nothing to do with Howard or any of his doctors," growled Marianne. "It's me. He was a bargaining chip with a demon who wanted my ass."

Wagstaff found a copy of the *Sacramento Bee* on the arm of Turnbow's chair. He opened it.

"Does he read? Request things to eat? Anything?"

Lorraine shook her head. "If I open up the paper, he'll stare at it, but he never turns a page. The store manager has been calling, the mayor's office has a million little problems to solve, and I don't know what to tell them."

"Hey, M, see this?" Wagstaff pointed out a story on the second page:

SHOPPING MALL TESTS NEGATIVE

The Valley River Mall in Roseville has been declared free of radioactivity following decontamination by federal hazmat teams. Mall businesses expressed concern after the parking lot became the site of a failed terrorist attack on Folsom Lake.

The EPA official in charge has assured the city that the "trace amounts" of americium 241 found there have been safely removed.

Marianne scanned the article and shrugged. Her interest in merely human terror was now blotted out by supernatural cares. "I'd park on the other side of town, myself," she said.

"Maybe the exorcism, or whatever you did, isn't finished yet," said Sergeant Sarzo. "What's in that book of yours?"

"Good question."

Marianne stalked off to the mansion's redwood deck, where she sat herself down beside the hot tub. Sergeant Sarzo followed and stood beside her.

Lorraine trailed after them. "What am I going to do?" she moaned.

Marianne reached into her bag for a loose leaf notebook. She opened it and pointed to the pages, a thick collection of computer printouts.

"Bagwell's translation of my old book. Let's see what my ancestors had in mind."

She donned black-frame glasses and buried her face in the ancient spells and potions.

Wagstaff joined his anxious mother, put an arm around her. They watched Marianne slowly examining the cryptic text. After five minutes it became clear that they were in for a long wait. Lorraine drifted off to the kitchen for lemonade.

She returned with tall glasses and little sandwiches. Marianne waved the snacks away. Time passed.

"Whoa, here's something," she said at length, skimming a set of magical instructions. She showed them to her father. "What do you think?"

"Might work. Better get his attention first."

"You're right, you're right. How about this?" She backtracked through the chapters to locate a minor spell.

"Good. Try that before you fire the big guns."

She kept her finger on the page to hold her place and flipped back to her new discovery. Abruptly she stood up.

"I've got it."

By now Lorraine was back in the kitchen, and Wagstaff was busy texting on his smartphone.

"Hey guys?"

She marched across the grass to Turnbow, still settled in his lawn chair, oblivious to everything. Lorraine and Wagstaff hurried to catch up, both skeptical about any of Marianne's enchantments.

"What are you doing?" demanded Lorraine.

"I'm going to try a spell or two."

"Oh my God, you're going to kill him."

Dad noted Lorraine's frazzled expression. "It's okay, Mrs. Turnbow. Strange as it seems, my daughter actually knows what she's doing."

Lorraine's shoulders slumped. Wagstaff pulled her into a consoling hug.

Marianne leaned over the catatonic man. "Howard? Golden Girl on the horn from Planet Earth. You in there?"

Turnbow hardly moved.

"Stop this, you know he's not," said Lorraine, offended by Marianne's casual tone.

"Just checking . . ." She opened her book and recited a spell:

> *Stop your doubts and douse your fears;*
> *Look at me and free your ears.*
> *Attend and hear my fervent plea;*
> *Thus I charge and order thee.*

Turnbow twitched. His head swiveled around toward Marianne. But his vacant stare remained unchanged.

Lorraine backed away. "What was that?"

"My *listen up* song."

"Oh."

"Now for the real thing." She riffled through the pages of her book and found another, more potent spell: *Recovery*. Summoning her most commanding voice for maximum authority, she read aloud:

> *Sad soul lost on sickness' sea,*
> *Set your sails and follow me.*
> *Selfhood lately cast away*
> *Floats here still; yours to belay.*
> *Brawn needs brains to catch a fish;*
> *To catch your mind is my good wish.*
> *Troll a net and look alive!*
> *Snare your thoughts and thereby thrive.*
> *Shake thy body!*
> *Wake thy heart!*
> *Heal thyself by my sure art!*

Turnbow blinked. He shook himself. He stared straight ahead and swallowed. He leaned forward and gripped the arms of his chair with white knuckles. He remained in that pose for a long time.

"Howard?" ventured Lorraine.

He didn't answer.

"Oh, Marianne, look what you've done," she blurted.

"Hold your horses. Give him a minute . . ."

After another interminable interval, suddenly Turnbow turned around and leveled a perfectly alert gaze on the anxious group.

"Jesus, how long was I out?" he wondered.

Tears sprang into Lorraine's eyes. She bent down and kissed him tenderly. "A week, love. We have been frantic."

"Never had a dream like that. Went on forever."

Marianne was very curious about his 'dream.' "What did you see?"

Turnbow gave her an ironic grin. "Well, it was terrible. You were in it. I don't suppose you remember?"

"I'll take your word for it," she said, secretly glad to hear him confirm her otherworldly trial at the Golden Egg ranch.

"There were giants . . . and . . . and, those damn little people."

"Little people?"

Turnbow stood up.

"Or maybe they were squirrels. Christ, I need a drink."

57

WAGSTAFF was pacing restlessly around his office. The latest issue of the *Courier* was languishing unfinished on his computer. His assistant, Kari, was gone for the day. He was alone with his fiancée and mother-to-be, and neither one of them was very cheerful.

"So the name. I might have been consulted, you know," complained Wagstaff.

"Me too, when you think about it, right?"

"I dunno, M. You say a two-month-old fetus picked out his own moniker. How do I know that? Maybe that's what you're telling me, just to make sure I can't object."

Marianne was stung by the accusation, impossible to refute. "I didn't lie about it," she pouted.

"Okay, say I believe you. But it's tough to be dragged along for the ride. I'm supposed to be your life partner."

"You are."

"And some of that is mutually agreed-upon behavior, right? We commingle our funds and discuss our expenditures, we negotiate our vacation spots, all that stuff you read in the magazines."

"We will."

"Except I have very little influence. Here you are, pregnant, and you're off risking your life and the life of our son on a harebrained manhunt for a psychotic maniac. Did I get to advise you? No, I did not."

"I had to do it for Howard . . . and your mom."

"So you said, and you explained it all, but I don't really understand the problem."

"What about that blur in the mirror?"

"Yeah, I saw it. I did, I admit."

"Well, buster, that's the surface of a deep ocean. I can swim in it. Not my fault that you can't."

Wagstaff came to a halt. He took her hand. "Good metaphor, points for that. So, Officer Sarzeau, here's what I'm afraid of — you're going to drown yourself."

Marianne snatched her hand away. "You're still on about my powers and how to lose them."

"I thought you just wanted to be a mom, Mrs. Ordinary Human Unit."

"I did, and now I don't. Is that so bad? Be who I am? Go with the weirdness?"

Wagstaff puffed out an exasperated sigh. "No, it's all up to you."

"'Cause if you want ordinary, there are other possibilities. Lots of ordinary women out there."

"What's that supposed to mean?"

"If you're so unhappy about me — about us — we can still call it off."

Wagstaff's turn to feel a sting. "What are you talking about?"

"If this is how it's going to be with us, angry shit all the time, maybe we'd be better off."

Wagstaff registered the bitterness, mulled the challenge, took some thought before offering an answer.

"Well?" she prompted.

"No way, babe. We're having a kid together, we make the best of it."

"If you say so."

"I do. I say, be legal, if not blessed. Obey the forces of *this* world to some degree."

"We've got two weeks," said Marianne. "I think it would be a good idea for me to stay at my place until the big day, if that's okay with you."

"I'm tired of arguing."

They glared at each other.

58

IN MID-AUGUST, foothill weather was dependably hot and dry. Allowing for that, the Sarzeau-Wagstaff wedding was scheduled for 5:00 PM. However, in this summer of unusual events, a Pacific hurricane off Baja was delivering moisture into California in the form of towering thunderheads, and measurable rain had been falling on the Golden Hills Tri-Town Special District all week long.

When it became obvious that her son and future daughter-in-law were incapable of any serious planning, Lorraine rolled up her sleeves and made all the arrangements, including an emergency order for tents and canopies, just in case Mother Nature decided to frown on the affair.

By Saturday Lorraine was exhausted, but all goods and services were ready in the kitchen and on the spacious lawn at the Turnbow residence.

At noon clouds began to gather. By three o'clock an enormous white mass loomed above Tarvolo, piling high into the stratosphere. The rumble of thunder was heard. Lorraine was beside herself. But no rain fell. By four the clouds were melting away, and by five, the appointed hour, the sky had cleared. Lorraine steadied herself with a margarita.

Guests began arriving. They strolled through the opulent house, out across the deck, and on into the garden and terraced grass, walking at leisure under bouquets of flowers strung up on tall iron poles.

The décor was, in fact, identical to that attending the earlier marriage of Lorraine and Turnbow, and the same caterers were on hand, crisply dressed, ready with canapés, champagne flutes, and foaming glasses of beer.

Several of Marianne's college buddies appeared, fellow members of her soccer team and glee club. Likewise many of Wagstaff's friends and family, including Bob Osborne, the neuroscience researcher.

The cool afternoon encouraged finery. Lieutenant Kazmarek and Dez Otis arrived in their police outfits. Sergeant Sarzo was there with Aunt Imogen on his arm. Major Ray Bagwell showed up unexpectedly, having just flown in from Turkey. He and Dad were both wearing their dress uniforms with badges and medals and stripes on display.

Ricky Moss and Wade Gawley were again pressed into action as ushers, and on this occasion they also were in uniform. They went about seating the guests in the rows of white wooden folding chairs with brisk efficiency.

Finally, Chief Fabriano strode out across the yard and stood in the little white gazebo with hands folded, ready once again for ceremonial duty. He too was in full dress, looking very spiff with gold braid on his arm and a gold band around the brim of a jaunty hat. Everyone who could do so seemed eager to pay respects to Marianne, their fellow officer and military adjunct.

The Tailings country rock band was set up under one of the tents, with speakers placed all around the grounds. Fabriano raised his hands, and the keyboardist launched a surprisingly delicate rendition of Mozart's *Piano Sonata Number 16 in C Major.*

As the piano piece veered into the minor key rondo, Howard Turnbow led Tom Wagstaff to the gazebo. Turnbow was resplendent in a white suit and sky blue tie. Wagstaff wore a dove-gray jacket over a bright red tie, with a red carnation in his lapel. But in good-natured defiance of convention, his pants were khaki cargo shorts. Knee-high red socks flashed boldly above hiking shoes.

Upstairs, Marianne was fidgeting while Lorraine attempted to set a veil in place.

"Hold still, kiddo, while I pin this thing."

Marianne exhaled, stood at attention.

"You seem tense. Everything okay?"

Marianne made a choppy little head bob.

"Everything is fine."

Lorraine frowned. "You don't sound so fine."

"I'm fine, Tom's fine, we're both fine. Fine, fine, fine."

"Whoa, what's wrong? Everybody has last minute jitters."

"Nothing is wrong. But you should know, as my friend and mother-in-law — we're not the perfect couple."

Lorraine did her best to glide over a spasm of alarm. "Nobody is, dear. You work at it, is all."

"Right. There'll be some heavy lifting, I can tell you that."

Lorraine gave up on the veil. "What's the problem? Should we not be getting you two hitched?"

"No, no. We're good for it. I just wonder . . . how long we'll last."

Lorraine poked a finger into Marianne's belly. "You're going to have a child. I'd plan for a long future together, if you want my advice."

"Yeah, I know, the standard rap."

Lorraine looked closely at her young friend. "Do I see a tear forming?"

"Not a chance. I am a china doll. I could be the wedding cake topper."

"Well, I need to finish becoming a bridesmaid, and I'll see you downstairs. No makeup running, hear me?"

"I'm not wearing any."

Lorraine made a *whatever* wave and left the room. Marianne picked up her bridal bouquet from a vase on the dresser and hefted it experimentally. She looked at herself in the mirror.

"Whiskeyjack, you there? We should talk."

No ripples, no smoke, no otherworldly image altered Marianne's glum expression.

"Far away somewhere, huh? And on my wedding day. For shame."

A prickly feeling came over her. A small voice popped into her head.

"Hi, Mom. Me again, your son. I'm glad you're getting married."

"Aren't you nice."

" I know you're not sure about Dad. Not sure how things will work out. And I want to tell you — stick together."

"I'll give it my best shot, you've got my word on that."

"No shots. Always. Forever. Never part. I know you love each other. And I am NOT growing up in a broken home."

Marianne blinked misty eyes. "Okay, wise guy, I'll try my hardest."

"Promise me."

"Cross my heart."

Downstairs, Marianne joined Lorraine at the door.

"Feeling better?"

Marianne nodded.

Outside, Chief Fabriano pointed to the musicians. A thunderous chord blared through the speakers, and a hard-rock version of *Here Comes The Bride* signaled the start of festivities.

"Okay, Mom, this is it. Don't screw up."

"You are an annoying little nag, know that?"

"Sorry to get in your way. But we need to talk now, because once I'm born we won't be able to do this anymore."

"Okay, kid. Now, excuse me, I've got a date."

The gathered guests rose together as Lorraine paraded Marianne out across the lawn. The bridesmaid was resplendent in a lavender top and black skirt. In spite of a slight swelling in her middle, visible only to the most penetrating eye, Marianne was the virgin bride, a goddess in white taffeta. The peachy roses in her hair and bouquet matched her complexion, flushed by all the *oohs* and *ahhs* she was hearing.

Wagstaff watched her approach, awed by the celestial beauty arriving at his side, and amazed by the magical transformation from law enforcement pro. She in turn eyed his ridiculous pants with a scowl and a wry grin.

Hannah Crowfoot had been invited to participate, but declined, pleading old age. Instead she suggested a text that Fabriano seized upon for his invocation.

"Dearly beloved," intoned the police chief. "To every thing there is a season, and a time to every purpose under Heaven. A time to cast away stones, a time to gather stones together. Today is the time for a wedding.

"Two people we all know well, very different from each other, are going to join and craft a life together. We are here to speed them on their way. Who gives this woman in marriage?"

Sergeant Sarzo stood up, beaming with pride. "Her father."

"Love is patient, love is kind," continued Fabriano. "It is not proud, it keeps no record of wrongs. Love bears all, believes all, hopes all, endures all. It never fails."

He paused and smiled to concede the foibles of mere mortals.

"Friends," he said, "we cannot mold a marriage. Only they who dare to undertake this solemn obligation can set the terms. Now, in their own words, let's hear their vision for a future together. Tom? What have you got to say for yourself?"

Wagstaff turned toward Marianne, took both of her hands in his, and in a halting voice thick with emotion, recited an oath he had rehearsed twenty times.

"Marianne, I promise to honor and cherish, in sickness and in health, you and our family with love and kindness — to be forgiving and tolerant of our faults, and our differences, to uphold our union, to secure our fortunes, to be faithful and true . . . to the end of our days."

"You heard it here, folks. Now, Marianne, your turn . . ."

Marianne gulped, caught her breath, and recited her own oath as if it were one of her many spells. (And it might have been, since Ray Bagwell helped her write it.)

"Tom, dearest love, I hereby swear to honor and cherish you and ours whatever the future holds, in freedom tempered by our common goals and mutual regard, to solve life's problems with love and respect, to faithfully cleave unto you only" — here she improvised slightly — "always . . . forever . . . never part . . . to . . . to . . . the end of our days."

"Marianne, do you take this man to be your lawfully wedded husband?"

Marianne nodded and just managed to croak out an "I do."

"And Tom, do you so take this woman?"

"I sure do."

"Are there rings?"

Turnbow held out a small velvet box and presented a gold band. Wagstaff slipped it on the third finger of Marianne's left hand, which was shaking.

"And . . ?"

Lorraine held out an identical ring to Marianne. She placed it on Wagstaff's hand, shaking as badly as her own.

"I now pronounce you man and wife. Tom, kiss the bride already."

Wagstaff leaned over, ostentatiously tore off Marianne's veil, and planted a ceremonial kiss that turned into a big smooch. For both, it was like an electric shock passing between them. The guests were stirred to murmurs of approval.

"See, that's what I'm talking about," said Dez Otis in a loud voice. The rest of the assembly burst into laughter.

"Ladies and gentlemen," said Fabriano, "I present to you Marianne Sarzeau and Thomas Wagstaff, married today in the sight of Heaven and Earth."

Huge round of applause. The Tailings blasted into an enthusiastic cover of The Byrds old hit, *Turn, Turn, Turn,* and the newlyweds marched away hand in hand, waving and grinning.

▼

At 7:00 PM the festivities resumed down beside the Tarvolo golf course at Rossi's Fine Italian Dining. Lorraine knew all about the restaurant's sentimental history and, using her husband's good credit, hired the place for the occasion. Chairs and tables were cleared off the deck, the Tailings were ready with their guitars and amps, and after a sitdown meal inside, dancing under plumes of wisteria was the business of the evening.

Marianne and Wagstaff kicked things off to a lush version of Billy Joel's *Just The Way You Are.* They parted at the first chorus, Wagstaff to dance with his mother, the maid of honor, and Marianne with Turnbow, best man.

"Don't you let go of that girl," admonished Mom.

"Don't worry, I'm hip."

"It's not going to be an easy life for you two."

"I know all about her, I'm fully informed."

"Bless you both." She kissed her son on the forehead.

Turnbow was wearing a troubled expression. "Lorraine tells me you two were fighting even before you put rings on your fingers. What gives, Golden Girl?"

"We have our ups and downs. I made a promise. I'll keep it. Tell Lorraine not to worry."

"You make it sound like hard work."

"Relax. Once we calm down, I'll hop in his lap."

When the band broke into *Footloose,* Marianne retired to the sidelines. Wagstaff did likewise. Their electric moment during the ceremony was fading as the reception wore on, and the two of them were standing at opposite ends of the dance floor, casually ignoring each other. The guests, fueled by excellent food and drink, probably didn't notice and, in any case, paid no heed. They were here for fun and were having plenty of it.

After quickstep instrumental renditions of the standards *It Had To Be You* and *The Way You Look Tonight,* followed closely by guitars grinding out a ferocious heavy-metal take on *You Do Something To Me,* the band settled into a mellow mood with *Unchained Melody.* This old Righteous Brothers tune, slow enough for the slowest feet, brought the entire assembly onto the dance floor.

Wagstaff circled around to his new bride and led her into the crowd. They moved slowly to the beat, holding each other close, silent lest harsh words should ruin the evening. At the end of the first verse, Wagstaff leaned into Marianne's ear.

"I've been giving it some consideration," he said, "and I just want you to know that I think *Gabriel* is a great name for our son."

"Unh-huh, me too," she replied with cool diffidence.

"And, even more important, I'm glad *he* suggested it."

A little ripple ran up Marianne's spine.

"Mean it?"

"Every word."

She gave him a big squeeze. They stopped and shared a delirious kiss, causing giggles and applause. Then they danced and danced, rubbing elbows with their friends and families until the band packed up at midnight.

59

"SO WHERE'S the honeymoon?"

Wagstaff, Marianne, her father, Aunt Imogen, and Ray Bagwell were gathered in Placerville's Buttercup Pantry for a late brunch. Marianne was on duty and in uniform, with her Glock strapped to her hip. It was two days after the wedding, the newlyweds were still in town, and their companions wanted to know the reason why.

"I'm making up time after chasing that damn train," said Marianne.

"And I'm whipping up a new woodworking project for the course I teach down in Lodi," added Wagstaff.

"But," continued Marianne, "we're joining Howard and Lorraine — Tom's mom and our mayor — down in Cancun come October. Our weddings kind of overlapped."

"Milo says you're pregnant," said Aunt Imogen.

"I was wondering about that," chimed Bagwell. "What's going on?"

"It's true, the modern age and all," said Marianne without a hint of embarrassment. "Our son *Gabriel* will arrive in February, not quite the proper nine months after this" — she held up her left hand, showing off her ring.

They all ordered pancakes and omelets. Once food was on the table, Sergeant Sarzo brought up a sore subject. "Okay, Angel, when you talk to me, your aura is blue."

"As it better be."

"When you talk to Gen . . . well . . ." He waggled his hand to indicate ambiguity.

Marianne blushed crimson. "Oh my God, don't tell me it's red."

"No, greenish yellow, mostly. Occasional cyan flashes."

Marianne reached across the table and grasped Aunt Imogen's hand. "I'm really sorry I've been carrying such a grudge all these years."

"She's good at that," said Wagstaff, with an ironic grin.

"You know the story, I think," said Aunt Imogen.

"Yes, Dad explained everything. So here's my apology — I'm truly sorry. You were great to watch over me back in my high school days after Mom left — what a nightmare! I don't blame you, but I forgive you anyway."

"Thank you," said her aunt. "Apology accepted, hon. Of course."

Marianne turned to her father. "How do I look?"

Sergeant Sarzo smiled. "Not bad. True blue, all the way."

"See? I'm learning," said Marianne, much relieved.

Tom looked at each of the women. "Here's what I'm wondering — does the strange stuff Marianne can do come from Dad's line only, or . . . both sides of the family?"

"What do you mean?" asked Aunt Imogen.

"Just, um, do you see auras, have any special abilities with animals, summon people at will, or, you know, do any other witchy stuff?"

"I can tell when the meat is done in the oven," said Aunt Imogen. "I know when it's going to rain."

"That's all?"

"Sorry, Marianne is Dad's little girl."

"So it seems."

Marianne nuzzled her husband. "Gabriel will be Gabriel."

Wagstaff sighed. "I don't doubt it."

Bagwell finished off his short stack, wiped his mouth, and lifted a piece of paper from his pocket. "Here's something of interest, I think. It was released to the media, but no one ran it. I got a memo . . ."

Marianne unfolded the printout. Wagstaff peered over her shoulder while she read it:

```
ACTION MEMO                        DA 621-01
PERSONNEL ASSIGNMENT NOTICE
RE: Jaromir Pavlov

1. Following detachment with commendations from his
post at the Department of Homeland Security, Jaromir
Pavlov has rejoined the Army at his former rank of
captain, per DA PPG.

2. Captain Pavlov is assigned to the FULTAP program
at Fort Benning, Georgia, as an intelligence analyst
starting 1 September.
```

Marianne's jaw dropped. "Ray? You did this."

Bagwell beamed. "Milo and me. Seemed like a good idea. We've been working with him for a while, and he burned the trail at Homeland with you, so we got General Weaver to pull a few strings . . ."

"Well, *boy howdy* to Jerry when you see him."

Marianne remembered noticing her former Tri-Town police colleague Wade Gawley and Chief Fabriano talking shop at the bar during her wedding reception. As a result, on her first day off she motored down to Jackson to check on her impression. Sure enough, Gawley was happy to report he was resigning from the force in order to pursue his now-flourishing U-Haul franchise full time.

"I've got another location lined up in Ione, and if that comes through, I can't be a cop anymore."

Marianne clapped her hands.

"I know what you're thinking, Sarzeau," said Gawley.

She gave him a big high five. "You're reading my mind."

"By the way, see this?" Gawley opened the day's *Bee* to an article in the regional news section:

OSTRICH FARM SOLD

Golden Egg Family Farms in Jackson, together with its flock of ostriches, has been sold to a ranch based in Marana, Arizona, following the murder of the owner, Alejandro Muñoz, in what federal investigators have determined was a lucrative human smuggling operation gone wrong.

Shipping containers that were used to bring undocumented aliens into the country have been impounded. Law enforcement officials contacted for this story believe Muñoz was himself a murderer, responsible for the death of several Mexican nationals and at least one investigator in order to conceal his illegal activities.

▼

Marianne waited a week, discussed all her options with Wagstaff, and then, at the end of a long shift, worked up her nerve and knocked on Lieutenant Kazmarek's door.

"Hi, Nina, I've got some news, bad or good, depending on how you look at it."

Kazmarek scowled, pretty sure she knew what was coming. "Oh?"

"I'm resigning."

Kazmarek nodded. "I was talking to Fabriano at your wedding, and I heard the gossip about Officer Gawley . . . so, not a big surprise."

"You warned me, and you were right. It's hard to juggle FULTAP with police work. Back in Tri-Town I can sub in whenever, and the chief is down with me playing hooky now and then."

"Good fit."

Marianne was overcome with relief at her boss' mild reaction, causing her to natter on.

"Right, so . . . no commute. And, I won't have to wear this damn Glock any more, or drive that stupid Charger. I can strap on my Beretta."

Kazmarek sighed. "All I ever hear are complaints. Does Otis know?"

"Not yet. You first."

"There's a courtesy. How's the mom-to-be? Still sick? Any more seizures?"

"No, all gone. You heard? You knew?"

"Honey, I'm not running the shop by accident."

"You could have grounded me."

"But I didn't. Executive decision. Now, take a look at this, a blast from your recent past, if I'm not mistaken." She tossed a copy of the *Roseville Reporter* across her desk:

WOULD-BE TERRORIST DIES

Yannick Brunel, whose failed attempt to poison Folsom Lake ended explosively in a Roseville parking lot, has died in prison while awaiting trial in federal court. The cause is said to be acute pneumonia brought on by inhaling some of the radioactive dust he planned to mix into the lake water.

His co-conspirator, Simon Hatch, remains in critical condition in the state prison hospital with third degree burns.

▼

By mid-September Wagstaff had carpentered a wall to divide the *Courier* workspace from his old loft-like living area, which was now the newlyweds' home. Marianne busied herself on a day off by mudding seams in the drywall she had helped tack up over the wooden studs.

It was hot, and the building was without air conditioning, so after working long enough to feel virtuous, she laid trowel aside and fetched beer and lemonade from the fridge. She carried them through an unfinished doorway and handed the beer to her husband.

"Hey, M, here's what I'm setting up." Wagstaff pointed at his computer monitor. Marianne glanced over his shoulder at a modest headline on the third page:

SARZEAU REJOINS TRI-TOWN POLICE

"That's me, local cop."

"Any news from over the border?"

"You mean my so-called guardian spook?"

"What else?"

"Haven't seen him since he blew up. Looks like I'm just an Ordinary Human Unit now, Pregnant Variety. But . . . give me six months, I'll be as weird as I ever was."

Wagstaff tilted his head up, twisted around, and brushed his lips against her breasts.

Cancun in October was warm and mild. A hurricane that threatened the combined honeymoons of Marianne, Wagstaff, Lorraine, and Turnbow veered east at the last minute and dumped six inches of rain on Florida.

While her companions were sipping margaritas under a wide umbrella, Marianne had a look at her smartphone, buzzing on the table beside her glass of iced tea. A text message had arrived:

Take a gander at the link. — xo — Jerry

She touched the URL on the screen, opening a blog item on *DC Daily,* an obscure east coast political website:

HOME TEAM SHAKEUP

Homeland Secretary Quincy has a new playbook today, shuffling his team into new positions on the anti-terror field. To this sports fan, it's all because of Senator Daggett's blistering criticism in committee last week. The guy is still sore about Homeland's failure to anticipate an attack that came close to choking the water supply of California's capital city — in a drought yet.

Permanently sidelined is Assistant Deputy Jameson Sizemore, who some pundits had picked to be quarterbacking Homeland within a year. Instead, it looks like he'll be taking the snaps at *Blackball, Inc.,* a private security contractor.

Marianne chuckled and tapped out a single word — *Revenge*. She added a smiley face emoji, hit send, and headed for the water with her snorkel and a little waterproof digital camera from the hotel gift shop.

She hiked across the wide white beach with an awkward gait due to the growing bump that already made her feel like a whale. She waded out into the shallows and launched herself into the bay. She was paddling face down, looking for colorful fish to photograph.

And she found some; luminous parrotfish and wiggly little wrasses. Soon she was daydreaming, happily immersed in buoyant seawater where her bump was invisible.

Twenty feet below her on the sandy floor of the bay, small plants and anemones were growing. Crabs were scuttling here and there. She paddled on and on. Suddenly the sand beneath her shifted and began to blur. A cloud bloomed in the water. She shook her head, momentarily fearful that a seizure was in progress, two hundred yards from the safety of dry land.

But no. An enormous manta ray was shaking itself free of a hiding place. It rose beneath her, a huge creature at least fifteen feet wide from wingtip to wingtip. Marianne coughed, spitting out her snorkel and a stream of bubbles. She pulled her face out of the water, wheezing and sneezing.

The manta ray flapped slowly away toward the open ocean, a sovereign monster of the ordinary world, benign and indifferent.

60

IN THE BITTER COLD of late February, Marianne, although very pregnant, was still on active duty, still patrolling in spite of her mountainous abdominal bulge.

She waddled uncomfortably through the leafless apple trees in Applefield's quaint town park in search of drug paraphernalia. Now that heroin was a cheap high, syringes and needles had become a problem, even in her picturesque little corner of California.

She was careful on the brick sidewalk, which was still slick at 2:00 PM. Snow had fallen the day before, and although most of it had melted, patches could be seen in the shadows. She longed for a quick and painless birth, a brief period of total immersion in motherhood, and then the chance to turn the kid over to Lorraine for a winter getaway involving snow, snowboards, and a glass of wine with Tom.

At the bronze prospector statue in the middle of the park she peered into the little pool at the miner's feet. A thin sheet of ice covered most of the basin. She swept it aside with her baton, revealing coins in the pool, but, thankfully, no needles.

She was there looking for trouble, but secretly hoping for a visit from her spiritual guardian. In the months since her last encounter she had tried to raise him several times with zero success. It occurred to her that, without her special acorn, the various mirrors she had already tried might not be sending the proper signals. With a glance around to be sure she was alone, she hauled her stony amulet out from under her jacket and held it tight.

Whiskeyjack, Whiskeyjack...

She recited the *named spirit* chant in a hoarse whisper, puffing out a cloud of chilly vapor with each word. She waited for more than a minute, but standing still made her shiver, and seeing no supernatural ripples or shadows on the water, at length she turned away.

"Wherever you are, buddy — hey, call me sometime, okay?"

She had her fingers on the door of her police cruiser, an old reliable Crown Vic, when her water burst, flooding her pants. Then the pains hit.

"Hi, mom. Me again. It's time."

Marianne did her best to breathe regularly and stay calm.

"You little rascal. Go easy on me."

▼

Gabriel Sarzeau Wagstaff was born at 1:30 AM the next day in the obstetric unit of Sutter Amador Hospital in Jackson. Tom Wagstaff stood by, crushing Marianne's hand in his as she pushed and pushed. The little guy finally emerged, red and gooey and howling. Wagstaff cut the cord. He was nineteen inches long and weighed seven pounds.

▼

Ten months later.

An hour before Marianne was scheduled for her radio show, she was sitting with Lorraine in a glassed-in porch at the Turnbow mansion, sharing a pizza and planning next week's thanksgiving dinner.

Between bites, she pulled small pieces of crust free and stuffed them into little Gabe, who was fastened into a portable car seat on the table between the two women.

"If you're working tonight, why didn't you leave this cute little guy with Tom?" asked Lorraine.

"You know the drill — his dad is laying out a newspaper that's due at the printer tomorrow."

Marianne's son was now a strapping infant of twenty-one pounds, with an uncontrollable thatch of blond hair sprouting out of his scalp, and four little teeth visible when he smiled, giggled, or screeched in misery.

"Say anything yet?" asked Lorraine, attempting to smooth Gabe's locks.

"Not yet. Tom is predicting his first word will be 'Dada.' We have a bet."

"Your prediction?"

"Mama, natch."

▼

Marianne drove her little blue Mini a mile up the road to the KVIG property and rolled down to the station building. She parked beside Turnbow's Mercedes and was unbuckling Gabe's car seat when an unfamiliar mental voice spoke. She froze.

"Hi, Mom. It's me. Saying hello."

"Mom, is it? And who are you?"

"Your daughter. It's time we got to know each other. We have a lot to talk about."

Marianne was in shock. "I'll bet. But not tonight, if you don't mind. I've got a show to do."

"I understand. Totally."

Marianne laughed aloud at her new predicament.

"In bed by eight, hear me?"

"I'm in bed all the time. It is so borrrrring."

"Then go to sleep already. I'll play a song to send you off to dreamland. Don't scare me like that again."

Inside, Marianne ran into Turnbow, who was anxiously checking equipment that ran itself without human help for months on end.

"You're being superstitious, Howard," said Marianne, settling down in her DJ chair. She placed Gabe in his car seat on the desk in front of her.

"I know. Can't help it." He tousled Gabe's crazy hair. "How about you, kid? What have you got to say about this?"

"Nothing, that's what," said Marianne, puzzling over the new voice she had just heard.

"We should get him going. Gabe, my boy, can you say K-V-I-G? Or 'foothill favorites'?"

"No coaching, mister. Tom insists that his first word has to be 'Dada.'"

"Once he learns to speak, I'll audition him. He may talk you out of a job."

"Wouldn't that be nice."

"Right. Well, lights on the boxes are green, so I'll say goodnight. Break a leg, Mom . . . or more to the point, a tonsil."

Turnbow patted Marianne's hand and withdrew. She heard his car start up as she recorded the night's advertisements and slotted them into the playlist on the station's computer. She dug through a collection of audio files searching for a suitable intro, couldn't find anything she liked, and recorded a new one. She pasted it in place and sat back to watch the second hand of the big wall clock sweep around to showtime:

"Good evening, foothill folks out there. This is The Golden Girl of the Golden Hills. Thanksgiving next week. Got your turkey? Got a good recipe for pumpkin pie? Got some requests? Talk to me at *The Vig* — that's K-V-I-G — in Applefield, California, at ninety-three-point-one on your FM dial. It's seven o'clock."

Maroon Five's electropop hit *Love Somebody* jumped up between the arrows on her monitor. While it played, Marianne picked up her smartphone and thumbed Wagstaff's number.

"Oh my God, Tom, guess what just happened?"

"Hey, M, you're on the air, right? Everything okay?"

"Gabe is good, I'm good. And — now get this — our *daughter* is also good."

"What?" He groaned. "Didn't quite hear that. Must have wax in my ears."

"I'm pregnant."

"Hoo boy."

"I know. Who'da thunk it?"

Marianne heard Wagstaff chuckle.

"Has she picked out a *name?*"

"Not yet. All I know is how bored she is."

"I think there's some tequila around here somewhere," mumbled her husband. "I'm going to pour myself a drink. But not you — you're on the wagon again. See you at the witching hour."

Marianne looked through the impending music selections and advanced one to the top of the list.

"Here's a lullaby for someone who ought to be sound asleep. She didn't give me her ID . . ." Marianne touched a button and John Mayer's sonorous *Queen of California* rolled out over the air waves.

While the guitars rippled and the lyrics wailed, Marianne warmed a pot of water on the station's hot plate. She dunked a bottle of juice to take the chill off and poked the nipple into Gabe's mouth. He sucked merrily for a moment. Then he lost his grip, and the bottle tumbled to the floor.

Suddenly his car seat began to vibrate. It bounced around the desktop. Marianne clutched frantically to prevent it from toppling. Gabe's hands closed into fists. His eyes rolled up in his head. His mouth opened wide.

Snap!

The station lights blinked out. The song was cut off midway through the instrumental break.

"Whiskeyjack!" cried Gabriel.

▲ ▲ ▲